WISHFUL WISTERIA

Wisteria Witches Mysteries

BOOK #10

ANGELA PEPPER

CHAPTER 1

Wednesday Morning
First Week in August
Pacific Spirit Park, Wisteria

The man slumped on the park bench was motionless.

I approached the bench at a casual, disinterested pace, aware that someone could be watching. Magic pooled within my hands, at the ready. A wise witch had to be on high alert whenever anything broke the pattern of an ordinary day. Strange happenings and danger walked hand in hand.

Somewhere in the park, a dog barked. It was a tiny bark, more of a yip than a woof, and that yip resonated with approximately seven pounds of unholy terror. I knew that bark. Pippi Poplin, the Pomeranian. Danger was afoot, after all.

At the sound of the yip, the man slumped on the bench stirred. His head jerked up. He pushed back his hat and glanced around sleepily, rubbing his eyes.

I could let my guard down. The man wasn't dead after all, which meant I wouldn't be spending my day filling out incident reports.

The power level of the plasma in my hands dropped from Wallop Senseless all the way past various Day Ruining levels, and down to Mild Indigestion. As the tingling in my fingers dissipated, I breathed easier. Good ol' Harry wasn't dead yet.

Even with his hat tipped over his face, I had recognized the figure on the park bench as Harry Blackstone. He was a regular at the Wisteria Public Library. He loved dozing in the cozy reading corner that caught the mid-afternoon sun. Harry had learned our routine, and had his own. He knew to get comfortable by one o'clock so he could get enjoy a full sleep cycle before we did the 2:00 pm patrol, also known as The Nap O'Clock Wakeup.

As I watched him, Harry removed his hat and ran his hand through his hair, which was as thick and unruly as it was entirely black. He was only in his early fifties, which was young for such a prolific public napper. His eyes were large, brown, and continuously scanning, more out of curiosity than anxiety. His nose was large, with a hump on the bridge, and a pointed tip. He had small, square teeth, with a gap in the middle. His features weren't perfectly balanced, but his warm personality and heartfelt smile made him handsome, all the same. I might have set him up with my aunt, if it wasn't for one small issue: He could be dead by the end of the year, according to him.

He'd explained to me that he napped frequently because, despite appearances, he wasn't well. He was currently enjoying a surprise respite from his unexplained illness, but the good health wouldn't be permanent. And that was okay, as far as he was concerned. He had big plans for his afterlife, he'd told me with a wink. He was an inventor, and he'd only just begun his greatest work. As for his days on earth, he'd already done some creative refinancing to get his affairs in order, and would simply live out his remaining days with what he called *graceful surrender.*

"Good morning, Mr. Blackstone," I called out cheerfully. "That bench doesn't look nearly as comfortable as a nice leather club chair!"

He flashed his smile of small, square teeth with a sizable gap, and retorted, "A hard bench is not my favorite spot to rest my eyes, but at least I don't get in trouble for snoring!" He chuckled. "And call me Harry! Mr. Blackstone is my boring, uptight brother."

"Okay, Harry. But if your brother's anything like you, I doubt he's boring."

"Oh, he's pretty dull, but people change." Harry smirked. "People change," he repeated.

I stopped in front of the bench. My back was damp with perspiration from the bright late-summer sunshine. On any other day, I might have taken a break on the bench next to Harry, but that particular morning I was running late due to some issues at the house with our protective wards.

Making polite conversation, as one ought to in a small town, I said, "Great weather for the end of summer." I gestured to the edge of the forest, where some of the deciduous trees were sporting orange and red hints of a pending wardrobe change. "I can't wait to see the leaves turn. I hear the fall foliage is stunning."

"Ah, yes," Harry said with a knowing eyebrow-raise, his large, brown eyes roving around, scanning our surroundings tirelessly. "But we must not be in too much of a rush to see the seasons change. We have to enjoy this beautiful last month of summer while it lasts."

I winced inwardly as I realized my faux pas. Mentioning the passage of time in a positive, anticipatory manner was not the best choice for idle chatter with the terminally ill.

Harry, seemingly unperturbed, replaced his floppy hat on his thick black hair and continued talking. "As soon as the September rain begins to fall, it won't stop until October."

I nodded. I'd heard that warning from several longtime Wisterians, but didn't believe it.

Harry stretched his arms across the back of the bench and loosely crossed one leg over the other. "I've got a secret for you," he said in a fatherly tone. "Stock up on umbrellas right away. Once the rain starts up, you won't be able to find a decent one anywhere in town."

"That's a great tip," I said. "I'll return the favor with a secret of my own." I leaned forward, held my hand to the side of my mouth, and said, "You don't actually snore. That's something we tell everyone, whether they snore or not, to discourage napping in the library."

He started chuckling, and soon he was laughing so hard, he had to uncross his legs and slap both knees to get it all out.

I shouldn't have divulged one of the library's secrets, but it made my heart sing to see a dying man so happy.

"Have a great day," I said, stepping backward onto the path. "Maybe I'll see you later."

He stopped laughing, and his expression quickly turned serious. "You will be seeing me," he said. "Sooner than you think." His gaze meandered over to the forest, where it suddenly froze. He frowned, looking at the point where the path I stood on disappeared into darkness.

The grave tone of his voice, combined with his expression, gave me the same ominous feeling I'd gotten from the sight of his limp body.

I considered sitting on the bench after all, and finding out more about his illness, using magic or my natural charm. I could get whatever information I wanted, if I tried.

But then Harry's big, brown eyes returned to their usual scanning, and his focus shifted away from the forest. His expression relaxed, and he waved at someone behind me. I turned to find the source of the yip I'd heard earlier. Pippi Poplin, the Pomeranian, was dragging her owner, Patricia Poplin, toward us.

Floopy Double Doops!

I muttered another hasty goodbye, and took off before the duo could engage.

Pacific Spirit Forest was noticeably cooler than the open park had been, thanks to the shady leaves. After the perspiration on my back evaporated, I buttoned my cardigans—both of them—against the chill.

The forest was peaceful. Too peaceful. The birds weren't chirping.

The back of my head tingled. Was it just my skin contracting in the cool forest air, or was something magical afoot?

Using minimal hand motions, I cast a basic threat detection spell. The shadows to my left inversed, darkness turning to light.

Thanks to the spell, now I saw what had been there the whole time. *Who* had been there.

The threat glowed like a lantern. It continued moving alongside me, unaware of the spell that shone a spotlight upon it.

CHAPTER 2

The threat in the woods was a danger, all right. A danger to both my patience and my sanity. It was my father, in his sneakiest form: a red fox.

In a commanding voice, I said, "Rhys Quarry, you might as well stop slinking around in those bushes and come out. I know you're following me." I also knew he'd been listening in on my private conversation earlier that morning, thanks to the protective wards on my house.

A red fox emerged from the underbrush and stepped onto the path in front of me, hanging its head—*his* head—sheepishly.

The fox was him, all right. I recognized the gold-green eyes. As we locked gazes, I remembered a previous time we'd met in those same woods. He'd been hurt badly. At the time, I'd had no idea my father could turn into a fox, let alone the one I anxiously bundled into my coat and rushed to a veterinarian.

That had been in June, two months ago. I'd saved his life that day. I hadn't seen the man—in any form—since the night he returned the favor by leaving me for dead. Our father-daughter relationship was, in a word, complicated.

The fox stood before me, motionless on the path.

He couldn't speak in shifter form, so I would have to do the talking. I surreptitiously prepared a spell in my hand as I asked, "Are you hurt?"

He shook his head, his pointy sable ears swivelling as he did.

"Good." I opened my hand and let the spell take flight.

A transparent blue bird fluttered up from my palm, took aim, and launched itself at the fox. The bird exploded like a miniature fireworks display on my father's wet, black nose. A ripple of light passed over Rhys-Fox, sparking one last time as it flared out at the white tip of his bushy tail.

Rhys-Fox let out a confused yip, and shook himself. He blinked at me, then shook his whole body again. He sat back on his haunches and tilted his head questioningly.

"It's a form-locking spell," I explained. "You can stay in that form a little while longer, because I don't want to see your face."

He pawed one side of his face, as though nervously playing with his whiskers the way some people twist their hair.

"I haven't been your biggest fan," I said. "Not since you abandoned me and Zoey and Zinnia to be eaten by that monstrosity." The anger rose within me like a different type of spell. "And Boa! You used our sweet little cat as bait. What kind of person does something like that? Poor Boa never did anything to you."

He stopped swiping at his whiskers and used his paw to partially cover his eyes. If the red fox had been anyone else, my heart would have melted from cuteness. But it was my dear ol' dad. My fair-weather father. My boundaries were stronger than his adorability.

As I let him have it, my fury subsided a little. It felt good to get out the words I'd been saving up. Better still to not have him able to interrupt.

"Thanks for the car and everything," I said in a lighter tone. "But I'm not ready to interact with you. On some level, I do understand you had your reasons for doing what you did, and you probably underestimated the danger you put us in. But on another level, I just don't want to see your human face."

Another cute look from behind a sable paw. My heart threatened to melt its icy boundaries. Darn him for being so cute.

Avoiding direct eye contact, I continued. "So let's extend our cooling-off period a little longer. Things are good right now. Zoey's happy. She's dating a boy. And I'm dating someone, too. He's actually..." *A vampire.* "Good for me."

When I looked at Rhys-Fox again, he'd stopped with the cute routine and was simply looking alert. Was I projecting my emotions, or was he happy for me? I felt my anger ebbing, so I quickly made a fist to hold steady. *Zara is a good witch, with sensible, solid boundaries.*

"I'm sure Zoey wants to see you, but can you give us all some space? Not forever. Just for..."

The fox waited expectantly.

"A month or two," I finished.

The fox stood on all fours and bowed, like a dog inviting another to play, but slower. It was a gesture of acquiescence. He agreed to my demands.

Good, I thought. I'd won. So why didn't I feel happy?

He straightened up, winked one gold-green eye, and launched himself back into the side brush.

That was easy, I thought as I began walking. *Too easy.*

The leaves rustled, and a fox darted out in front of me. This one wasn't my father. It wasn't even red. It was covered in thick, bushy, glossy black fur. I'd never seen a black fox in person before.

I readied the same spell I'd used on my father, but hesitated.

The intricacies of witch-shifter relationships were complicated, but not so complicated that I didn't know casting a form-locking spell on the shifter would be a serious breach of etiquette. Especially since, unlike my father, the black fox hadn't committed any transgressions against me—that I knew of.

So I stood there, unmoving. I gave no outward sign of a reaction, yet I twirled my tongue inside my mouth, warming up a trio of defense spells. Just in case.

The black fox had big, dewy, dark eyes. Its stance was hesitant, one paw raised. Its body language was submissive—ears flat, bushy black tail tucked between its legs. A friend of my father's? I'd expect any companions of his to be as cocky as he was, but this fox was hesitant. Who was it? I stared into its big, brown eyes.

The fox broke eye contact first, its half-lidded gaze shifting to the ground between us.

There was a yip sound. Not Pippi the Pomeranian, but another fox. The yip came from somewhere else in the forest. It had to be my father, unless he was running with a whole pack—or a whole *skulk*, to be accurate. There was another yip, followed by excited dog barking. The latter I recognized as being Pippi. Trouble was on the loose, all right.

"Your friend's in trouble," I said to Black Fox.

Words came back inside my mind: *He's always in trouble.*

I did a double take. A psychic fox shifter? Things just got even more intriguing.

I chuckled and said, "You're not wrong about that."

Black Fox cowered and shrank back. The voice echoed in my mind again: *You heard me?*

I pointed to my temple. "Yes, I did." I started walking toward the trembling creature slowly. "Do I know you? I don't believe we've had proper introductions."

In the distance, there was more yipping, sounding frantic, and more barking, sounding bloodthirsty. Pippi was the most blood-thirsty Pomeranian I'd ever met.

I glanced in the direction of the noise. There was only the lush green woods, but I could see ferns shaking with activity beneath their fronds.

While I did wish for my father to back off for a bit, I didn't wish for him to be eaten by Pippi the Pomeranian. Good people don't leave their family members to be eaten. I pushed up my cardigan sleeves and pondered my battle options. Pippi was a tiny ball of fluff, but one must never underestimate their opponent.

The barking and yipping continued, and then poor Patricia Poplin howled fruitlessly for her dog to "Come back, Pippi! Get back here! It's just a stupid squirrel!"

I turned my attention to the Black Fox to gauge its reaction to the melee. There was only empty pathway. The creature was gone.

I stood still, opening my senses and enhancing my sight and hearing with a spell.

Seconds passed. The forest was silent. Then more yips echoed through the woods, further away than before. I couldn't see any ferns moving.

Pippi barked some more. I didn't speak Pomeranian—though I knew another witch who could—but even I could tell it was the bark of disappointment. The foxes had gotten away.

The danger seemed long gone, but I cast another threat-detection spell anyway. I would be able to assure my mentor I had been cautious, plus it was the sensible thing to do. *Zara tries to be a sensible witch.* The coast appeared to be clear, so I continued on my way to work.

My pace was quick, thanks to my eagerness to tell a coworker about my morning adventure. Soon, I had to unbutton my outer cardigan as well as my inner cardigan.

I couldn't wait to ask the library's resident shifter about psychic powers. Was that an undocumented feature of their kind? If Frank Wonder didn't have the answers, there were plenty of other resources. When it came to finding information, librarians didn't give up easily.

Whoever he or she was, Black Fox had pushed words into my mind. That was no small feat. I'd specifically worked on building up my mental defenses to keep other witches—*Maisy Nix, I'm talking about you, cough cough*—from walking all over me.

If that bushy-tailed critter could get through my defenses so easily, I had to know who it was.

CHAPTER 3

I didn't get a chance to tell my coworker about my strange encounter in the woods until coffee break.

Frank Wonder had been the children's librarian for ages, since long before I'd started there. He was both a regular fixture and a popular attraction. Kids loved everything about him, from his dyed pink hair to his storytime readings. Frank did a multitude of hilarious voices that elevated his books from readings to theatrical performances. In addition to the pink hair, Frank had quick-moving eyes that were small and hooded, wide-set in his triangular-shaped face. His jaw narrowed to a point that was slightly skewed to one side, like the point on a comma.

Frank would be considered fit and athletic for a man half his age. The mid-fifties looked good on him, as did his unconventional wardrobe of vintage cords and paisley shirts. That Wednesday, he'd reversed his usual attire. He wore a corduroy shirt with paisley trousers. And he wore it like nobody else could.

"Spill it," Frank said to me, speaking out of the side of his mouth in that slightly askew way of his. He put on his fake Southern drawl. "Zara Riddle, you've been busting at the seams all morning. You're positively dying to tell me something."

"I wouldn't say I'm *dying*, except possibly for one of those cinnamon buns Kathy was kind enough to supply." I wiggled my fingers impatiently, urging him to open the box already. The scent of vanilla plus cinnamon was already making my mouth water. Adventures in the woods always made me hungry.

He cracked the seal on the box. "That's odd," he said with a sniff. "There's still a full dozen in here. Normally you would have snuck into the break room already and helped yourself to at least one." It was not an inaccurate statement. "Something's got you rattled."

"I had kind of a strange encounter in the woods on my way to work."

"A strange encounter in the woods. That reminds me." He waved one finger in the air. "We need to have a serious talk about the Little Red Riding Hood mural in the children's reading nook. Perhaps later." He waved for me to continue. "What happened in the woods?"

"First, my father was following me."

Frank nodded. "That's disconcerting, considering how complicated things are with you two."

"I know, right? He thought he was being so sneaky, but I knew something was up. I swear he forgets I'm a witch. So I called him out, and then, get this, I cast a spell to keep him locked in fox form. He had to keep his big mouth shut the whole time, while I read him the riot act without interruption."

Frank frowned. "You cast a form-locking spell on a shifter?" He shook his head and made a tsk-tsk sound. "Zara Riddle, consider our friendship over."

"Frank." I raised my eyebrows. "It was my *father*. The one who left me for dead."

"Doesn't matter." He shook his head and tsk-tsked again. "This is exactly why shifters and witches don't get along."

"But you and I get along."

"Only because you haven't cast a form-locking spell on me." He gave me a dirty look. "Yet."

"And I won't. The only spells I've ever cast on you have been the exact opposite. I try to calm you down when you get overexcited, Frank. This break room would be covered in pink flamingo feathers if it wasn't for me."

He pursed his lips tightly, so that his whole face had an accusing point to it.

"It was my *faaaather*," I said. My voice sounded petulant, even to my own ears. As I heard myself, I realized I shouldn't have cast that spell, satisfying though it was.

Frank's pointy face continued accusing me.

"I screwed up," I said meekly.

"Why are you telling me about this, anyway? Are you looking for some kind of absolution?"

"What?"

"Zara Riddle, I love you like I love a firm pillow and a silk sleeping mask, but I am not going to lie and say it's okay for you witches to do whatever you want to other people, shifters or otherwise."

I cleared my throat and swished my hand between us, as though manually trying to clear the air. A spray of magic sparkled out of my fingers inadvertently. The spell did clear the air. The smell that had been wafting up from the box of cinnamon buns was now gone.

"Point taken," I said. "I hear you, and I understand what I did wrong. I appreciate you taking the time to point it out to me. I'm sorry."

Frank crossed his arms and tapped his foot. "You said *first. First, your father was following you.* Then what?"

"Oh." I flicked out my fingertips in a wait-for-it gesture. "The thing with my father was just the lead-up to what happened next."

"Did you turn someone into a horse and demand a ride to work?" He batted his eyelashes. "Don't make me report you to the PTB."

My jaw dropped. "The PTB? Who the heck is the PTB? Is there some new secret organization in town?"

He flashed his bright teeth in a crooked grin. "PTB stands for the Powers That Be. It's a joke." His expression grew serious. "You really are rattled about something."

"Yes. After I finished with my father, there was another fox. A black one. He or she knew Rhys, and they put words in my mind. Psychically. The shifter was psychic."

"No, they weren't."

"Yes, they were." I explained the exact exchange, and how Black Fox had seemed surprised at our psychic communication.

"Then it must not have been a shifter," Frank said when I'd finished. "Shifters aren't psychic."

"Then how do you communicate with each other in shifter form? Most of you can't talk that way."

He shrugged.

I pressed on. "Frank, when you're flying around with Rob and Knox, how do you keep from crashing into each other?"

"That's different."

"How?"

"It's a shifter thing. You wouldn't understand."

"Try me."

He took a deep breath, turned to the counter, and used a pair of tongs to transfer a cinnamon roll from the white bakery box to a plate. He then proceeded to lick the icing off the stubby silver tongs.

"Classy," I said flatly. "It's so much more hygienic to do that with the tongs than with your fingers."

"Waste not, want not." He narrowed his small, hooded eyes at me. "Don't look at me like that. I'm going to wash the tongs when I'm done." He turned on the water at the sink.

"You're so gross."

"Don't be cranky. I'll hurry so you can get your cinnamon bun, too."

"No need." I levitated a cinnamon bun from the box and floated it onto a plate. "Being a witch means you don't need tongs, or oven mitts, or—"

He cut me off with an imitation of me, in a high-pitched voice, "Being a witch means you don't need tongs, or oven mitts, or blah blah blah, because being a witch is the greatest!"

I put my hands on my hips. "Don't make me use my fireballs on you. I will ruin your day, Frank Wonder."

Frank finished cleaning the tongs, then rubbed his chin thoughtfully while he left the water running. "I wonder if it's true, what they say about witches melting if you get them wet." He used the sprayer attachment to direct the water my way.

I easily shielded the move with a wave of magic and tossed the water right back at him, soaking his corduroy shirt and paisley trousers.

He made a flamingo-like squawk of indignation.

I snorted.

"I regret nothing," he said. "Except not bringing a change of clothes."

"Tell me more about your secret shifter-communication powers, and I'll dry your pants with a spell."

"Deal." He held out his arms and grimaced as though bracing himself for a high-powered fan, which wasn't how the spell worked all.

"You're dry," I said casually.

He opened one eye and then the other. "Not bad." He patted himself. "A little shrinkage."

I snorted. "Your pants aren't shrinking. If you think they are, that's an issue you might want to take up with the cinnamon buns."

He gasped in mock horror.

I waved my hand impatiently. "Tell me about your communication magic."

"Try not to be disappointed. Honestly, it's not that fancy. You know how when it gets busy here, we can have as many as five people working the circulation desk, scrambling in every direction, and we don't bump into each other?"

It rarely got *that* busy at the Wisteria Public Library, but I nodded to show I got his point.

"It's like that," he said. "There's a rhythm. A knowing. You just *know* each other's intentions and movements, without having to verbalize."

"But you *could* verbalize into each other's minds if you needed to, right?"

He scrunched his face. "Not like your pet dragon."

"He's a *wyvern*, and he's not my pet. If he knew you'd said that, he'd go on a long rant about eviscerating you."

"Either way, he's the one you should be asking about this." Frank finished his pastry, licked his fingers, and washed his hands. "If you want, I can ask around about black foxes. Don't worry, I won't say a word to Rob. He's such a gossip."

I raised an eyebrow. Talk about the pot calling the kettle black.

Frank said, "But Knox knows how to keep things quiet. I can ask him."

"Thanks for the offer, but I'd rather keep this between the two of us for now."

Frank raised an eyebrow. "Because you don't want anyone to know your father's in town?"

I pretended to be deeply interested in my cinnamon roll, which wasn't difficult. It was both heavy and light at the same time, in that magical way of cinnamon buns, thanks to a practically illegal amount of butter baked in.

"Forget I brought it up," I said. "I was probably on edge this morning from dealing with my father. I must have imagined the fox was talking to me."

"It might have been a regular fox that you made talk with one of your spells. Poor creature. Nasty witch magic takes another innocent victim."

I didn't like where the conversation was going. In an upbeat tone, I asked, "How are things with your sister, Bellatrix?"

"Oh, good." He lolled his head from side to side. "We took some flights together. Everything's changing. Before, she was just my sister. And now, she's... I don't know how to explain it."

I took another bite and waited for Frank to gather his thoughts. In the silence, I felt a warm wave of gratitude. Despite the stories about witches and shifters being natural enemies, my coworker and I had clicked from the start. We had our tiffs, but I was thankful to have him as a friend, and as a second conscience.

He finally finished his thought. "Bellatrix was always my sister, but now she's a *person*."

"When you found out your sister could turn into a swan, she finally became a person to you?"

"See, I told you I couldn't explain it right."

I waved my hand. "No, no. It's wrong of me to judge. I don't have any siblings, so I wouldn't know. But I do understand that us supernatural folk have a lot more going on than what's visible on the surface."

He nodded. "We sure do."

We chatted about life while I finished my cinnamon bun. Frank headed to the door, and I asked him to cover me for a few minutes while I made a phone call.

"Don't be long," he said. "It looks positively frantic out there again. We have a line forming."

"A line?"

He grinned. "Two people qualifies as a line, right?" He winked and left the break room.

I grabbed my phone and put in a call to my other main shifter resource, my neighbor, Chet Moore.

A female voice answered. "Yes?"

I assumed it was Chet's fiancée, Chessa. My stomach threatened to reject its recently-acquired cinnamon bun. I swallowed hard and lied, "Chessa! How lovely to hear your voice."

"You don't have to lie," came a playful reply. "It's Charlize. The less terrifying, more fun sister."

I exhaled in relief, then asked, "What are you doing with Chet's phone? Is everything okay?"

"Uh... I can't talk right now. In the middle of something. How about lunch? I'll pick you up. My treat."

"Oh, Charlize. I could never say no to you, or free lunch."

"Figured as much."

"Parking's tight mid-day, so you can text me when you get close."

She made a hissing sound. I pictured the blonde gorgon's hair snakes doing their excited dance. "I'll do sssssssomething better than text you."

"Please don't honk," I said with a groan. "When people honk, everyone in the library looks up and scowls at whoever's heading for the door. It's so obvious."

"I won't honk," she said. "You'll ssssssee."

We confirmed the time and said goodbye. As I was putting my phone away, the door to the break room opened quickly. Frank ran in, chest heaving in his tight corduroy shirt.

"The fox," he said breathlessly. "The fox is here. In the library!"

"My father?" I shook my head. "I knew it. This morning was way too easy."

"Not your father," Frank said. "The other one. The black fox. See for yourself." He waved me over to peer through the door.

I looked through the crack. I saw the head librarian, Kathy Carmichael, chatting with one of our regulars. It was Harry Blackstone, the man I'd seen on my way in that morning. He didn't see me, but he did remove his hat and run his hand over his hair.

His black, bushy, shiny hair.

I pulled back, closed the door, and whirled to face Frank. When I'd told Frank about my strange encounter in the woods, I hadn't mentioned I'd also seen Harry just moments before.

"How did you know?" I asked, almost as breathless as Frank had been.

"He has a fox on his key chain," Frank said. "I saw it when he was digging around for money to pay an overdue fee. Plus, look at his hair. No man over fifty has that much hair."

My excitement faded. "That's certainly *something*, but it's not exactly a smoking gun. You didn't happen to see him shift, did you?"

Frank looked me dead in the eyes. "He tapped the key chain with the fox on the counter, gave me a knowing look, and asked if I'd seen any unusual birds flying around the town lately."

"Okay." I nodded slowly. We were getting somewhere. Supernaturals could be very subtle, speaking in code to each other before proper introductions had been made.

"Also, he asked to see you. He asked for you by name."

"He asked for me by name," I repeated. "And *his* name is Harry Blackstone." I grimaced. "Blackstone, for a black fox. It's a bit obvious, don't you think?"

Frank shrugged. "I have pink hair. My sister has weird chicken feet."

He had a point. Magic had a mind of its own, and a warped sense of humor.

I went out to see what the man wanted.

CHAPTER 4

Harry Blackstone fidgeted with his floppy hat, putting it on his head when he saw me approaching, then yanking it off, folding it into a triangular shape, and tucking it into his jacket pocket.

I looked at his thick, bushy black hair and compared it with my memory of the black fox in the woods. Shifters in human form didn't always resemble their animal counterparts, but, once you knew, there was always a detail or two that matched perfectly, such as my father's gold-green eyes. Harry's hair was as black and full as the fox's, and yet not as silky or well organized. Still, it was close enough for me to make the same assumption Frank had, and connect the two.

"Zara Riddle," he said warmly. "I warned you I'd be seeing you soon."

"It's always nice when you drop in, Mr. Blackstone. I mean Harry. Did you have fun at the park this morning?"

"I did." His big, brown eyes roved left and right continuously, taking in the environment. "Until that racket with a certain red-haired fellow that you and I both know."

"Oh?" I decided to play dumb. "And who would that be, this mutual acquaintance of ours?"

He continued on as though I hadn't asked a question. "For a while, I didn't know you were Rhys Quarry's daughter." His brows dropped limply, shadowing his big eyes as they slowed. "For a while, I didn't know much of anything. I was very ill."

"But you're better now, right?"

"Thanks to Ankh's serum, but it won't last."

Ankh's serum. He was talking about the good doctor's simulated plasma, the one that both my vampire mother and my vampire boyfriend were taking so they wouldn't need to eat people. I shouldn't have been too surprised. My neighbor Don Moore had been taking it as well, and it was reversing his memory issues.

Ankh's Special Magic Blood Serum. It cures what ails you! You've never seen anything work like this, not even genuine Omega-rich snake oil. Why, it slices, it dices, it keeps you from forgetting your own name. Say goodbye to mindlessly snacking on friends and family like a zombie. Say hello to a Whole New You!

Harry was staring at me expectantly. He'd been saying something about his recovery, but my mind had wandered. It did that sometimes.

For lack of a better idea about how to proceed, I reached across the circulation desk counter and offered him my hand. "Consider this our formal introduction. Since you know my father, you must know all about me."

It was awkward to shake hands over the high counter, so Harry squeezed my fingertips in lieu of a full shake.

"And Rhys must have told you all about me," he said. "And what I can do."

"You might think that, but my father and I don't exactly..." I trailed off, aware of a person lingering nearby, moving in the holding-pattern sequence of small, insignificant movements that betrayed the person's true intention of eavesdropping.

It was the head librarian, Kathy Carmichael. Since she'd revealed her powers on the previous Monday, she'd been hovering and lingering more than usual.

Kathy wasn't a gossip hound, really. She wasn't any type of hound. She was a sprite, with an insanely long retractable tongue that would make an African anteater jealous. She was older than me, yet she acted like a pesky tag-along little sister who didn't want to be left out of any interesting developments, magical or otherwise.

I liked and respected Kathy, but I still didn't want her listening to my conversation with my father's associate. How could I get rid of my nosy boss? A non-magical solution came to me immediately.

I turned to the head librarian and said casually, "Frank cracked open that box of cinnamon buns. Isn't it about time for your break?"

She hooted excitedly, and skipped toward the break room.

Like shooting fish in a barrel.

I turned back to Harry Blackstone and said, "Thanks for helping my father this morning in the woods so I didn't have to."

"Oh, I didn't do much. By the time I got there, they'd already gotten away."

"They? Is there a whole pack of you folks?"

His brow wrinkled as he looked down at his keys on the counter. There was a fox pendant on the key chain, just like Frank had said.

"A whole pack of us folks," he said slowly, as though confused. "I, uh, it might be time for me to take my medicine." He looked up at me, then through me, his eyes dazing out of focus. "I get a little tired sometimes." He thumped his chest twice with his fist while clearing his throat. "Plus, I believe something in my diet is giving me heartburn. The peppers, maybe."

"Sorry to hear that. Can I get you something?"

"I wouldn't want to trouble you, but I'd kill for a cup of coffee."

"Coffee?" I'd been thinking of a glass of water, or an antacid tablet. We didn't provide patrons with coffee; we didn't even allow coffee outside the break room, because it smelled too good, and the aroma spread through the library faster than burned microwave popcorn.

I told Harry to take a seat over at the Information Services kiosk, and I'd join him in a moment, after I got clearance from the boss.

* * *

"This is the best coffee I've ever had," Harry Blackstone said. We were seated comfortably across from each other with a round table between us. We both had a mug full of fresh coffee. Kathy had authorized my extra break with the implication I'd share what I learned.

Harry's big, brown eyes were getting bigger with each sip. "So good," he said.

"The beans are from Dreamland," I said. There were two locations in Wisteria, and most residents were familiar with the local brand.

"Best coffee ever," he repeated.

"You wouldn't say that if you saw the cheap little brewer we use. It's actually a Frankensteined unit, made from other broken machines. The carafe is too small for the percolation unit, so we have a wedge under one side to change the angle of the drip to line up with the hole in the lid."

Harry let out another big laugh, like he had that morning when I'd tipped him off about our snoring trick. He smacked both of his knees.

"Your coffee pot sounds like a certain car I put together from a variety of sources." He gave me a knowing look. "I believe your father dubbed it Foxy Pumpkin."

"You made my car?"

He laughed again. "*Your* car? Rhys said he loaned it to you."

I snorted. "He didn't loan it to me. It's my car now. He's not getting it back. I love that car."

Harry grinned. "Hearing that makes me very happy. Do you know about all of the aftermarket modifications?" He leaned forward and spoke in a hushed tone. "I designed the system myself." He winked. "I'm sure you've noticed that the vehicle's fuel efficiency is not exactly average for the year and model."

He wasn't wrong about the efficiency. "I can't remember the last time I had to visit a gas station," I said. "Except to buy emergency late-night potato chips after the grocery store's closed. Speaking of healthy eating habits, how's that heartburn?"

He tapped his sternum once. "Much better now, thank you. I should stop eating those red peppers, but they taste so good, and my local supplier would be offended."

Just then, a pair of ladies from the knitting group emerged from the shelves near the Information Services kiosk. Both turned their heads and gave us a curious look as they walked past. One lady muttered to the other that it was "high time" we'd started serving coffee in the library.

I rolled my eyes. We loved the knitters, but they could be a bit territorial.

Harry said, "Thanks to that car of yours, I suppose you understand my life's work as well as anyone."

"Your life's work? You're some sort of... special mechanic?"

"An inventor," he said proudly.

"That's cool," I said. Most of the people I'd met who called themselves inventors were conspiracy nuts who invented new ways to use tinfoil.

Harry looked down, and his smile faded. "It's a shame I won't be able to finish my final project. Not unless..." He kept looking down, at the busy-patterned industrial carpet, and then at his socks. The hems of his pant legs had risen to mid-calf, thanks to the ultra-low seats at Information Services. His socks were argyle, with shades of purple and green.

"What is it, Harry? Can I help you with some research? The computer's right here." I waved to the unit we kept locked down on the table.

Without looking up, he said, "Zara, you may be the only person you can help me with my greatest work yet."

"Mm-hmm." I'd heard this line a few times at that very table. From the conspiracy nuts. I was starting to get a bad feeling about this conversation.

Harry said, "It's not really my area of expertise, but, based on my research, I believe you could—"

Just then, a warm breeze passed over us and fluttered some nearby magazines. A gust had come in with the opening of the front doors. Harry jerked his head up and craned his neck, looking at the library's entrance. I followed his gaze to find a pair of familiar people entering.

One was a pleasant sight: my boyfriend, Detective Bentley.

His companion was the last person I expected to see walking around freely: disgraced WPD administrator Persephone Rose.

What were those two up to?

I turned back to my new friend. "Harry, you were saying?"

His expression was frozen, his gaze locked on the newcomers.

"Harry?"

He placed both hands on the chair armrests and noisily hoisted himself upright. "I, uh, let's continue this chat some other time," he said, barely meeting my eyes.

Probably for the best, I thought.

He'd been about to ask me for a favor, by the sound of it. Normally I would have been eager to help a dying man, especially one as pleasant as Harry Blackstone, but given he was an associate of my father's, I had to be on guard. I had to take everything he said with a grain of salt. Was he even sick at all?

"Sure," I said lightly. "We can chat another time."

"I can help you with the car," he said, his big, brown eyes roving continuously, taking in everything. "I'll show you a few tricks."

"That would be great." I got to my feet and smoothed down the magazines that had rustled in the breeze of the door. "You know where to find me."

He pulled the folded hat from his pocket and put it on his head. With his black hair covered, he looked both older and more tired.

I picked up our empty coffee mugs. His had left a ring on the table. Kathy wouldn't like that. I swiped my hand over the ring, using magic to clean it. The spell wasn't one of my favorites. It didn't make spills disappear into some magical void, but instead transferred the offending matter to the bottom of the spellcaster's socks. I'd found that out the hard way after using it on a big spill of melted popcorn butter.

Harry paused, saying over his shoulder, "I wouldn't mind giving Foxy Pumpkin one last tune-up before..."

I tilted my head, waiting. Before what? Before he passed away from whatever illness he might or might not have? Or before the next phase of some scheme he'd concocted with my father?

He didn't finish. He gave me a quick nod, and then made a bee-line for the exit, avoiding eye contact with Bentley and Persephone.

As I watched him walk away, I imagined him changing form, and using a bushy black tail to wave goodbye. The mental image made me smile.

Now, let me make something perfectly clear.

In that particular moment, I did have questions about Harry Blackstone and his motivations, but one thing I was absolutely certain of was that the man was a shifter. Not just any shifter, but the same black fox I'd seen that morning in the forest.

I wasn't the only one who'd made that leap in logic. My coworker Frank had made the connection first, and with less information.

And then, when I'd spoken to Harry, he had seemingly confirmed this hypothesis. He had offered only the smallest hint otherwise by way of his bout of confusion, which I'd excused due to his illness.

Eventually, I would learn of my error and make corrections, but it would take a while. A whopping fifty-five days.

I would kick myself for not seeing it sooner. *Zara tries to be a smart witch who doesn't make assumptions.*

But for the moment, the pieces seemed to fit together, and, if anything, I was rather pleased with myself.

CHAPTER 5

The WPD duo had split by the time I finished talking to Harry.

Persephone Rose appeared to be lost. She probably didn't know what a library was. I offered her some helpful suggestions, and she busied herself looking over the new arrivals and staff picks.

I went over to Bentley, who coolly suggested we head upstairs to the children's reading area for some privacy. Except for visits by a few preschoolers, it was a quiet place on weekday mornings.

"But it's not *that* private," I said, waggling my eyebrows. "Not like the stacks."

"I wanted somewhere private to *talk*," he said.

"Right." I led the way upstairs.

We reached the storytime corner, and Bentley stopped in his tracks, transfixed by the new mural on the wall. And who could blame him? It was quite the mural.

"That is... quite the mural," Bentley said neutrally, as though fishing for my uninfluenced reaction.

"It sure is," I said, also neutrally, enjoying the drawn-out tension of Bentley's unsatisfied curiosity about my uninfluenced reaction. Having a boyfriend was fun.

A moment of silence passed as we faced the mural, holding our hands behind our backs like polite visitors at a museum.

The artwork depicted a terrified young woman in a red dress fleeing a giant beast of a wolf with an enormous head and glistening fangs. The rendering was so realistic and dynamic, it practically screamed.

Frank, Kathy, and I all had mixed feelings about the mural. It *was* an artistic masterpiece, and yet it was not exactly what one would call "appropriate for taxpayer-funded premises," especially in a zone designated for children.

"But why?" Bentley waved one hand at the slobbering wolf-beast. "How? Who did this?"

I smiled, enjoying his distress. "*Someone*, by which I mean *Frank Wonder*, thought it would be a good idea to allow Carrot to channel her creative energy into a Little Red Riding Hood mural."

"Carrot Greyson? The tattooist?"

"How many Carrots do you know?"

He frowned and walked along the wall, examining the details. Carrot Greyson had recently left her job at City Hall to open her own tattoo studio. She was a talented artist who didn't limit her canvas to human flesh. She was also working through some things. *Exorcising her personal demons*, one might say. Carrot didn't have the best taste in boyfriends. She'd been through some dark times that year. We all hoped the mural might turn things around for her, and that her next boyfriend might not be a murderer.

"But..." My own boyfriend—a good one, as far as I could tell—looked utterly mystified. "How is this Little Red Riding Hood? There's no cloak. No hood. The girl is just wearing a red dress."

"That's your main issue with the mural? The lack of a red hooded cloak? Not the fact that the wolf is drooling blood? Or that his glowing eyes follow you wherever you go? Or that the fangs and mouth are so detailed you can see the creature's gingivitis?"

He took a step back to observe the mural's full glory, and then shrugged. "I don't mind the realism. And it's accurate. The original fairy tales were quite violent compared to children's entertainment today."

"All true. And I'm all for it." I waved a hand emphatically. "Beheadings, rolling people down waterfalls inside knife-filled barrels, and all the juicy Medieval torture—minus the witch-burning stuff, of course—but this painting may be a teensy weensy bit ahead of its time." I brushed my fingertips over the textured paint near the wolf's extended claws. "Our last storytime session was an unmitigated disaster. Between Frank's dramatic reading style, and Carrot's mural, five kids wet their pants."

Bentley, who'd been about to seat himself on an upholstered stool, immediately reversed course and straightened up again.

I elaborated. "Five kids *that we know of*."

He nodded grimly and glanced around. At least we were alone in the area. The Big Bad Wolf had created a zone of privacy by scaring people away.

I remembered what we'd come there to discuss.

"What's up with your new partner?" I asked, thumbing in the direction of the stairs. "Is this some new WPD program, where they pair up the good employees with the ones who don't understand basic rules about security and privacy?"

"I told you last night. Rose was working undercover for the Department. She was authorized to send the photos to Krinkle through her work account. She's been cleared of all charges, and she's getting promoted. Don't you remember? I told you all about it last night."

"Oh." I lightly smacked my forehead. "I should have listened to the words coming out of your mouth when we were at the beach. I guess I didn't care about what your lips were doing when they weren't..." I took a step toward the detective, closing the distance between us. Out of the corner of my eye, I sensed the wolf on the mural watching and salivating. *Kissing me*, I finished in my head.

Bentley's cool, detached expression broke. A flash of guilty pleasure crossed his face. He swayed forward, closing the gap between us without moving his feet, as though his body was magnetically attracted to mine—which it was. In a deep growl, he said, "Zara." It was both a warning and an invitation.

I took a step back. "Don't you dare use your sexy voice on me." I flashed my eyes and whisper-yelled, "I'm at work!"

He swayed his body back and shook his head. "I should have phoned you with the news."

"What news? About your new partner? Wait. Is she your partner?" I'd been joking about the young woman being his partner, but now I feared my intuition had spoken through humor, as intuition often did.

"She is my partner now."

Ba dump dump, as the comedians say.

Bentley continued, "But that's not why I came here."

"Are you serious?" I waved at the stairs as though accusing them. "Does she even know about you-know-what?" It was a dumb question. If she worked undercover for the Department, she knew more than most people.

He locked his silver-eyed gaze on me. "She knows."

"Since when?"

"Since forever, Zara. She comes from an old family." *An old family* was a euphemism for supernatural bloodlines.

"What kind? She's not a witch, is she?" I snorted and pushed up the sleeves on my double layer of cardigans.

He said nothing.

I glared at him for withholding, but I understood. He couldn't say what she was. It was Persephone Rose's secret to share.

And yet, because she worked for the DWM—apparently, according to what I'd just learned—she had access to information on all the supernaturals in town, including me and my friends. She knew all about my private life, but I didn't know about hers.

What kind of last name was Rose, anyway? I didn't know anyone else in town by that name, so I couldn't even guess at her abilities. She could be a shifter, or a mage, or a sprite, or a gnome, or any number of things.

Since the DWM didn't trust witches—except when they needed a witch to do their dirty work—she probably wasn't a witch. That narrowed it down, but not by much.

What else did I know about the girl? Not much, except that I'd taken an immediate dislike to her. I had bristled at the first mention of her name, and her voice alone. I didn't like her one bit. That had to mean something, but what?

Bentley spoke, pulling me from my thoughts. "Ms. Rose would probably tell you everything herself, if you could manage to be civil to her for all of five seconds."

He was being so melodramatic. I'd been plenty civil to the young detective. Why, just moments earlier, I had thoughtfully steered her toward the new releases for reluctant readers, suggesting that the shorter books might be appropriate for someone at her reading level.

Bentley waved a hand. "But that's not why I'm here." He looked me dead in the eyes and said, "Zara, your father's been spotted in town."

"I know. I saw him this morning."

"You did?"

With a weary sigh, as though this were an everyday occurrence, I listed off my points on my fingers. "Saw him, spelled him, sent him on his way."

"You *spelled* him?"

To answer his question, I showed him. I conjured the form-locking bird in my palm, illuminated it specifically so Bentley could see it, then explained what had happened, including the part where Harry Blackstone had spoken to me briefly as Black Fox.

"Shifters aren't supposed to be psychic," Bentley said. "There's nothing in the resources about that."

"I've got news for you, my tall, dark, and handsome detective." I made air quotes. "*The resources* aren't exactly reliable. My Monster Manual says that a single line of pink Himalayan salt drawn across a doorway keeps out flying magical creatures, but all the salt in the world hasn't kept Ribbons from raiding my refrigerator. I understand that the definition of doorway may or may not apply to a refrigerator, but we have to understand that when those spells were first documented, things like refrigerators didn't exist. Maybe it's just me, but I feel like anything that's called a door has to fit into a doorway. That means cars have doorways and cupboards, too. The text is very clear about creatures not being able to pass the line of pink salt, and yet, all my orange juice was gone this morning. It was a new carton, too. He didn't even open the top! It looked untouched, but then I picked it up and nearly fell over backwards, because it was just an empty box. That was when I saw the two tell-tale fang holes on the bottom. He sucked it dry like some sort of..." I suddenly realized the word I'd been about to say, and stopped my tirade.

"Vampire," Bentley finished. "Ribbons sucked your orange juice dry like some sort of vampire."

"No offence," I said.

"None taken."

We stared at each other a moment.

In his very serious, professional tone, the vampire detective said, "I'm sorry to hear about your orange juice, ma'am. Would you like to press charges?"

I swatted him on the shoulder. "My point is that *the resources* don't get everything right. Some shifters might be psychic. Harry said his powers only worked with family members, so he's probably related to me somehow. He's a fox, and my father's a fox, and they're friends, so they've probably got a number of people in common, possibly family members. Harry might be my distant uncle." I rubbed my chin. "I wonder if he has a will." I shook my head. "That was dark. Forget I said it."

"What were you two talking about when I came in? He had a guilty look on his face when he saw me."

"He was trying to ask me for a favor."

Bentley raised an eyebrow. "Beware of new friends asking favors."

"I didn't fall off the turnip truck yesterday, Detective."

He pressed his lips together in that cute way of his.

I said, "We might trade favors sometime." I explained how Harry was familiar with my vehicle, and how he'd offered to give Foxy Pumpkin a tune-up.

"It's my fault for scaring him off this morning," Bentley said. "Before I knew about this town's secrets, he was one of the people I questioned about his family's connection with all the Wakeful businesses that disappeared a few decades back. He comes from a long line of inventors and mechanical engineers, though they weren't always called that." Bentley gave me a press-me-for-more look.

I batted my eyelashes. "Is that so? Tell me more."

"Arvus Blackstone claimed to have the formula for turning lead into gold."

I rolled my eyes. "That's easy. It's just three protons. Everyone knows that. The problem is that the energy input required to make the transformation exceeds the value of the gold. At current rates, anyway."

He gave me an amused look. "I know I shouldn't be surprised at what's in that librarian head of yours, and yet I am."

I beamed at him.

There was the swish-swish of corduroy pants, size small. A preschool-aged child had wandered into the reading nook. He looked up at Little Red Riding Hood with big eyes, whimpered, and ran away in terror.

"I should get going," Bentley said. "I just wanted to let you know about your father being in town, plus one other thing."

"Your new partner?"

He glanced down and kicked at a patch of stray glitter on the carpet, spreading it like a comet streak. "Something else," he said.

I didn't like the sound of his reluctance. "Now what?"

"My ex-wife," he said. "She's actually, technically..."

My stomach clenched. "What?"

"Still my wife," he said.

My legs were suddenly weak. I took a seat on one of the upholstered stools. It was safe enough; We'd had them all steam-cleaned following the storytime incident.

"It's just a formality," Bentley said. "Until I sign some paperwork."

I almost laughed. "Is that all?" I stood again. "For a minute there, I thought it was something serious."

He tugged at his ear, avoiding eye contact. "The thing about my wife is—"

"Don't," I said, cutting him off. "You might think I want to know all about her, but, believe me, I do not."

"I want to be completely transparent. There are things you should know."

"Do you have kids with her?"

"No."

"Do you own a charming Bed and Breakfast together? Or some other ongoing business?"

"What? No."

"Do you still..." *Love her?* "Share a pet? Maybe a goldfish, or a Bichon Frise? I know it seems weirdly specific, but I've noticed there are an awful lot of fluffy white dogs at the heart of pet custody disputes."

"No pets," he said. "No children, businesses, or pets."

"Then we're good," I said. "I don't need to know any more. Not even her name. For the purposes of future discussions, which I hope will be infrequent, she shall be referred to as X. The letter X."

He frowned.

"One more question," I said. "Does X live around here?"

"No."

I already knew that from our previous conversations, but figured it didn't hurt to make sure.

"Zara, the thing is..." His gaze flicked over to focus on something or someone behind me.

I turned to find Persephone Rose standing behind me, her hand partly covering her face as she nervously smoothed her thick, dark bangs. How long had she been standing there? The area was carpeted, but even so, I was surprised at how silent she'd been. I hadn't experienced someone sneaking up on me unnoticed in a long time. I sniffed the air between us. My nose wasn't nearly as sensitive as my fox shifter daughter's, but my sensory powers had all improved with witchhood. The young woman had no scent whatsoever that I could detect. She was as scentless as Boa's fur after a nap in the sun.

"You don't smell," I said to her. "What are you?"

Her big, brown eyes widened, and a deep blush spread across her whole face. Her jaw dropped and she half-stammered, half-croaked, "Wh-a-a-?"

I prepared to cast a bluffing spell. She would tell me, if I applied a little pressure. She didn't strike me as the toughest walnut to crack.

But then Bentley placed a warm hand on my shoulder and murmured, "Don't."

I muttered back at him, "I wasn't going to do anything."

He gave me the look that said he knew better.

I nodded and let the magic tingling inside me dissipate. *Zara tries to be a good witch. A patient witch.*

Zara doesn't crack people like walnuts unless they really deserve it.

Persephone Rose apologized for interrupting our conversation, and gave her new partner an update on an ongoing case.

Bentley thanked her, gave me a quick peck on the cheek goodbye, and told me to call him immediately if my father turned up again.

Persephone did that thing where she pretended to not be interested in our conversation, which only made it more obvious she was dying to know more. So obvious. Like I said, not the toughest walnut.

* * *

At lunch time, right when Charlize was due to stop by, I suddenly received a vision. Only I didn't realize it was a vision at first. I was updating the database with some new items, and the keyboard melted under my fingers. As I stared down in horror, the computer monitor melted. The acrid smell of burning plastic made my eyes water. Before I could cast a single spell, everything around me melted. Every book and shelf in the library. Melted. Into... rivers of lava?

Then I blinked, and everything was back to normal.

That was odd.

I turn to ask Kathy if she'd noticed anything unusual; but then, everything melted again.

This time it was different. Instead of one long melt, there were only two short bursts—like the way someone might honk a horn if they were waiting outside to pick you up.

Charlize. The gorgon was there for our lunch date, and that was her special "honk."

Life was never dull when you had supernatural friends.

CHAPTER 6

I slid into the passenger seat of the Beetle named Bugsy. Fast food bags and wrappers crumpled under my shoes. I could be messy, too, but the level of chaos inside Bugsy was alarming. The usual flotsam and jetsam that lived in the back seat of the gorgon's vehicle had expanded like some sort of ecological disaster.

Under my butt, something made a whoopee cushion sound, and no, it wasn't my bum. Or even a whoopee cushion. I reached underneath my buttocks and pulled out a flattened cream puff. I set the mangled pastry into the debris forming a nest by my feet, and used magic to transfer the stain from my skirt to the bottom of my socks.

Charlize, oblivious to my issue with the state of her vehicle, said, "How'd you like my special honk?"

Her special honk? I struggled to find the words. "Like it? I thought the world was ending."

"It's good, right?"

"If you mean good as in powerful, then yes."

"You weren't impressed?"

"Oh, I was impressed. But next time you come pick me up, I'd rather you honk the car horn. Forget what I said about not honking."

"Yes, ma'am." She hit the gas and gave me a soldier's salute while she used one elbow to steer the car. The tires spun, kicking up loose gravel, as she pulled into traffic without so much as a shoulder check. Behind us, a big black truck honked as the driver slammed on the brakes to avoid rear-ending us.

"Charlize!" I stared at her in horror. The debris in the back seat rustled as it slid around, and something living chittered in displeasure. I didn't dare look.

"What?" She kept facing ahead as she chewed on two fingernails at the same time—one from each hand—while continuing to steer with her elbows. Her other, visible nails were ragged. Had she always been a nail biter? I couldn't remember the condition of her nails before. I wasn't a manicure sort of gal, so it wasn't a thing I paid much attention to.

I asked, "Is everything okay? You look a bit..."

I stared at her as I struggled to finish the question. The blonde gorgon's usually-pretty ringlets hung limply, except for a patch near the back of her head, which was on its way to becoming a matted clump, or a single dreadlock. Her blue eyes were framed by purple shadows. She was wearing one of her favorite silver jumpsuits, but it was wrinkled and stained.

She looked like garbage. Like stewed garbage on a stale cracker.

I said delicately, "You look like they've been working you too hard at the Department."

She said nothing as she cut off another driver.

I asked, "Is something big going on?"

"Something big?" She spat out her words. "I wouldn't know if there was. I'm on leave." The magical snakes within the gorgon's hair stirred and hissed at me half-heartedly. Charlize scoffed and spat out more words. "Management felt that it would be in everyone's interest for me to go on leave for a while. Management felt that some time away from the office would be good for me."

"Because of what happened with your computer program?" I was a touch hazy on the details about Codex, but I'd gotten the gist through my usual sources.

Charlize snorted. "First, they hail you as a genius. They give you unlimited resources. The sky's the limit! Literally. They put a sky ceiling in your office." She laughed bitterly.

"It's a nice sky ceiling," I said.

"When you're their darling, their whiz kid, everything's peachy keen. Until one little thing goes slightly wrong. Then you're the pariah. Or worse. You're nobody." She muttered what felt like swear words, but in an ancient language I didn't speak. Her hair snakes snapped at each other, infighting and leaving red marks on her pale cheeks.

What I should have said was nothing. But because we were good friends now, and I figured she needed the perspective only a good friend could provide, I didn't say nothing.

I said, "Charlize, your crazy computer program summoned an ancient goddess who was going to bring on the apocalypse so she could remake humanity and the world the way she wanted it. I wouldn't call that *one little thing going slightly wrong*."

The blonde with the matted, snake-filled hair pressed her mouth into a grim line, hit the gas, and sped through an intersection's red light. More vehicles honked.

Zara delivers the tough love because she's a good friend. However, Zara could be less about the tough and more about the love.

"So you're taking some time off," I said in a gentler tone. "Time off can be nice. You can spend more time with Jordan Junior. Last night at Chet's house, I noticed he's growing like a weed." Or like something far more deadly than a weed. "Where is Chet, anyway? Why do you have his phone?"

"I don't have his phone. We had his number forwarded to mine. As for where he is, he's up there." She pulled one chewed, red fingertip from her mouth and pointed upward through the windshield at the sky.

In heaven? Dead? No. My body turned cold and heavy, as though I was turning into one of Charlize's granite statues. Chet Moore couldn't be dead. I'd seen him last night and he'd been fine. Happy, even. Really happy. Perhaps I'd hallucinated the whole thing.

My words came out squeaky. "He's up where, exactly?"

"Flying to London," Charlize said. "In a plane. Not as a bird or anything." She laughed hollowly. "He's still just a wolf."

"Oh." I let out a breath I hadn't realize I was holding. "I didn't know he had a trip today. Is it Department business, or is he scouting a place for the family to live?"

"He's gone, Zara." She jerked upright and took a break from punching the gas to hit the brakes.

"Gone?" I braced my palms on the dash to keep from flying through the windshield as we screeched to a halt. I'd forgotten to buckle my seat belt when I'd climbed into Bugsy, and the sticky pastries that were still under my butt were not effective at holding me in place. Not even the jam tarts.

"Their stuff is getting packed up by the movers today," Charlize said with a note of bitterness. "The four of them left this morning with a couple of suitcases. Just like that. 'See ya later, alligator!' Lucky me, I get to hang out at the house all day and supervise the movers because I have literally nothing else going on."

I couldn't imagine the Moore house without its people. "Grampa Don is gone? And Corvin?"

"They're all gone." Another hollow chuckle. "Gone for good, gone for bad, who knows."

My insides felt as cavernous as the gorgon's laugh. "But they didn't say anything last night at the barbecue.

They said they would be moving before the new school year started, but... If I had known, I wouldn't have ducked out early. I would have stayed and said goodbye. I would have..."

I trailed off, and in the silence, I completely understood.

"Yup," Charlize said dryly.

"I would have made leaving more difficult," I said.

We screeched to a halt in front of a Mexican restaurant.

My body, now motionless after the roller coaster ride, felt heavier than ever.

The Moores were gone.

CHAPTER 7

Inside the restaurant, Charlize made the switch from chewing on her abused fingernails to chewing on the "bottomless" nacho chips the Mexican restaurant offered.

I cast the sound bubble for privacy. With a little prodding, she went into more detail about exactly what happened with her creation, the Artificial Intelligence known as Codex. I reviewed my experience with the goddess Mahra. Charlize kept yawning. She was slightly more interested in hearing about Bentley's efforts to make sure everything on my body was working properly, but even then, she wasn't terribly interested.

She kept looking up at the television screen that was mounted on the wall in between the giant sombreros.

I switched topics, telling her instead about encountering my father that morning.

Charlize said, "You know, Zara, your father isn't a bad guy."

"I never said he was. But he does bad things."

"Only for good reasons. He's been secretly working for the DWM for years."

I sat back in my chair, feeling lighter. I had figured as much, but it was sobering to have it confirmed.

Charlize grabbed a fistful of nachos, destroyed them in no time, and signaled the waiter to bring more as she continued. "Rhys was only operating as a go-between on Project Buttercup because Tansy Wick didn't trust the DWM. She was a paranoid woman."

"Was she? Really? Paranoid?"

Charlize guffawed as she leaned back and grabbed a basket of nachos from a waiter who'd been heading toward a different table. The waiter took one look at her and hurried back to the kitchen to get more.

I went on. "You have to admit, the lines between the good guys and the bad guys are pretty hazy."

"She set her dogs loose on your father. She could have killed him. Who's the bad person in this scenario? From where I'm sitting, it looks like it's the lady who knowingly tried to kill a shifter."

I looked away. "Yeah, well, her karma came due in the end, didn't it?"

Charlize laughed. "Karma. That's cute. You witches are so fascinating, with your archaic, demonic superstitions."

"Whatever." I waved both hands to show I was about finished with the topic of conversation. I didn't even care if she knew anything about what business my father had in town.

Charlize said, "Good guy or not, your father didn't leave you for dead. He was smart enough to know he was in over his head. He called me, which was why I was there to save your life."

"Thanks again for killing me and unkilling me."

"No prob." She blinked, then slowly brought her thumbnail to her lips. She bit the white of the nail away, and it didn't grow back. I was fascinated. Magic certainly had a mind of its own. The gorgon could spontaneously heal from injuries. So why did she have chewed-up fingernails and now chapped lips, too? Was she willfully shutting down her healing powers, or did fingernails have some magical exemption?

She asked, "Did Rhys say why he was in town?"

"I told you. He didn't say anything. I thought you'd know."

She shrugged. Either she didn't know, or wasn't authorized to tell me.

I tried to engage her in conversation about other topics, but she kept looking at the TV on the wall.

Charlize interrupted me mid-sentence, as though I was just background noise, and said, "Her life must be perfect." She was looking at the TV.

"Who?" I didn't turn to look.

"Her." The gorgon narrowed her eyes. The air crackled with energy, and her blue eyes lost their blue, turning a shade of granite.

I waved my hand in front of her face. "Easy now," I said. "Don't crack that screen with your gorgon death ray."

She kept staring at the image on the television.

I turned and followed her gaze. The woman on TV was a famous actress named Larissa Lang. She was a Chinese-Canadian woman who'd gotten her start in Hollywood playing a teenager on the TV comedy-drama series *Wicked Wives*. I'd been a huge fan of both her and the show as a teenager. I'd been watching a double-length pre-finale episode the night I went into labor with Zoey.

My aunt, who knew *an awful lot* about *Wicked Wives* for someone who claimed to have never watched it regularly, suspected the series had actual witches on the writing staff. At the very least, they had supernaturals consulting. The details about the magic system were too accurate to be mere coincidence. Plus there was the giant red flag that the four main characters were named after the Four Eves: Quenya, the warrior queen; Dinara, the thinker; Amora, the lover; and last but far from least, Mahra, the mother and destroyer.

On the screen, Larissa Lang laughed at some unseen interviewer's question. I couldn't hear what she was saying due to the TV being muted, but suddenly I wanted to know what the segment was about.

I could have cast a spell to boost my ability to read lips, but I would need a warm pebble from a hen's nest, and hen's nests were never handy when you needed them. It was much easier for me to use simple telekinesis to press the volume button.

The volume came up as Larissa Lang said, "And that's exactly why I'm so excited about the remake! Now that Mahra's daughter Mahrissa is all grown up with children of her own, it's going to be so fascinating to see how the characters have evolved."

Larissa Lang played Mahrissa. The similar names led to some continuity errors within the show, where the character was occasionally called by the actress's name and the editors missed it.

The screen cut to the interviewer. He was dimple-chinned and evidently smitten with Larissa Lang, judging by the puppy-dog eyes he was making at her.

He asked, "What about romance? At the end of the first series, fans got quite the cliffhanger. Your character was having a baby, but it wasn't clear with whom."

Larissa fluttered her thick, dark eyelashes. "Did you have anyone specific in mind?"

The dimple-chinned man's cheeks flushed under his on-camera makeup as he let out a laugh.

Larissa's focus shifted toward the camera, and she looked directly at the camera lens. It felt like she was looking at me. Darkness shadowed her eyes. The curve of her flirty smile drooped. I knew she was facing a camera lens, and not seeing little ol' me, sitting under a piñata-strung ceiling in a Mexican restaurant, but I felt the connection anyway. Her eyes drooped, as though she was suddenly overwhelmed with sadness and regret. Or because the dark purple eye shadow weighed too much.

She's exhausted, I thought. The woman was on a press junket, and that had to be grueling. The show was currently in production. In the midst of a hectic shooting schedule, she had to sit on a stool in a hotel room and answer the same five questions from every entertainment reporter in the city.

I felt bad for her, but not for more than a few seconds. Any sympathy I had for the woman's exhaustion was quickly overridden by my own selfish desires. She was on the TV screen for one reason only, and it was a good one.

I turned to Charlize and said breathlessly, "They're actually rebooting *Wicked Wives*? I have not been informed about this development! What is the point of having all these powers and connections of ours if we don't receive updates about important, life-changing news?"

Charlize visibly relaxed, and let out the first chuckle of the day that wasn't darkly ironic.

The sound of a commercial for yogurt blasted on. I muted the TV volume before the restaurant staff came to investigate the noise competing with the contemporary Mariachi music.

"You make a good point about our intel sources," she said. "Who cares about the monster of the week?" She thrust one chewed finger in the direction at the TV. "*This* is *something*."

"It's not nothing."

"We have to watch the premiere together."

"We have to," I agreed.

"With Chloe." Chloe was her sister, also a gorgon. Chloe was a baker, and had probably lovingly baked the pastries that were now trash inside Bugsy or stuck to the bottoms of my socks.

"All three of us will watch the premiere," I said. I liked the ring of that.

"We'll have wine?"

Was that an actual question? I held out a hand and gave her a perplexed look. "We're not going to *not* have wine."

She wrinkled her nose. "I wish we didn't have to wait. It's not going to start airing for two months." She glared at the screen. I turned and saw that she was right. According to the graphics on the screen, the premiere of the *Wicked Wives* reboot wasn't scheduled to run until a few days before Halloween. It was good marketing for the network to hold back a show about witches until Halloween, but that didn't make it any less annoying.

I groaned. "What about that screening program you guys have at the Department? Where you get the movies before they come out so you can make sure the magic isn't too accurate?" I knew about the boxes because my neighbor, Ishmael Greyson, had been in possession of one, back when his head had still been attached to his body.

The gorgon slumped in her chair. "I'm on leave, remember? I can't get access to *anything*."

"That's not fair. I can understand why you'd be punished, but what about me? I didn't do anything wrong. Now I have to wait and watch the premiere with all *the regular people*." I shook an accusing finger her way. "You're the one whose baby turned out evil. Why should I have to suffer?"

Charlize gasped in mock outrage and tossed a nacho chip at me.

I caught the chip and ate it while I enjoyed the improvement in the gorgon's mood. It wouldn't last long, and she'd be back to chewing her fingers before our entrees arrived, but at least we had a girls' night to look forward to. And all those plot twists!

What I couldn't have known then was the plot twist that actress Larissa Lang had in store. The one that was just for me.

CHAPTER 8

I got home just as a 1986 Nissan 300ZX, custom-painted orange, pulled up to the curb. Neighbors walking their dogs all turned their heads to admire the classic vehicle. We didn't call the car Foxy Pumpkin for nothing!

My sixteen-year-old daughter hopped out of the driver's side, flung back her red hair, and ran to give me a hug right there on the sidewalk.

"Fancy meeting you here," I joked as she squeezed me tight. When she didn't release me from the hug, I asked, "Rough day at the museum?" She was working at the town's museum for the summer, in a temporary position that would end when high school started in the fall.

"Not too rough," she said. "More like a really *long* day."

"Tell me about it," I joked.

My day had started with the security wards being triggered at the house. Then I'd had a double fox encounter in the woods, a surprise visit at work from a sexy vampire and his new partner, followed by lunch with an angry gorgon. Then things really blew up in the afternoon. The head librarian received news of an impending budget cut, via a phone call from her old nemesis Vincent Wick. The minute she ended the call, Kathy flew into the worst tantrum I'd seen yet. Worse than when she had to spend her whole lunch break waiting in line at the bank. And even worse than the time some hacker set the public computers to play the Mexican Hat Dance at full volume randomly throughout the day for a whole week.

Frank and I had to use magic to subdue Kathy and put her in the Grumpy Corner for a timeout. She muttered about budgets and Vincent Wick while demolishing nine cinnamon buns from a distance of ten feet, thanks to her prehensile tongue. After an hour, she'd calmed enough to report back to work, albeit with a crooked, strained expression on her face. She was helping a patron named Helen Highbury with something, and handling it remarkably well—Helen was a known complainer—when suddenly a half-dozen of the public computers began playing the Mexican Hat Dance.

Frank ran interference, getting Helen Highbury clear of Kathy's blast radius, while I subdued her with three types of calming spells.

It had been quite the day.

Zoey, still hugging me, said, "I should have taken a job somewhere calm and peaceful, like the library."

I practically chortled at the irony.

She finally released me from the hug, and we walked up to the house.

She said, "Thanks for letting me take Foxy Pumpkin today."

"No problem." She could take the bus to her job, but, due to the universal cruelty of bus schedules, the bus tended to drop her off exactly one minute late for her shift, which didn't work for my punctual daughter.

I said, "It was a good thing I walked into work this morning, anyway." I paused to take in enough breath to finish with a breezy tone. "I happened to bump into your grandfather."

"Pawpaw?" She squealed and clapped her hands. When it came to the man she lovingly called Pawpaw while he called her Zozo, my sophisticated teenager lost all her cool.

"Don't get too excited." I opened the front door using magic instead of my key. "He's probably here on some kind of business. Charlize doesn't know what he's up to, but I'm sure it's something secret. You might not see him this time around."

"Is that what he told you?"

"Um. He didn't actually say anything. He was in fox form, and he, um, didn't shift."

We were inside the cool, dark house. She flicked on the light and leaned back against the closed door, her hazel eyes wide with concern. "Why? Was he hurt?"

"He's fine." I ruffled her hair.

She swatted my hand away. "Why didn't he change and talk to you? Is he afraid of you?"

"I sure hope so. He'd better be."

She put her hands on her hips and frowned. "What did you do?"

Busted. "I kinda, sorta cast a form-locking spell on him."

Her eyes bulged and her arms went limp at her sides. "You did not."

We were still in the entryway, and the foyer space felt claustrophobic. I kicked off my shoes and traded them for a pair of soft-soled ballerina flats I used as house slippers. I could do the Shoe Dance without looking, but I kept my eyes down to avoid the accusatory look my daughter was shooting at me.

Finally, I waved my fingers like a white flag. "I know, I know," I said. "Frank already prosecuted me on behalf of all shifters everywhere when I told him."

She snorted and muttered, "A form-locking spell. Poor Pawpaw."

Poor Pawpaw? I straightened up and gave her a look of my own. The wise, motherly one. While she did have a point about my breach of supernatural etiquette, there had been a valid reason for it.

"Your grandfather is a dangerous influence," I said. "Have you forgotten what he did to us? Maybe we need to get your brain checked. I know that *my* brain is working, because I sure haven't forgotten." *Or forgiven.*

"But we were okay, Mom. It all worked out." Her eyes glistened. Her lower lip trembled slightly. We were standing so close, I could almost feel the raw teenaged emotions radiating at me. She'd had a long day, and her mother had only comforted her for as long as it took to walk from the sidewalk to the house before delivering news that made the day worse. And it wouldn't get better for a while. I still had to tell her about the Moores being gone.

"You're right," I said softly. "We were okay, and it did all work out. You came into your powers, and you saved the day."

I reached out and tucked a strand of her red hair behind her ear. She didn't swat me away.

"There's more," I said. "Charlize told me some other stuff. Let's go to the kitchen and talk."

* * *

When I was done relaying what I'd learned about my father, Zoey smiled and said, "I knew it."

"You did not."

"Pawpaw is one of the good guys."

I made a face. People being called "the good guys" was one of my pet peeves, like when salespeople say "trust me," or when anyone says "calm down."

The floorboard squeaked as another member of the family entered the kitchen.

It was Boa, the fluffy cat who was the manufacturer of all the white hairs that now decorated every single thing I owned, wore, or ate. She looked up and meowed at us. The meow could be interpreted as "hello," or as "I see that you have been home for more than thirty seconds, and yet you have not begun preparations of my evening meal, so what is the deal with that?"

Zoey scooped up the fluffball and apologized for the slow service while I prepared her meal.

We were new at being cat owners—or cat *parents*, as some people would say, although neither term really explained the employer/employee nature of the relationship—but I had learned that begging forgiveness while preparing a cat's meal was not uncommon.

The food smelled terrible to my nostrils, but the cat meowed with excitement. She knocked the dish from my hand as I was setting it down. I used magic to catch the plate. It's never fun cleaning up a broken dish, but it's worse when there's an agitated cat watching with the how-could-you eyes.

The plate landed safely, and Boa happily munched away on the food.

Over the rhythmic sound of the dish rattling on the floor, I told Zoey about my day, including my walk that morning, and meeting the black fox in the woods.

"I knew it," she said, for the second time.

"You did not," I said again. "You're a smart kid, but you don't know *everything*."

"A black fox? That makes perfect sense. I knew I smelled another shifter around the house. Corvin did, too. We agreed it was a fox, but not Pawpaw."

"You smelled this shifter around the house?" This worried me. Harry Blackstone seemed like a nice enough man, but if he'd been skulking around the house, that changed things.

She shrugged. "Not just around the house, but everywhere. When there's a new smell in town, you notice, even if you can't put your finger on what it is, exactly. You wouldn't understand. It's a shifter thing."

"No, I get it. You have a feeling for each other, like an extra sense."

She glanced in the direction of the Moore house. "That's funny," she said. "Speaking of that sense, I can't sense Corvin."

She couldn't sense Corvin, because he was gone. He'd left the country. Without a last goodbye.

My stomach clenched, and not just from the dank smell coming from Boa's cat food.

This was the conversation that I'd been dreading ever since I'd learned the news. I had to break it to my daughter that spooky little Corvin Moore, who'd become like a kid brother to her, was gone for good.

She already knew about the family's plans, but she had assumed, like I had, that we had until the end of summer.

I told her.

She... did not take the news well. After a long day of scraping gum off the undersides of benches at the museum, Zoey was in no mood to hear about a friend abandoning her. But who would take such a thing well?

I bit my tongue and let her process the information.

Her process included shooting the proverbial messenger, me. She blamed us for their abrupt departure, but mostly me. I took the flack for a while, because mothers were nothing if not resilient to a bit of undeserved flack, but eventually I had to point out that Dr. Bob was the guilty party to blame. He was the one who had imprisoned Chessa and soured her on the whole town. He'd started everything. Plus he was dead, and why not blame the dead guy?

"I'm sorry," Zoey said, wiping her cheeks. "I shouldn't take it out on you. I know it's not your fault, but I feel so sad, and you're the only one here."

"It's hard to lose someone," I said.

"Life sucks," she said.

Her sniffling slowed.

After a moment, I asked, "Are you ready to be cheered up, or do you want to sulk for a while longer?"

She put one finger to the corner of her mouth. "I don't know."

"If you're ready to be cheered up, I do have some amazing, wonderful news," I said.

The redness in her eyes disappeared instantly.

"They're rebooting *Wicked Wives*."

She rolled her eyes. "That show is so old, Mom. It went off the air when I was a baby. Why would you think that would cheer me up?"

"It's a show about witches."

She stared at me like I'd just started eating Boa's dank-smelling cat food.

"Oh," I said, picking up a clue from the passing Clue Train. "You're still lacking in cheer because the show is about witches, not shifters. At least there's magic. And a few shifters. I remember some wolf and cat shifters."

She raised her eyebrows higher.

"Oh," I said again, as the Clue Train passed in the other direction. "Now I remember. The shifters on the show were all villains and monsters."

"Yeah," she said acidly. "Enjoy your cool show, Mom."

"Things might be different this time around with the reboot," I said. "The world is changing. It has already changed so much in the last sixteen years. Time sure flies. It seems like it was only yesterday when you waltzed out of my womb, shook hands with the taxi driver who delivered you, and corrected my pronunciation of the name of the hospital we didn't make it to."

She stared at me like I had just grown a prehensile sprite tongue and was wagging it around.

Bad timing, I thought. Some days she enjoyed the retelling of her birth. Today was not one of those days.

Just then, the doorbell rang.

"Doorbell," I said.

"Doorbell," my daughter agreed.

"Did I order a bunch of pizzas and forget? That doesn't sound like me. The forgetting part, that is."

"It's not pizza," Zoey said, heading toward the front door. "Mr. Caine is here."

Mr. Caine, as in Archer Caine, her genie father.

"Wait," I said. "You're still calling him Mr. Caine?"

"Would you rather I called him Dad?" She paused on her way to the door, looked at me, and wrinkled her nose. "Or *Daddy*?"

I shuddered. "Mr. Caine it is."

CHAPTER 9

It was quickly explained to me that Archer Caine was there to take my daughter out for dinner.

The two had met for an official father-daughter lunch less than a week earlier, and already another visit was happening? When I'd given my daughter my blessing to see the man, I figured they would take their time getting to know each other. This new weekly date thing was a surprise to me.

But what did I know? I'd grown up seeing my father once a year. My perspective on paternal involvement wasn't exactly normal. Also, my own father wasn't a genie who'd been trapped in a metaphorical bottle for most of my first sixteen years.

The three of us stood chatting on the front porch.

"Great weather," Archer said, ruffling the dark brown hair he'd cloned for himself from Chet Moore.

"For now," I said. "I hear it rains a lot in September."

"I've heard that, too," he said. "The whole month."

"People like to exaggerate about the weather," I said.

"They sure do."

"People like to exaggerate about everything," I said knowingly.

"Such as?"

"Oh, the usual." I looked around for a change of topic. The wisteria vines lining the porch were particularly lovely in the evening light.

"Plans for the weekend?"

"Laundry," I said.

"Laundry. Is that the thing where you apply water to old clothes instead of buying new ones?"

I snorted. "You weren't out of circulation *that* long."

He grinned at me. "And you haven't lost *all* of your sense of humor."

I shook my head, then we both turned to Zoey. She was in charge of ending this exchange.

Zoey said, "Oh! Wait here. I need to run back to my room for something." She asked me, "Is it okay if I show Mr. Caine some old photos?" We had a few shoeboxes full of pictures from before we'd fully switched to digital.

"Perfectly okay," I said. "But not any of the ones where I'm wearing a corset."

"How about the Halloween ones?"

"*Especially* not the Halloween ones," I said.

Zoey darted back through the front door, pausing to say, "I'll just be a few minutes."

"Take your time," Archer said.

"Hurry back," I said.

Zoey scowled at me and mouthed the words *be nice*.

Once she was gone, Archer raised an eyebrow at me and said, "You have to be nice to me. Zoey's orders."

"I'm always nice."

"Plans for the weekend?" Archer asked.

"Laundry. We covered that already. And you?"

"I'm thinking about joining a bowling league. You should, too."

"Hah! That'll be the day."

I looked down and kicked a lumpy pebble. It stuck in the crack between the porch's wooden floorboards. I tried to kick it back out again without using magic. It just dug itself in deeper. When I finally looked up again at my fellow parent, he was grinning at me.

His grin rubbed me the wrong way. Or maybe it was his face.

When Archer Caine had gotten himself back into the physical world, he'd cloned a body using Chet Moore. That meant he had Chet's body and face, as though the two were identical twins. It had been confusing at first, but the fact that Archer was usually grinning and looking pleased about life made it easy to tell them apart. Chet had always looked uncomfortable. Perpetually awkward. Like someone who had no idea how he'd gotten to where he was, and desperately wanted to be anywhere else.

Whatever he was doing in London at that moment, I imagined Chet frowning.

Archer, however, was lazily leaning against my porch post as though he owned the Red Witch House and I was the visitor.

I kicked the pebble deeper into the floorboards, then cast the form-locking spell in my hand as a sort of nervous tic. Charlize bit her fingernails; I cast glowing birds.

"That's pretty," Archer said. "It's like a steadfast spell, but for living forms?"

"You can see this?" I released the bird. It fluttered up from my hand and winged toward the tree branches before dissipating.

Archer's gaze followed the bird the whole way. He could see it.

His gaze flicked to the open front door, then back to me.

"Zoey's a great kid," he said.

"Yes. She is."

"A great kid," he repeated.

"And she'd better stay that way," I warned. My capacity for small talk had been exceeded, and the words started flowing. "You might think she's all grown up, because she has a driver's license and she's wearing the clothes of an adult woman, but she's barely sixteen. I'm sure it's hilarious for you to flirt with waitresses in front of her, Mr. Caine, and joke about getting her a new stepmom, but you have to remember there's a part of her that's still a child, and children are impressionable, like damp clay. You might forget this, and say one dumb thing as a joke, a throw-away comment, and they'll hold it inside. They'll stew on it, and stew on it some more, and then one day, out of the blue, three years later, they'll toss your dumb throw-away comment back in your face. You'll find out they've been hurting over it the whole time. Then you'll think back over all the many, many, many careless things you've said over the years and wonder how badly you've—"

His fingers were touching my cheek. He'd closed the distance between us, and I hadn't even seen it. Not even a blur. He'd been leaning on the porch post and now he was touching my face. He seemed to move like a vampire, but he wasn't a vampire, and he didn't move that fast. He'd frozen me, stuck me in time, while he'd snuck up on me at regular speed.

"Don't!" I jumped back, pulling free of his caress. I flicked both hands, tossing a Day Ruining zap at his center of mass.

He should have sizzled, or at least yelped.

Instead, he effortlessly caught my blue plasma in his hand. He made a fist, and when he opened his hand again, he was holding a sparkling glass marble.

Archer Caine had created mass from pure energy. Without batting an eyelash. The books hadn't said anything about genies doing that.

"Zara, I didn't mean to scare you," he said, his voice strong and powerful despite being quiet.

"Scare me? You didn't scare me. You jumped out at me like a maniac, and you got yourself a warning, fair and square. The next time, I won't go easy." I lifted my chin.

"Consider this your first and last warning. Don't freeze me and sneak up on me, and don't you dare touch me. Never again."

"But I just—"

I waved my hand for him to zip it. "And don't you ever, ever, ever touch my daughter. If you harm one single hair on her head, so help me, you will never see her again."

He gave me a hurt look, his pretty face crumpling.

I wondered if I might be overreacting. There's nothing quite like someone with a pretty face giving you a hurt look to make you feel like you might be the crazy person in the equation.

I said nothing. I wasn't going to apologize for being a mother.

After a moment, he said, "You've changed."

"Since the castle? No, I haven't changed one bit. When I met you, I thought you were someone else. I thought you were Chet, or his long-lost brother." My chin had been retreating, so I lifted it again to show I meant what I said. "Don't ever lie to me again."

Gently, he said, "I mean you've changed since we were kids. Don't you remember how it was?" He reached for my face again, but then wisely pulled his hand back and tucked it in his pocket. "Of course you don't remember," he said, looking down and shuffling his feet. "It's been a lot longer for you than for me."

I said nothing. Where was Zoey? How long did it take a person to grab a couple shoeboxes full of pictures?

Archer asked, "Do you remember the Ferris wheel?"

I answered quickly. "No."

As the word came out of my mouth, it became a lie after the fact. I did remember the Ferris wheel. The pressure of pushing up through the air on the great machine. The shift and sudden weightlessness at the peak. The airy sensation of floating down. I remembered the scent of frying donuts, generator exhaust, and kicked-up dust. I remembered the laughter over the roar of all the machinery.

"I tried to meet you that night," he said. "I really tried."

I pressed my lips together and tried not to remember. The cotton candy. The warm and moisture of his palm in mine. The feeling of cool water on bare legs.

"But you didn't try hard enough," I said. "I waited, and you never came."

"Oh, Zara. You must know why. You must have figured it out by now."

You didn't want me, I thought. "Yeah, I know," I said. "Whatever. The past is the past."

His green eyes were locked on mine, unwavering. Behind his head, the wisteria leaves fluttered and filtered the sun. And then the leaves were gone, and there were only his eyes.

He said, "The only reason I didn't meet you that night by the Ferris wheel was because my deranged sister broke me down and bottled me. I was primordial goo. That's why I didn't meet you. You must know I never meant to leave you waiting."

But I had been left waiting. And nothing he could say would change that.

"You should have warned me," I said. "About what you were."

He took a step back, but his eyes still blocked out the rest of the world. "How could I? I didn't even know what I was. I hadn't grown into my memories from my previous lives. Being with you was helping me break through, but I didn't understand what was happening with me."

I squinted at him. "You know what's weird? I can't remember what your face looked like back then." His hair had been fair, I thought, but that part of my memory was blurry now, messed up by my new memories. His old name had similarly been lost. My memory for everything else was excellent, so I knew his genie magic was to blame.

He shook his head slowly, ruefully. "If I'd known then what I know now, I would have run screaming from the woman I knew as Crazy Aunt Morganna. I would have met you by the Ferris wheel that night, and we would have run away together like you wanted to."

I almost smiled. "Like *I* wanted to? I believe running away together was *your* idea."

He smirked. The tension between us had changed, and he was pleased.

I tried to summon my rage again, but it was gone. I didn't hate the man who'd fathered my daughter. Hating him was pointless.

He said, "After all this time, I still feel flattered that you wanted to run away with me."

I snorted. " My interest in you had nothing to do with you. I would have run away with anyone who had a car."

"You mean that Nate guy?"

"Nate?" I smacked my forehead. "Why didn't I think of that? My mother would have had a fit. She would have killed him."

At the mention of my mother, Archer stepped back.

"Your mother," he said hoarsely, rubbing his neck where she'd sunk her vampire fangs into him.

Seeing the genie cower at the mention of my mother put a big, proud smile on my face.

"Let that be a lesson to you," I said breezily. "Don't mess with the Riddles."

That was when Zoey reemerged with an armload of shoeboxes and photo albums.

"What's going on?" She gave me a stern look. "I told you to be nice."

"She was being nice," Archer said. "Nice enough."

Zoey looked unconvinced.

Archer said, "Not as nice as she used to be when we were younger, but we'll get there."

"Haw haw," I fake-laughed.

Being nice to the genie had only gotten me into trouble. That, plus a few too many Barberrian wine coolers. And possibly an ancient prophecy.

My daughter and her father wished me a good evening, and the two of them left for dinner.

* * *

That interaction on my front porch happened during the first week in August.

Life for the next four weeks continued with its usual ups and downs.

The weather was gorgeous.

Aunt Zinnia was still on vacation.

My father kept his word about staying away.

Mr. Blackstone came by the library a few times, but didn't bring up whatever favor he had in mind. I didn't ask.

Charlize spent her leave of absence haunting the Moore house next door, drinking tequila, and goading me into casting spells that were far above my level.

My own house was up to something, but I didn't know what. The attic joists creaked and groaned in the middle of the night, but I couldn't see any changes from the street. *All things in time*, I told myself, and left the house to its business.

Zoey and Archer kept meeting once a week, and our co-parenting interactions on the porch continued to be fraught with all kinds of tension.

Bentley was a sweetheart. The perfect vampire detective boyfriend.

Zoey finished working at the museum, and prepared to return to school.

Life was good.

The calendar changed to September.

Then, one day, the clouds rolled in and the rain started.

And everything changed.

CHAPTER 10

One Month Later

~

Monday Afternoon
First Week in September

The sky flashed with sheet lightning. I was driving Foxy Pumpkin to pick up my daughter from the high school. I had the car radio on, and thunder rolled ominously around while the DJs on the local radio station cracked jokes about the gods bowling in the clouds. The DJs were Kaytlen and Kozmo, local celebrities who were known for their zany behavior. I had to give those two ding-dongs credit, because the thunder really did sound like a giant bowling alley. Especially after they'd put the idea in my head.

I got to the school and parked, mindful to keep my classic—by some collectors' standards—car within the boundaries of the student pick-up zone. It was the first day of a new school year for my daughter, and I didn't want to mar the year by getting a lecture about parking from the school staff.

There was no shortage of parking around the school, thus no need for the pick-up zone enforcers to be so persnickety; but, as a fellow enforcer of seemingly arbitrary rules, I did understand. Rules were rules, and they existed for a reason. Whenever I found myself in trouble, it was usually because I'd ignored some rule that had seemed arbitrary at the time but turned out to exist solely for my own protection. Wasn't life funny that way?

I turned off the engine, as per the no-idling rules of the pick-up zone. Foxy Pumpkin made a sputter of protest, as though she didn't want her engine shut off.

I patted the dashboard. "What's wrong, girl? Do you need that tune up?"

Another sputter, and the engine went quiet.

"Was that a yes or a no?"

The car didn't respond further.

I wondered about the man who'd built the car from parts, Mr. Harry Blackstone. I hadn't seen him in several weeks. Had the man already passed away? Was that why I hadn't seen him?

I pulled out my phone, clicked a bookmark, and checked the local obituaries. I should have been checking them regularly, to be prepared for any visits by spirits with unfinished business, but the ghost business had been slow lately.

There was no mention of Mr. Blackstone in the obituaries.

"Your creator's not dead yet," I said to the car, patting the dashboard again. "But here's something interesting." I read the item from the police blotter, and then summarized it for the car. "Someone spotted a black fox in their garden, menacing a trio of pugs. Sounds like quite the standoff. Just picture all those bulging pug eyes." I cackled, and the sound startled me. I sounded just like a witch who talked to her car.

I put the phone away before things got really weird.

The rain started with a few splats on the windshield. They were the sort of big, juicy splats that told you the bowling-alley-of-the-gods thunder you'd been hearing was not an audio test of the Emergency Broadcast System. Rain was coming.

After a minute of splatting, the proverbial heavens opened, and then the water really came down.

It was only once the downpour had begun that I realized how pleasant and rain-free our time thus far in Wisteria had been.

Zoey and I had relocated there from a large city on the East Coast known for short but intense rainfall, as well as flash flooding. I had not missed the rain at all. The bagels, yes. The rain, no.

The passenger door opened. The temperature inside the vehicle dropped as the humidity rose.

A damp and miserable teenager grumbled as she slumped in her seat and closed the door. She didn't even look over as she gave me an impatient "Well?"

"Well, what? How was the first day of school?"

She used the side of her hand to wipe rain from her cheeks. "Okay, I guess. We didn't even get any homework."

"Aw," I said, then, brightly, "Maybe tomorrow!"

"What do we know about this rain?"

"That it'll be here for a month. I've heard from everyone that Septembers in Wisteria are very rainy."

"I haven't heard anything about that."

"Of course you wouldn't have. You're a teenager. People don't talk to you about the weather. When you become an adult, you'll learn a lot more about the weather. Everything from what the weather is currently doing, to what it did yesterday, to what it might do tomorrow, and how any of that may or may not affect a person's bursitis."

She grumpily swept more rain from her cheeks.

In a librarian tone, I explained, "*Bursitis* is the inflammation and swelling of a bursa." I smiled knowingly. "You'll learn more about that, as well as other skin, bone, ligament, and joint issues, when you become a full-fledged adult."

"Can't wait." She sniffed miserably. "I hate the rain."

"Don't say that. You used to love the rain. You said it was nice for staying indoors and reading."

"Why don't we have bubbles over our cities yet? We have the technology."

"I'm not sure that would be such a good idea."

"Stupid rain," she muttered.

I sniffed the air. "Do you smell wet dog? I smell wet dog."

"Not funny," said the fox shifter who was in no mood for fur-based jokes.

"It might not be funny right now, but if what the locals say about the rain is true, I'll have the whole month of September to work on my wet dog jokes."

She turned her head slowly and stared at me. If looks could kill, I'd be triple dead. A single rain drop fell from her lightly freckled nose.

"This rain has put a real damper on your mood," I said. "Get it? Damper?"

She pursed her lips.

I pressed on. "What do you call a soaking wet member of the Ursidae family?"

She blinked. "If I guess correctly, will you stop?"

"You know any sort of reaction to puns is a form of encouragement."

She frowned and narrowed her eyes at me.

"The answer is *drizzly bear*," I said.

More death rays.

I checked that nobody was looking directly into the vehicle, then cast a spell to dry the rain from Zoey's hair and clothes. That was probably what her initial "Well?" had been about.

"Thank you," she said flatly, the way my mother thanked a waiter for bringing the wine she'd been waiting ten excruciating seconds too long for.

"Yeah, well, try not to drag in so much water next time. It's not good for the vintage upholstery."

Another sullen look.

I put on the turn signal and started us rolling.

As we drove, I tried again to make conversation a few times, with similar results. I lost track of how many times I could have been killed by her deadly looks.

So, being the cool mom I was, instead of heading straight home, I changed course and pulled into the parking lot for Kin Khao.

"Takeout or eat in?" I asked.

My daughter quietly looked down at her hands.

I asked the question again.

She looked up at me, tears in her eyes. "Why are you even being nice to me? I've been so rude to you. Why do you even like me? I'm a monster."

"You're not a monster, Zoey. Trust me. I've seen monsters, and you are not one of them."

She sniffed.

"You're having a rough time," I said. "You love school. You should be smiling, because today is usually the happiest day of the year for you. But you miss that boyfriend of yours. He's ruined your happy day." I shook my head. "Silly boyfriend. Shame on him for being so smart and getting into that good college."

She wrinkled her nose. "He's not my boyfriend."

"Right. He's just your friend who happens to be a boy, with whom you've been hanging out every single day for the last month."

She turned and gazed out the rain-streaked passenger window. "And he's the boy who happens to not even live here anymore."

The boy had left for college over the weekend, and now my sweet kid was suffering her first romantic heartbreak. She didn't think heartbreak would be able to find her. She'd been careful. But no amount of denial, planning, or abstaining from labels had spared her young heart.

"I guess we could go straight home," I said. "There's no amount of *pad kee mao* that will help with a problem big enough to merit a sigh like that." I put the car back in gear. "It's a bit early for dinner, anyway. What are we, retired? It's not even four o'clock."

She whipped her head and gave me a panicked look. "I think we should at least *try* the *pad kee mao*."

"Will it help with the loud sighing?"

"It can't hurt."

I turned off the engine. I reached for the handle but didn't open the door yet. Another thunderous bowling ball rolled overhead.

We sat in the warm, cozy car, listening to the rain pour down.

In a moment, we would take deep breaths, as though preparing to dive into a swimming pool, and exit the car like synchronized swimmers. We would squeal as we darted around newly formed puddles.

Inside Kin Khao, we would be warmly greeted by May Meesang, who would comment on the rain, and how it would be there all month.

That September, the rain would be omnipresent, alternating between heavy downpour and light drizzle. The sky would remain gray until one morning, when dawn would finally break, golden and beautiful, over my very changed family.

CHAPTER 11

Tuesday Morning

It was raining again, so I offered to drive Zoey to school.

As we drove, she brooded over her phone the whole time.

"What's wrong?" I asked, glancing over from the driver's side seat. "Has Griffin not been returning your text messages?"

She answered in a clipped tone. "He writes back."

"Then why are you breathing so furiously? You're steaming up your side of the car. I've got the air vents cranked to maximum and they can't keep up."

She looked up at the glass and saw that it was true. She gave me a helpless look.

"What's wrong?" I asked again. "Besides the obvious."

"It's his birthday today."

"Okay. That's understandable. He's turning eighteen, which is a big milestone, and it's sad that you won't be there."

"Exactly."

"Poor kid. He probably misses all his friends from here. It serves him right for taking all those extra courses and graduating a year before his buddies. I guess he'll be eating that cake we sent him all by himself, alone in his dorm room. Speaking of which, did the cake get there okay? Chloe will want to know if the packaging held up."

She wrinkled her brow and pouted. "That's the thing. He won't be alone. He's been sending me these long messages about all the amazing new friends he's making."

"Amazing new friends? Is that a bad thing?"

"I don't know. It's weird. He hasn't even been there a week."

"He's an extrovert, Zoey. You knew that when you met him. He got you the job at the museum so you could hang out with him and his entire group of friends."

She wrinkled her nose. "He's like some kind of pack animal who can't be separated from the herd for a minute."

"It may seem strange to you, but I'm sure all of us introverts seem equally strange to extroverts."

"You're not an introvert, Mom."

"What are you talking about? Of course I'm an introvert. I'm a librarian. I love books."

"But you like *people*."

"You don't like people?"

"I like *some* people."

I pulled up in front of the high school. "Why would you say I'm not an introver—"

A rain-soaked figure in a fluorescent safety vest jumped in front of the car, waving desperately. Through the pattering of the rain on the windshield, I heard the figure lecturing me about the boundaries of the pick-up zone.

I flickered the headlights in apology, put the car in reverse, and backed up three feet so that I was within the zone.

I returned to my question. "Why would you say I'm not an introvert?" I had always assumed I was an introvert, because so many of my colleagues in the library services realm were. But there were times when I'd been eager to make scads of new friends, such as when we'd moved to Wisteria. I enjoyed being around people, and having them inside my home, even if some of them were wyverns or cats and not typical people. As my house had filled with life forms, my heart had filled with happiness.

"Maybe I'm an extrovert after all," I mused. "Sort of a stealth extrovert."

"You're more of an ambivert," Zoey said.

"Ambivert?" I stuck out my tongue. "I've never liked that word. It sounds like a sleeping pill, or a new drug for treating mold allergies."

"Don't get all weird about it."

"Who's getting weird? You're the weird one, with your labels."

"I'm sorry if I just shattered your whole image of yourself, but look on the bright side. It's probably a good thing you're an ambivert. You can go either way. You're more flexible."

"Ambivert," I said, feeling more comfortable with the label by the minute. I thought of my most extroverted ghost, Winona Vander Zalm, and my most introverted ghost, Tansy Wick, and pictured myself falling on the social spectrum between the two of them.

"Ambivert," I repeated, in my TV announcer voice. "Take two as needed for a good night's sleep, or pesky mold allergies. Side effects may include laughing out loud instead of typing LOL, talking to strangers at parties, or attending community theater productions that require audience participation."

My daughter didn't laugh. She was looking at her phone again, and not happy about it.

"Now what?" I asked.

"Griffin's new college friends are taking him out on a tour of all the places that give away free things if it's your birthday."

"That sounds nice," I said cautiously. "And perfectly normal, too. I thought you liked it when people do normal things. You keep telling me the best part about Griffin is how normal he is."

She snorted and glared at the phone, ignoring most of what I said. "His parents are paying all his tuition. He shouldn't be trying to get everything for free. It's not fair to the local businesses. He's such a scammer."

That was the first time I'd heard anything negative about the amazingly normal Griffin Yates. I had been waiting for this day, and the opportunity to suggest she look on the bright side. Without a boy taking up all her free time, she could put more effort into making friends— the regular kind who weren't romantic interests.

Zoey was a true introvert. She didn't need a large group of friends, but she needed a few. She was always happier when she had a deep bond with a couple of kids her age. I'd been suggesting she recruit a friend or two at her new school, or even through her job at the museum, but the latter hadn't worked out. Griffin Yates was normal, and his friends were normal. While she enjoyed Griffin's buddies when Griffin was at her side, she couldn't hang out with the museum gang without him, because they were "too normal," and made her feel like the odd one out.

The day before, over Thai food, I'd asked about other potential friends at the high school. Zoey reluctantly mentioned she'd noticed a girl who drove an old hearse around town. Her name was Ambrosia Abernathy. Her family ran a funeral home, which explained the hearse.

I suggested that Ambrosia might like to come over for a make-your-own-pizza night. Zoey said she'd think about it, but only if I promised to get normal toppings for a change. She loved my noodle-pickle-meatball-blue-cheese-dressing pizzas, but they were unsuitable for potential friends.

I had promised to source some "normal" pizza toppings, such as salami and peppers, and she had promised to chat with hearse-driving Ambrosia.

"Hey," I said, remembering the pizza conversation from the night before. "Remember to talk to that girl who drives a hearse."

"Yup."

"Do you have any classes with her today?"

"Maybe," she said distractedly.

It wasn't like my daughter to not know her schedule. She was really bothered by the whole Griffin business. I could relate. At her age, I'd been devastated when the boy who knocked me up had disappeared into thin air. The devastation hadn't lasted long, because I'd had a pregnancy to distract me. Thankfully that wasn't going to be an issue for Zoey. She had more sense than I'd had at her age. Plus, Griffin was just a normal boy, not a charming genie.

Griffin moving away was my daughter's second big loss in less than a month. She had been mopey about Corvin leaving for London, but at least the new romance with Griffin had been a positive distraction. Now, with Griffin gone, she was on her own again, or at least with nobody under twenty to hang out with.

I felt bad for her. I didn't want her to be so independent, or grow up so fast. That had been my path, and while I had turned out spectacular, I'd hoped for an easier path for my only child.

Zoey gave the phone one last dirty look before putting it in her backpack. She huffed, "I will never date an extrovert ever again."

"That seems a bit extreme. No extroverts whatsoever? I believe they're the majority. You're ruling out a lot of potential boyfriends."

"Good."

I checked the time. If she didn't get going, she'd be late for her second day of school.

I reached over and ruffled her hair. "Have a great day at school, sweetie!"

She gave me a pained look. "And have fun at the *library* with Mr. Wonderful and the Hooter."

"You bet your fluffernuts I will."

She stepped out into the rain and ran toward the school entrance. I waited until she was out of sight before I drove away.

I didn't go straight to the library. My schedule that week was light, so I had the morning free to run errands.

Despite the gray skies, I was in a sunny mood.

I wouldn't have turned up the radio and sung along happily to pop tunes if I'd known the afternoon would turn up a dead body.

CHAPTER 12

The thing about errands was the more trivial the tasks were, the more productive I felt.

I drove to three different stores to pick up the esoteric supplies I needed for a potion. It was a compound that would facilitate the removal of a dozen sticky spots from the surface of the car, where the neighborhood trees had dropped their sap.

Next, I dropped off some clothes for alterations—new finds from Mia's Kit and Kaboodle that needed to be taken in.

Then I went shopping for giant vats of foodstuffs from the town's warehouse store. I bought a five-month supply of "normal" pizza toppings, among other necessities, such as a decade's supply of dental floss. To my surprise, I loved buying things in bulk. There were so many great deals, and now that I lived in a house with adequate storage instead of a small apartment, I could really stock up.

When the cashier saw the quantity of pancake syrup in my shopping cart, she commented that I must have several growing boys at home.

"Just one growing boy with a sweet tooth," I said. *A sweet tooth and several sweet fangs.* Luckily for my budget, the store carried a line of maple-flavored syrup that contained no maple whatsoever and thus was quite reasonably priced. Ribbons couldn't tell the difference, or least he hadn't noticed that I'd been refilling an old container of genuine maple syrup with the fake stuff. I'd learned that little trick from an episode of *Wicked Wives*. When Quenya's husband lost his job as a lawyer, she had to stretch the family food budget using any means necessary. I had used the same trick on Zoey, refilling brand-name cereal boxes with cheap copycats, and claiming that such inventiveness was my idea of an "investment strategy."

I stopped by the house to unload the groceries, since the enormous vat of store-brand ice cream wouldn't keep well in the car while I worked my shift. Or, if it *did* happen to keep well and not change texture, I didn't want to know.

While I put the groceries away, I heard what sounded like Santa's reindeer landing on my roof, then having a party.

After cramming the ice cream into the freezer, I went outside to investigate the noise. I held my hand over my eyes to shield them from the rain, and stared up at the roof. Whatever aspect of my house was being magically remodeled, it wasn't visible to the naked eye.

"That's a lovely roofline," said a female voice.

I turned to find a woman in a conservative suit in front of the Moore house. She was in her thirties and pretty, with a button nose and bright green eyes. Her shoulder-length auburn hair must have been coated in waterproof hairspray, because the rain was sliding off her bob like water off a duck's back. She had a big mallet in one hand. A new For Sale sign was stuck in the grass in front of her.

The rain let up at that very moment, as though being courteous.

"Thanks," I said, dropping my hand from my forehead. "Did you happen to hear any banging just now? Or see anything out of the ordinary?"

Her eyes widened. She glanced around furtively and walked toward me. Her gait was ungainly because her narrow heels kept sinking into the lawn, aerating it as the mud coated her pumps.

In a hoarse whisper, she said, "Do you mean the squatter?"

I gave her a sidelong look. "Maybe. Which squatter are you referring to?"

She nodded at the blue house behind her, the Moore residence. "The one who's been leaving all the bottles inside my client's house."

I winced. "Tequila bottles?"

Her eyes widened. "You heard?"

"That's not a squatter," I explained. "That sounds like the work of..." *Charlize* "the house sitter."

"Really? A house sitter? It's not just the bottles. There's garbage, and wrappers from packaged foods, plus a smell I can only describe as *feral*. Is the house sitter a teenaged boy?"

I bit back a laugh. Charlize would have taken great delight at this woman's dismay.

"The house sitter is an adult who should be tidying up after herself," I said. "I will speak to her about keeping the house in showable condition."

"It's a woman?" The agent's pretty upper lip curled in disgust. "I'm not sure what value she's offering as a house sitter. A family of raccoons would do a better job." There was a twinkle in the woman's eye at the mention of raccoons. "How long do you think she'll need to make the house presentable?"

"Not long if I help tidy up. Give us a day or two."

"The sooner the better." The agent glanced over at the blue house. "The market's been slower than a tortoise walking to work lately, but you never know." As she turned toward me again, a sly smile spread across her face. "You never know when your luck's about to change."

"Life is like that," I agreed. "It can turn on a dime."

As if on cue, the rain started again, with a light drizzle. Hilarious.

"I'm Zara Riddle." I offered her my damp hand. "I live next door, in the red house."

"The Red Witch House?"

I pretended to be surprised by my home's name and reputation. "It is red," I said slowly, confusedly.

"I'm so sorry," the woman said. "You know how it is in small towns. We Wisterians say a lot of silly things. It's all in good fun." She took my hand and pumped it hard. "You're not a witch," she said. "In fact, you seem like a perfectly lovely person." Her eyes flicked to the house, then back at me, with a hungry, eager look. "You must have known Dorothy Tibbits. She sold that house shortly before her unfortunate passing."

"She did sell me the house. Yes."

"Dreadful woman." The real estate agent shuddered dramatically. "And so terrible at her job."

I laughed. I liked this brunette. "Dorothy Tibbits *was* a terrible real estate agent," I agreed.

She pretended to slap herself across the cheek. "Shame on you, Reyna. We mustn't speak ill of the dead."

Her name rang a bell. "Did you say your name was Reyna?" *As in Reyna Drinkwater?*

"Yes. Reyna Drinkwater." She jerked her head in the direction of the For Sale sign. I read it fully for the first time. The house was being marketed by a local company called Akorn Realty, which had to be a sister company to Akorn Development. And the woman with the dark auburn, rain-proof bob standing before me had her photo on the sign. She was Reyna Drinkwater. We'd never met, but I'd definitely heard of her, and not for good reasons.

I kept a mask of a smile on my face as she handed me a soggy business card.

I thanked her, and we made small talk about the weather for a while before agreeing it was best to head for shelter before the rain got serious. I scarcely heard a word she said, because my mind was reeling from the mention of her name.

Reyna Drinkwater. I had a great memory for the names of known troublemakers.

Back when my father had first showed his foxy nose in town, I'd suspected his business was connected to a woman named Reyna Drinkwater. It turned out she wasn't involved, but I discovered she did have a history of malicious mischief. It was suspected—but never proven—that she was the party responsible for releasing a number of wild animals—plus a tame donkey—inside a property that Akorn Development was trying to acquire below market rates.

Reyna Drinkwater, criminal or not, was definitely trouble. And now she was in charge of selling Chet Moore's house? Chet was the same one who'd hired Dorothy Tibbits to take care of his deceased neighbor's estate.

Way to pick 'em, Chet.

* * *

"Drinkwater is small time," Bentley said over the tiny speaker in my phone.

I was in Foxy Pumpkin heading toward the library, talking to him on speakerphone while I drove.

"Everyone's small time until they pull off a big caper," I said.

"Caper?" He sounded confused. "What's this about a big caper? I thought you said she was the listing agent for the Moore house."

Another voice piped in. "We can look into Drinkwater's recent business dealings, if that makes you feel more comfortable, Zara."

"Thank you, Ms. Rose," I said flatly, then, haughtily, "I didn't realize I was speaking to multiple people on this call. I certainly didn't mean to trouble half of the Wisteria

Police Department with any of my petty concerns as a citizen."

"Oh, it's no trouble," Bentley's annoying new partner replied brightly. "I like it when you call us. You always have such interesting news."

I clenched my jaw. The worst thing about Persephone Rose was her niceness. The worse I was to her, the nicer she got. It almost made me feel bad.

Bentley cut in. "I'll call you back later," he said. *When I'm alone* was implied. "Have a great afternoon at work."

"I'll try."

"Shush some people for me. Shush them *real good.*"

I couldn't help but crack a grin. Bentley and I had developed a number of inside jokes during our weeks of dating. The whole Sexy Librarian routine was perhaps the most obvious of our games, but you know what they say: Stereotypes exist for a reason. I loved hearing about Bentley threatening to charge citizens with misdemeanors, and he loved hearing about me shushing library patrons. A little bit of power wielded unjustly was always a turn-on.

We said goodbye, and I clicked on the turn signal as I approached the library's staff parking lot.

The car's horn spontaneously began honking. A warning? I looked around. Everything looked rainy but otherwise normal. I rolled into a staff parking spot slowly. I cast a threat-detection spell, but nothing lit up. The car kept honking. A few people walking by with umbrellas were staring my way. The honking rose in pitch. I held my hands up so they could see it wasn't me honking. *It's the car*, I mouthed—not that they cared.

I turned the keys to kill the engine. The honk died slowly and dramatically, like a new actor milking their first death scene for maximum screen time.

It finished with a final death gasp. BOOOOP-PHWEEEEEEEEP-EEP-EEp-eeeep.

"That was a bit over the top," I said to the car when all was said and done. "What's the matter, Foxy Pumpkin? Do you hate the rain, too?"

No response, which was typical. The car had never communicated with me before, much less talked back.

"You'll be okay, ol' gal." I patted the dashboard. "Maybe it's time I track down Mr. Blackstone and get him to name his price for a tune-up."

I didn't know about the car, but the promise of taking action made me feel better.

I grabbed my purse, exited the car, and made the dash through the rain to the library.

I entered through the staff door at the side. I was setting my pink leather purse on the staff lunch table and magically drying the rain off myself when I heard screaming coming from the public area of the library.

A lot of screaming.

I ran out, fingers tingling.

One of the junior staff members ran toward me, her face ashen and her eyes bulging. "Zara, I thought he was sleeping, but he wasn't. He wasn't sleeping. He's dead, Zara. Dead. He died in his chair."

I reined in my power so I didn't zap the young woman by accident, and grabbed her hands. I looked into her frightened eyes and asked, "Who?"

As her mouth opened to form the first syllable of his name, my heart sunk. I already knew by the shape of her lips what she was going to say.

Harry Blackstone.

"Ha—" The name choked in her throat. Her eyes flooded and overflowed with tears.

Gently, I asked, "Mr. Blackstone?"

She nodded.

I folded her into my arms as though she was my daughter. She was young, and she was someone's daughter. I stroked her hair.

"It's okay," I said. "He was quite sick. It was bound to happen eventually."

"But Harry was so... nice."

"I know. Even nice people die sometimes."

Our touching moment was interrupted by fresh screaming as another person discovered the dead body in the library.

CHAPTER 13

Harry Blackstone was dead.

Frank and I ushered out all the patrons and junior staff members, and then closed early for the day. People would be upset over the short hours, but they'd be more upset to check out their cookbooks and such in the presence of the recently deceased.

The first person to arrive at the library in an official capacity was Dr. Jerry Lund. He was the DWM's Medical Examiner, who not only knew about magic but was researching the physical evidence of magical abilities. He could be creepy, such as when he talked excitedly about autopsies, but his relaxed, egalitarian manner usually put me at ease. He was curious and inquisitive, like his colleague Dr. Ankh, but without her prejudices about "indiscriminate interbreeding." I was glad the Department had sent Lund and not Ankh. It was always easier to be around people who didn't refer to my family as "mutts."

I met Jerry Lund by the front door, where he had stopped in the lobby to check the supplies he'd carried in. His assistants were still outside, unloading a gurney from the unmarked van in the rain. Lund was low to the ground, crouched over an open bag of medical instruments. The man never looked more like a bullfrog than when he was squatting.

He looked up, saw it was me, and said, "Ms. Riddle! Who have you killed now?"

"Harry Blackstone," I said.

Lund's wide-set, light-blue eyes bulged. I couldn't be sure if he was reacting to the deceased's name. His eyes were always bulging.

"Harry Blackstone," he repeated neutrally, still squatting. "Is that so?"

"Yes. But to be clear, I didn't kill him."

"How can you be sure about that?" A smile spread across his wide, bullfrog mouth, making it even wider. "A spell of yours may have interacted with one of Harry's pre-existing conditions. The man was riddled with brainweevil holes—even worse than poor ol' Don Moore."

"I understand he had been ill."

Lund paused thoughtfully, then rose up to his full height, which was shorter than my own. "Mr. Blackstone was ill, until quite recently. Luckily for some of our more experienced field agents, Dr. Ankh's trusty new serum has been approved for off-label use." His fingers twitched excitedly. "I saw the remarkable results myself. Just a few drops of that elixir had quite the restorative effect. I understand Harry was getting back to his research. He told me himself he was working on his greatest invention yet."

"Any idea what that was?"

Lund's expression darkened. "He didn't say. And it was a personal project, not on Department records."

"I guess we'll never know. Not unless you've found a way to suck a person's memories out of their brain."

"Not yet," Lund said, sounding disappointed in himself. "So, what spells did you use on him? Did you shush him with magic? Was he being too noisy?"

"I didn't cast one single spell on the guy." I held up one hand. "My word is my bond."

"If you say so. But you did know all about his health and his treatment protocols."

"Barely. He only mentioned something about a serum once. Other than that, I don't know anything about it."

The squat, bowlegged Medical Examiner gave me a knowing look. "I'm sure you know *plenty* about the serum. It is, after all, the only thing keeping your boyfriend, the tall and handsome detective, from devouring you while you sleep." He flicked his tongue over his plump lips. "Or so I assume."

"Oh, *that* serum," I said with a sarcastic eye flash. "All hail the miracles of modern medical magic." I could have said more, but didn't. People were naturally curious about a relationship between a witch and a vampire, but it wasn't my job to satisfy that curiosity.

Lund picked up his bag of supplies and looked through the lobby's interior doors. "Would you take me to the body, please? Or shall I sniff my way to it?"

Fighting a gag at the idea of Lund sniffing his way to the body, I led the way.

We hadn't moved Harry from the spot where he'd died.

As we walked, I could hear the krish-krish sound of Lund's shoes on the low-pile commercial carpet behind me. The whole library was more hushed than it ever was at that time of day, thanks to being cleared of the public. There was only the rustling of our clothes, and the patter of rain on the windows, which became more prominent when we reached the nook and the body.

Lund approached the figure slumped in the chair.

"That is, indeed, Harry Blackstone," he said resignedly. "I would know. We worked together on a few projects." Lund gave me a quick glance. "All confidential, of course."

"I'm sorry for your loss," I said. "Were you close?"

"We worked together," Lund said neutrally.

He began examining the body, lifting first one arm and then the other. When the movement of Harry's arms caused Harry's head to loll to one side, the man appeared to be reanimating. For a fleeting moment, I felt a surge of hope that he might be waking from a deep slumber. But his eyelashes did not flutter open; he remained dead.

"Interesting," Lund said. "Look at that. The socks don't match."

It was true. Harry's socks were different colors and patterns.

"Laundry day?" I guessed.

"Or he left the house in a hurry this morning." Lund ran his fingertips over Harry's cheek with a gesture that was almost tender. "But not before shaving."

"Poor Harry," I said, trying to look away out of respect but unable to.

Lund breathed heavily and poked at the body with quick, jabbing motions, almost too fast for me to see.

I asked with interest, "What are you checking him for?"

"Lividity."

"The normal kind, or something magical?"

"I won't know until I check, will I?"

"Ooh-kay," I said, in that passive aggressive tone people used when they knew they were being talked down to.

I stayed where I was, watching.

The rain pelted the window, and the nook darkened.

I should have left the good doctor to his business, yet I couldn't walk away. I kept giving Harry's lifeless face an expression of pity. *I'm sorry*, I thought.

One of the staff members had informed me, between messy sobs, that when Harry had arrived at the library a few hours prior, he had asked to see me. I'd probably been across town at the bulk warehouse at that time. When Harry learned I wasn't due in the library until after lunch, he'd announced that he would do some "reading" in his favorite chair until I arrived.

The man had died while waiting to see me. Because of that, I felt an obligation to not leave him just yet.

Standing there for no reason felt awkward, so I asked, "Say, Doc. Do shifters ever change after they die?"

Lund, who preferred *not* to be called Doc because it brought to mind a certain Disney dwarf, shot me an amused look. "That would make for some rather startling crime scenes, don't you think?"

"And a lot of memory wipes, I bet."

He continued to look amused. "Is that your way of making a request, Ms. Riddle? Would you like to have the memory of this unpleasant afternoon removed from your memory?"

"No!" I took a step back. "Not at all." I wiped my palms on my hips. "And I'm sorry I called you Doc."

Outside, the wind surged, and the rain crashed against the window like a trapped bird.

Lund returned his attention to the body, pushing up the man's eyelids to examine his eyes.

As he worked, he began speaking to me as though I was an intern taking notes. "I'm checking for petechiae now. None present. That alone doesn't rule out death by asphyxiation, but it does help paint a picture."

"What sort of picture?" I stepped in closer. "Do you mean the cause of death? Do you know what killed him?"

Lund chuckled. "Since the subject of my first hypothesis—Death By Hex of Witch—swears it wasn't her, I'll have to earn my paycheck this week. I'll be conducting a full examination back at the Department."

"What did he have, anyway? I mean, besides brainweevil damage."

"That, I cannot say."

"Whatever it was, it was probably what killed him."

"Probably," Lund agreed. "Unless it was Death By Hex of Witch after all." He raised an eyebrow. "Perhaps a member of your coven?"

I snorted. "What have you got against witches, anyway? You didn't have a problem with our witcher-i-doo ways when you were dating Maisy Nix."

Lund jerked his oversized head and gave me a surprised look. "You know about that?"

"I know plenty of things," I said airily. Maisy had told me about it herself, though I didn't know why. Dating the pale, squat DWM doctor didn't seem like something to brag about. But, then again, he was still a doctor, not to mention the least creepy of all the Department doctors I'd met.

Lund changed the topic. "What do you know about Blackstone?"

"He knew my father."

"Everyone knows your father."

"That's what I'm finding out."

"What else?"

I shrugged. "He liked to nap right here, by the window." I gestured at the gray beyond the rain-rippled glass. "When it's not raining, this is a nice place to sit."

Lund looked out the window. It offered very little view compared to the magical windows in his underground morgue. If we'd been having this conversation there, we could have enjoyed a sunny Alpine meadow, complete with a cow that looked back at us.

After a moment of contemplating the rain, Lund said, "There are worse places to die. I imagine it was peaceful."

Then he turned and looked at me as though I was one of his subjects. His pale, bulging eyes seemed to be drinking me in.

I scratched my neck self-consciously and scanned for something positive to focus on. I didn't like having the Medical Examiner's full attention. Avoiding eye contact reduced the eerie sensation he was planning my dissection.

I scanned the tops of the nearby bookshelves. Some of the houseplants were looking less than robust. And we had cobwebs.

There was a zipping sound.

When I looked down at Harry's chair again—it would always be Harry's chair from that point on—it was empty. Two of Lund's assistants were rolling away a gurney, topped by a full-looking body bag. I hadn't even heard the activity over the rain on the window. *Harry's window.*

The assistants disappeared with the body. Lund was sniffing the air over and around the chair with great interest.

"That was fast," I commented. "I didn't even get to say goodbye."

Lund stopped sniffing and closed his medical bag with a crisp snap. "You can say goodbye at the funeral, assuming there is one. The man didn't have much for next of kin. No wife or kids. Just a brother. I believe the brother works in the private sector."

"That's a good idea about attending the funeral. I'll bring a few of my coworkers, so it doesn't look suspicious."

"I promise he'll appear to be intact." Lund's fingers twitched eagerly. "From the outside."

Fighting another gag, I stared in the direction the gurney had disappeared.

Lund followed my gaze and said, tiredly, "Please don't track this one down and unzip it inside the transport vehicle."

Aghast, I said, "I wouldn't dream of it."

"But you *did* tamper with the Pressman body, at Castle Wyvern."

"Did I?" I feigned confusion. "Tamper is such an ugly word."

He stared at me, those pale eyes bulging expectantly.

I threw my hands in the air. "All I wanted was a sample of her hair, for testing. You, of all people, should understand. I didn't know she was going to, you know..." I made a sound effect with my tongue.

"Yes, well, sometimes a corpse that's been killed by poison will go..." He made the same raspberry noise, imitating me. "And since Blackstone was poisoned, it is a concern."

My hands flew to my heart. "You think Blackstone was poisoned?"

"I *know* he was poisoned."

My mouth went as dry as a bag of chalk dust.

"But not in the same manner as the Pressman girl," Lund said. "I believe it was a series of poisonings that slowly built to a fatal dose."

"How do you know?"

"I can smell it on the chair. Can't you?"

I shook my head. "Your sense of smell must be much better than mine." I tilted my head. "Why is that, Dr. Lund?"

"Aren't we a curious one today." He glanced around. "Well, since you asked, I'll show you."

Lund cocked his head, dropped his jaw, and flicked a long, prehensile tongue into the space between us. The tip of it missed my chin by less than an inch. I felt the moist heat on the lower part of my face. He flicked the tongue left and right. And then, just as quickly as the tongue had appeared, it reeled back into his mouth. His mouth was large, but there was no way the whole tongue could have coiled back inside there without magic. He was a sprite.

I noted with pride that I hadn't flinched. I might have screamed in a very uncool way if I hadn't already seen my sprite coworker, Kathy, do the same tongue trick more than once.

"You're a sprite," I said.

He chuckled. "That is what we're calling ourselves these days."

We chatted for a few minutes about the challenges of being a sprite, and special dietary concerns for their kind. When the conversation ebbed, we both found ourselves looking at Harry's empty chair.

"You're sure it was poison?" I asked.

"Positive."

"Any idea what kind? I'd like to avoid the same fate."

"A type of vegetable, I'd guess. People think plants are simply food, but plants do not wish to be harmed, let alone eaten. Every plant alive today is a survivor. And, since they can't run away from predators, plants must resort to other means. They make themselves toxic. People worry so much about the sprays that are put on the outsides of their leafy greens and sweet fruits, but they don't consider the neurotoxins, protease inhibitors, and sharp crystals produced by the plants themselves."

"Ah. The paradox of the plant-based diet. We've been getting a lot more of those books lately. You're talking about the oxylates, phytates, and lectins. Not to mention all the magical compounds that aren't in the books for the public."

Lund rubbed his chin thoughtfully. "I don't believe it was an overdose of any of the well-known antinutrients that killed Harry. I believe it was something novel— possibly magical, or perhaps a new, lab-designed compound."

"Harry did mention something about having heartburn from eating peppers."

Lund practically jumped with glee. "Peppers! That's exactly what I smelled. Thank you for helping me place the aroma." He shook his head. "Always the nightshades living up to their name."

"You're welcome for the tip. Remember to make a note in your case file that one of the local wicked witches was very helpful today. Unfortunately, Harry didn't tell me where he was getting his deadly nightshades."

"At least the detectives will have a lead," Lund said.

"The detectives? You're saying this is a homicide? Harry could have poisoned himself by accident. People do it all the time on those wacky juice cleanses."

"Harry was smarter than that. His death was no accident." The Medical Examiner gave me a deadly serious look and said, "The perpetrator picked a peck of poisoned peppers."

CHAPTER 14

Wednesday Morning
Wisteria Public Library

The woman's voice was high and irritating, like the buzz of a mosquito in a hot bedroom after the lights go off.

"They should give people some notice about these things, so that people can change their plans and not take a bus halfway across town only to have to bus right back again!" The woman thrust her small, white-haired head forward, her chin lifted as though she was looking down through bifocals, though she wasn't wearing any glasses. The tendons on her neck strained visibly. She'd apparently come by the previous afternoon, only to find the library closed due to "unforeseen circumstances."

The woman's name was Helen Highbury, and this wasn't the first time we'd tangled. She had last given me a hard time the month before, after one of our Mexican Hat Dance incidents. That particular afternoon, she'd given me a long lecture about the public computers, and how the people using them ought to be given more supervision. I explained that several other libraries had also been hacked by the same entity, and the Mexican Hat

Dance virus had likely infected our system through remote access over the internet, not within the facility. She had replied "Exactly!" as though I had unwittingly proven her point.

Now Helen was back, with a new bone to pick about yesterday's closure.

Rather than use facts and logic, which she'd only wield against me with her verbal judo, I played dumb.

I glanced behind me, then back at Helen. "I'm sorry," I said, sounding mystified. "Were you talking to me?"

She repeated herself, almost verbatim, but slower, and with a lot of emphasis on key words. "They should give people *notice*. Some people might change their *plans*. Some people don't want to take a bus *halfway across town* only to—"

I twitched my baby finger and cast a micro spell. I was breaking my rule about casting magic at work, but heaven help me, the woman was asking for a bite on the buttocks. Begging for it.

Helen jerked her head upright and blinked three times. Had I bitten too hard?

The woman recovered, continuing her tirade. "Only to have to, er, take the bus, uh, back home again." She coughed, and then dropped both of her clenched hands, which she'd been flailing for emphasis, from my view. I couldn't see what she was doing on the other side of the circulation desk. I assumed she was checking to see if her underwear had ridden up, and if the underwear was the cause of the discomfort she'd just experienced. She would never guess in a million years that the nip on her butt had been a spell, cast by the woman she was unjustly castigating.

As her cheeks flushed, I almost felt bad. In my defense, not only had Helen Highbury been asking for it, but I'd shown great restraint by casting a micro dose of the spell. At that power level, the effects were quite subtle. Barely a nibble.

I felt eyes on me. I glanced over to find my boss, Kathy, watching the interaction with interest.

Floopy doops, as my aunt would say. Busted.

The head librarian was often watching with her owlish eyes whenever I did something naughty. Kath was a sprite, like Dr. Lund, but being a sprite didn't give Kathy psychic powers—that I knew of. Yet she had quite the knack for catching me whenever I was the slightest bit rude to a library patron.

I returned my attention to the woman before me. The woman I had bitten, technically.

Helen Highbury, apparently satisfied that her underwear wasn't attacking her hiney, resumed her diatribe. "The library should not have been closed for the entire afternoon! It was raining. What kind of a library is closed when it's raining?"

"Ms. Highbury," I said patiently. "On behalf of the entire Wisteria Public Library, I apologize for any inconvenience our unscheduled closure caused you yesterday."

"I'm not looking for an apology." Helen's small head strained up and forward, bobbing like the head of a pigeon. "What I want is an explanation."

"There was a medical emergency," I said, holding out open palms.

"Medical emergency? What does that mean?" She gasped. "Did someone die? On the premises?" She stopped thrusting her head forward, and it rose up by an inch. The tendons at her neck strained. "I thought I saw the Medical Examiner's van pull up outside."

I shot a look over at Kathy. Kathy raised her eyebrows knowingly. We both understood exactly what was happening. Helen Highbury was only feigning outrage about yesterday's inconvenience. Her real mission was to rustle up information that she could report to the other busybodies who spread rumors around the town.

Kathy tilted her head, as though giving me permission to do as I pleased with Ms. Highbury, then walked away. Kathy didn't have time for gossip, unless it was gossip she didn't already know about—which technically made her a perfectly normal person.

Nosy Helen was bobbing her pigeon head in anticipation of my response.

"It was a medical emergency, and I really shouldn't comment further," I said. "Thank you for understanding."

Helen sputtered, "That's it?"

The life seemed to go straight out of her. Her head drooped, and she clutched the edge of the counter tiredly. I noticed the swelling in the joints of her fingers. I hadn't cast a magic spell to allow me to feel her pain, and yet I caught a wave of it all the same. That was the power of empathy. I felt the ache of her hands in my own joints.

Poor dear, I thought. Finding out the cause of yesterday's library closure had given her some purpose, some distraction from her personal pain and worries. I was also happier when I had a mission. Helen Highbury and I were not so different.

I looked left and right, though I already knew the coast was clear, and gestured for her to lean in. I would give her a little more distraction. She'd put in the effort, after all. Not many patrons riled me to the point of biting them.

"Yes?" Her cheeks grew rosy. She clasped her bony fingers together.

"Someone did pass away on the premises," I said in a gossipy, breathless tone.

"Ooh!"

"A man. He died peacefully, while napping."

She gasped, as though she'd misheard me say something much more interesting.

"How shocking that must have been," she said.

"It did surprise a few of the junior staff members."

"Yes, yes," she said excitedly. "How very unusual to have someone pass away in your midst."

"Very unusual," I said. It wasn't unusual for me, but I couldn't tell her that.

"Is there more?" Her mouth remained open, as though she might better suck in gossip that way, like a sturdy vacuum cleaner.

"Hmm." I gave it some thought, or at least pretended to. "Now that I think about it, the poor fellow did say something odd before he passed."

"Something odd?" She all but stopped breathing.

I savored what I was about to do, pausing for dramatic effect. "Before his nap, the man complained of... a strange pain in the buttocks."

She completely stopped breathing.

I waved one hand casually. "I'm sure it was nothing. It was probably natural causes, and not that new virus that's going around. The one that starts off with tiny cramps in the gluteus maximus."

Once she started breathing again, it took all of ten seconds for Helen Highbury to abandon her reference materials and exit the library at top speed, using her elbows on the door handle so she didn't touch anything with her bare hands.

That'll keep you busy for the day, I thought happily. *You're welcome, Helen!*

I sensed that I had an audience again. I turned to my right, smiling, expecting to see Frank Wonder offering a silent golf clap.

Except Frank wasn't there.

No one was.

Eerie.

* * *

The feeling I was being watched lasted all morning and through lunch.

It could have been nerves from having had a death on the premises the day before, or it could have been something new. Specifically, it could have been Harry's ghost. If Lund's theory was right, and Harry had been murdered, his spirit would be around for a while.

I didn't see Harry, but that didn't mean he wasn't there.

For the next hour, I cast several spells to reveal concealed secrets, hexes, curses, and pesky jinxes.

I found very little out of the ordinary. There were some plastic slabs of fake bacon, hidden in books as bookmarks, and placed where Kathy would eventually find them and freak out—the work of Mr. Frank Wonder —but nothing more sinister than that.

Mid-afternoon, I was performing the the 2:00 pm patrol, The Nap O'Clock Wakeup, when I noticed that someone was sleeping in Harry's chair, by Harry's window.

It was a man with thick, dark, bushy hair. He wore neutral-colored clothes, and mismatched socks.

"Harry!" I exclaimed, a little too loudly for a library. I coughed and muttered an apology in case anyone was listening.

I approached the sleeping ghost. The streaky gray light from the rain-soaked window disguised his wispiness, making him look so lifelike and solid.

Excitement flared in my chest, the way Helen's excitement must have flared when I'd offered gossip. Life was better when it had purpose, no matter what that purpose was. My ghost business over the last month had been slow, but now it appeared business was picking up again.

I knelt at the man's ghostly feet, by his mismatched socks, and pretended to be adjusting my shoelaces.

"Mr. Blackstone? It's me," I said, whispering now. "Zara Riddle. You wanted to see me about something?"

His eyes remained closed. He was as still as he had been the day before, when he'd been a lifeless corpse.

Was he sleeping?

Did ghosts even sleep?

I didn't have a lot of experience with "free range ghosts." My early encounters with the deceased had quickly escalated into possessions. It was only thanks to my clever rezoning spell that I had eventually gained some degree of control over my Spirit Charmed specialty. Even so, things didn't always go as planned. Communication was a big challenge. Direct contact through spellwork could cause a flowback of energy from the noncorporeal realm. Even chatting with them in a normal, albeit one-sided—ghosts were mute—conversation was dangerous. If there was one thing you didn't want to ever tell a ghost, it was the key fact they *were* a ghost.

"Psst," I said. "Wake up, Harry."

I was careful to be gentle. Ghosts had difficulties with time and space. My aunt had told me to always be patient, because it had to be so confusing for the spirits, finding themselves somewhere, repeating some pattern from their former life, but not understanding why the living—besides some witches—couldn't see them.

"Harry? Mr. Blackstone?" I waved my hand in front of his face.

When that did nothing, I waved my hand *through* his face. Then through his brain. I used one hand to make a fist, and I squeezed the area where his heart would have been.

Ghost-Harry continued sleeping.

Behind me, someone hissed, "Zara, not when we're open to the public!"

I turned to find the head librarian looking horrified, her golden-brown eyes wide behind her round glasses. Her tight brown curls trembled as she continued admonishing me. "If you absolutely must do one of your rituals, at least wait until we're closed for the day."

"I was just..." I gestured at the ghost, as 'though doing so might make her able to see him, but she couldn't. In fact, when I looked back to the chair, the ghost was gone.

Kathy said, "You could have taken today off to recover from yesterday's events. I told you we could adjust your schedule."

"Thanks for that, but I'm fine, honestly."

She scrunched her lips, then said, "My cousin told me about the poisoned peppers."

"Your cousin?"

"Lund," she said. "The Medical Examiner."

"I didn't know Lund was your cousin. You have a lot of cousins."

"I do."

"Are all of them...?" *Sprites?*

"Not all of them." She shook her curls, then eyed the empty chair warily. "What was in Harry's chair?"

"Harry."

She jerked her folded arms in a flapping gesture. "That's not good."

We had been speaking in a hushed tone, but because whispers traveled surprisingly well in a quiet library, I cast a sound bubble around us.

Then I told her exactly what I'd seen. Harry Blackstone, napping.

Kathy had not been well acquainted with Mr. Blackstone, but she did agree that the presence of his ghost supported the idea that the death had not been accidental.

"You must need to help Harry," she said. "To avenge him."

"That's my plan."

"But not during your shift," she said quickly. "No shenanigans when you're clocked in."

"Me? Shenanigans? Never," I swore vehemently.

Since when did I get up to shenanigans while I was clocked in? Besides *all the time.*

CHAPTER 15

For the rest of that rainy week following his death, the ghost of Harry Blackstone manifested repeatedly throughout the library.

Sometimes it was me who saw him napping in his favorite chair, but other times it was a patron who reported a chilly breeze, or the sensation of being followed, or even a book falling off the shelf as they walked by.

I was off all weekend, but the staff reported multiple strange occurrences.

The following Monday, I expected to see Harry haunting around the place. And he did appear.

I was surprised to find the library was also visited by several unfamiliar faces. The were all living people, at least, but not our regular crowd.

It didn't take long for Kathy, who monitored the numbers closely, due to how they affected our budgets, to notice our foot traffic had doubled.

The mysterious newcomers were outsiders, not Wisterians. Judging by the unchanged circulation numbers, they weren't visiting to get library cards or check out books.

On Tuesday, with Kathy's permission, I cornered and questioned one. Thanks to the judicious use of a bluffing spell, I learned that the newcomers were part of an internet support group for people who saw ghosts. Someone had tipped them off about our library being freshly haunted, and the strangers had come from all over the country to partake in the paranormal. They were ghost groupies.

By Wednesday, eight days after the death of Harry Blackstone, the number of paranormal enthusiasts in the library at any given time outnumbered the locals by three to one. Emboldened by their numbers, they dropped the pretext of being in town to visit friends or family, and talked loudly and excitedly to each other about ghost sightings. Using their outdoor voices!

The funniest part—to me, anyway—was that most of these supposedly "sensitive" folks were *not*. They sensed nothing! They couldn't spot a ghost if it sat on their lap. They certainly didn't spot the ghost in Harry's chair before sitting on *his* lap. Harry Blackstone would wander through a pack of them discussing their recent "sighting," and none would bat an eyelash.

There were, however, moments when one of the bunch would actually sense Harry doing something. Either they had some legitimate empaths among them, or they were occasionally correct the way a stopped clock was accurate twice a day. And if two of them happened to witness something at the same time, they would shriek with excitement as they rushed to take photos and record the "event."

Friday came, and we were happier than usual to close at the end of the day and kick everyone out.

After we'd begged, cajoled, and threatened the last ghost enthusiast off the premises, Kathy called an emergency staff meeting.

Kathy, Frank, and I sat in the staff break room, grimly dividing a package of dry soup crackers.

It was a dark day, indeed.

Due to all the hullabaloo over the haunting, we had completely forgotten about Fresh Pastry Fridays. There had been no baked goods that day. We didn't even have any leftover stale ones, hence the soup crackers.

"This is serious," Frank said, nibbling a dry cracker.

"It's untenable," Kathy said.

Both of them looked at me expectantly.

"Well?" Frank asked, spraying cracker crumbs.

"Well?" Kathy asked, too, leaning away to avoid Frank's cracker spray.

"Well, what?" I asked. "Just because I'm the Spirit Charmed witch, that makes me the ghost exterminator?"

In unison, they said, "Yes."

I nodded and grabbed some crackers.

"You have to do something," Frank said. "These ghost hunters are creating trip hazards with all the extension cords for their recording equipment."

"We need everything returned to normal," Kathy said. "The staff is too distracted, and duties are not being performed in a timely manner. While our mandate is to serve the public, and these ghost hunter people are the public, I'm not sure this is the best use of library resources."

"Stop being so politically correct," Frank said to Kathy. "It's just the three of us." To me, he said, "The loony toons need to hit the road."

"Frank's right," Kathy said.

Frank continued, "And you need to do it fast. They're posing for selfies in front of the Little Red Riding Hood mural. It's all going viral, Zara. There are a bunch of hashtags and everything. People on the internet are mocking us."

"That is what people on the internet do," I said.

"Yes, but they're being unnecessarily cruel," he said. "They're making Wisteria sound like one of those eccentric small towns full of weirdos."

I bit my tongue.

"What about your ghost powers?" Kathy asked. "Are you broken? Did something happen to you?"

"I don't know," I said plainly. "Maybe I am broken. I've tried the page-finding spell on Harry a dozen times, and I can't access his memories."

"Must be the beetles," Frank said. "He was riddled with holes from some kind of beetles."

"You mean the brainworms," Kathy corrected. "It was worms, not beetles."

"It was brainweevils," I said, correcting them both. "And maybe that's why this one is so tricky. His spirit's brain might have holes in it."

"Hmm." Frank rubbed his chin.

"Hmm." Kathy removed her glasses and cleaned them.

"Guys, I don't know what to tell you," I said. "The DWM is investigating his death. I'm sure once they figure out who supplied Harry with the peck of poison peppers, Harry will move on." I paused, frowning. "You know what? I gave this exact same speech to the coven earlier this week."

And I had. The coven's response had been mixed. Some of the witches wanted to help me cast a few of Trinada's three-witch spells, dangerous though they were. Others felt strongly that the local shifters had gotten lazy, and were relying too much on the free labor of witches. Margaret Mills in particular had ranted about men in general, and their willingness to let women do all the work while they took all the credit. Margaret was going through a divorce, and her rants had a particular anti-male slant to them.

I filled in Kathy and Frank on the gist of my last coven meeting. Then they both complained some more about the ghost hunters. Frank enjoyed dancing around their questions, but worried he might accidentally spill the beans to one of the nicer, more attractive ones of the bunch. Kathy was concerned about a rise in our electricity bills. All that paranormal equipment was a drain on library resources, and we already had budget issues.

The complaining was interrupted by the sound of a gentle tapping at the door. It was likely someone we knew. Even the most persistent of library patrons usually left that door alone. Then again, things had been different lately.

Frank looked toward the door, then smirked as he said to me, "It must be your good friend Helen Highbury, wanting to borrow every medical textbook that deals with butt cramps."

"Ha ha," I said. "Maybe it's that cute ghost hunter who was asking you about local wineries."

"I wish," Frank said.

There was another tap, louder and more insistent. Someone was definitely knocking to be let in.

Frank said, "Rochambeau?"

Kathy and I nodded in agreement, and we held out our fists for the game most Americans call rock-paper-scissors.

Frank lost the round by default when he fumbled and made a non-legal, spider-like shape to my mighty rock and Kathy's fierce scissors.

He went to the door and cracked it open. The sound of rain hitting the side of the mostly concrete building filled the quiet room.

Frank didn't open the door all the way, so I could only see a sliver of the person who'd been knocking. It was a female, and she was dressed in gleaming, bright-yellow rain gear.

Frank said, "I'm afraid we're closed for browsing, Miss, but can I help you with something else?"

The bright yellow wavered from side to side. She was trying to see into the room, past Frank, which wasn't difficult given his slim frame.

Her head tilted sideways, and she caught my eye with one of hers. Her visible eye was large and spooky, like that of my former neighbor, Corvin's. She had thick, dark eyelashes, equally thick, black eyebrows, and a fringe of bleached-white hair sticking out from under her cap, which was as yellow as her rain slicker. She looked about sixteen, my daughter's age.

The girl said to Frank, "Is that your car? The orange one?"

"No, but it does belong to my coworker," Frank said. "Are you looking for a used car?"

I yelled out, "It's not for sale!"

If the girl had been interested in the car, it wouldn't have surprised me. Foxy Pumpkin had been attracting more attention than usual. I'd had an offer to purchase the old vehicle every day for ten days—ever since her creator had passed away.

The girl giggled in response to Frank's answer. "I don't want to buy that dirty old thing," she said.

I muttered to Kathy, "It's not dirty."

Kathy snorted. "And it's not old," she said, because my car wasn't old when compared to Kathy's ancient Honda Civic, currently rusting in the staff parking lot.

"Then what can I help you with?" Frank asked, sounding a touch impatient. "We are closed for the day, miss."

"I just wanted to tell you about something?" Her voice pitched up, turning every statement into a sort of question. "It's just that someone is tampering with the engine right now? I thought whoever owned it would want to know?"

Frank leaned out. One of his feet rose off the ground behind him for balance as he peered out into the rain. I gave Kathy a double eyebrow raise. Frank was standing like a flamingo again. Kathy smiled. We enjoyed noticing it when he did anything related to his shifter form.

Frank said to the teenager in yellow, "Is this some sort of shakedown? Who sent you? I don't see anyone."

She replied, still uptalking. "Of course you wouldn't see him? He's sort of a ghost?"

A ghost?

Kathy hooted, "Whooo is that girl?"

I jumped off my chair and ran to the door. I grabbed Frank by the hips, yanking him out of the way despite his squawks of protest.

CHAPTER 16

The teen girl's face was round, and her eyes were large and dark, thickly rimmed with black eyeliner and topped by bruise-purple eye shadow. Her skin was pale, uniformly coated in a concealer three shades too light. I tried not to judge a book by its cover, or a person by their surface, but she looked like the sort of kid who would claim to see a ghost whether she was an empath or not.

I looked past her, through the veil of rain, at my car.

There was a man in front of Foxy Pumpkin, and he was not solid. His back was to me, but his clothes were the same ones Harry-Ghost had been wearing. Harry's ghostly hands were out of view, beneath the closed hood. What was he up to?

I turned to the girl's pale moon-face and asked, "What is this alleged ghost doing right now?"

She glanced at my car and answered in more teen-girl upspeak. "I dunno? Something with the engine, maybe?"

"Are you here with the others?"

"The others?" She blinked her dark raccoon eyes repeatedly.

"From the internet forum," I said. "The group that's been here all week. Are you one of them?"

"I'm not one of anything," she said, her eyes glistening. Hoarsely, she added, "I'm all on my own."

We locked gazes, and I felt her sadness rise up within me. I broke eye contact to check my car. The ghost was gone, and there was only rain pouring down.

The girl followed my gaze and said, "He's gone now." Then she turned her sad eyes on me and said, "Mr. B is supposed to be resting in peace, but he isn't."

"You knew him?"

She nodded.

"Who are you?" I asked.

"Ambrosia," she said.

I knew that name. The muscles in my back realigned as I stood to full height.

"Ambrosia Abernathy?" I asked, certain she was the eccentric girl my daughter had mentioned.

The muscles in her face twitched. "You know about me?"

"Maybe," I said. "Are you the sort of girl who drives an old hearse around town and pretends she can see ghosts?"

She pursed her pale lips and narrowed her eyes. Her eyelids lowered, expanding the dark purple eye shadow, making the pale-faced girl look more like a skull by the second.

She said nothing.

I pressed on. "Or, are you the sort of girl who drives an old hearse around town and can actually see ghosts?"

She broke eye contact and looked down at her yellow rubber boots. "Everyone knows ghosts aren't real."

"So, you didn't see a ghost tinkering with my car just now?"

"Nope." She shrugged. "It was just a joke. A stupid joke."

"Ms. Abernathy, do you know something about what's been happening around here lately? You can tell me. I'm a pretty good listener."

"Never mind," she said, turning away.

"I'll be here on Monday," I called after her. "You should drop in."

"I've got school," she called over her shoulder.

"Come by after school!"

She tilted back her yellow umbrella and twirled it in the rain.

I watched her walk away, then reported back to my coworkers, who'd been listening the whole time but weren't able to see the ghost like I could. Or like Ambrosia Abernathy could.

Frank looked up the teenager's account in our system. She had a library card, but had never checked out any materials.

"I have other resources," I assured the others. "My daughter goes to school with the girl."

"She can see ghosts," Frank said. "She's been sent here to help with Harry."

"I don't need help *seeing* him," I said.

Frank pointed at the closed door. "That visit was a message from the Spirits of the Deep."

Kathy asked, "The Spirits of the Deep send messages via teenagers in yellow rain slickers?"

"The Spirits of the Deep work in mysterious ways," Frank said. "Why not a teenager? They send messages to my uncle, Felix, all the time. The Spirits of the Deep don't have the highest standards."

"Okay, Frank. I'll bite," I said. "What's the message?"

Frank frowned for a moment, then said matter-of-factly, "You need to finish what you started with Harry."

"Finish what?" Kathy asked on my behalf.

"He wanted to do something to your car," Frank said, with a *duh* tone, as though it should have been obvious. "That must be why he was digging around under the hood just now. That is what you saw him doing, right?"

"It did appear that way." I rubbed my chin thoughtfully. "You don't think he's sticking around to avenge his murder by poisoning?"

"Maybe it's all connected." Frank circled his finger in the air. "Your old car. Harry's poisoning. All the ghost hunters coming out of the woodwork. That spooky little girl. Maybe everything's connected."

"Hmm," Kathy said. Her stomach grumbled in a threatening manner.

We all looked at the empty cracker box.

If I knew Kathy's stomach grumbles—and I did—this executive staff meeting would be ending soon, one way or another.

"Okay," I said, clapping my hands together. "I'll do something with Harry and my car. I don't know what, but maybe it'll come to me."

"Or you could take the car to him," Frank said. "Did he have a garage at his house?"

"I don't even know if he had a house."

Frank ran to the computer and typed rapidly. "Here he is. That's not an apartment address." More typing. "That's odd. It's the same street as the spooky girl." A few clicks. "Right next door."

Kathy's stomach grumbled again. She also grumbled, "We shouldn't be using the library computers to spy on people. It's against the terms of our privacy policy."

Frank and I exchanged a look. Kathy's regard for the rules fluctuated with her hunger levels. Sprites commonly developed dysfunctional metabolic systems on the Standard American Diet. Actually, Kathy's regard for a great number of things fluctuated with her hunger levels.

Frank said, "I think you should go to Harry's house. Who knows? He might be receptive to your spells there, and maybe you'll be able to read him like a book, or whatever it is you do. Am I saying it right?"

I nodded. "Reading him like a book is exactly what I'm supposed to be able to do." I kept nodding. "I guess going to his house is worth a shot. We're not getting anything useful out of him here at the library. All he does here is take naps."

"Your detective beau won't mind? You're not stepping on his toes, are you?"

"He's a big, strong guy who can handle a little toe stepping." I grinned. "Besides, I don't think the Blackstone case is a high priority." Unlike Lund, Bentley wasn't convinced the death was a homicide.

I turned to Kathy for her input, but her chair was empty. Kathy was by the door, pulling on a rain slicker of her own, a mottled green and gray slicker that didn't offer much visibility for crossing sidewalks in the rain.

"I guess that wraps up the executive meeting," I said.

"Pretty much," Frank said.

Kathy sighed as she zipped up her rain slicker. "Honestly, I don't care what you do, as long as you do something. This whole situation is untenable. It's only going to get worse. We're going to be overrun with *those people*. They're like a plague of locusts, or a horde of something worse." She wrinkled her nose. "Like goblins."

"They're not *all* bad," Frank said.

"They are all equally bad," Kathy retorted. "I've had to assign extra staff for the weekend, which will drain our budget. I can squeeze a few more cents here and there, but if this heavy foot traffic without the support of circulation numbers goes on much longer, I'll have to make cuts. We won't be able to paint over the wolf mural. Or buy crayons and coloring books."

"Not the crayon budget!" Frank gasped and turned to me with pleading eyes. "You have to do something," he said.

Kathy flipped up her collar. With an air of formality, she said, "Harry Blackstone was not my favorite patron when he was alive, but it seems death has improved my sentiments toward the man, as death often does." She looked directly at me. "Zara, I hereby authorize you to do whatever you can to usher his troubled spirit... somewhere else. You may use any of the library resources, including your time on shift, however you see fit."

I pushed up my cardigan sleeves. Let the shenanigans begin!

Kathy left.

Frank and I looked at each other.

"We need to save the crayon budget," I said. "I'll drive by Harry's house over the weekend."

"Let's go there right now."

"Let's?"

"I'm coming with you."

"Oh, Frank." I waved a hand. "You don't want to get involved."

"I'm coming with you," he said, lifting his chin. "I'm always hearing about your adventures secondhand. Not anymore! This time, I want in."

"Careful what you wish for," I said.

"Ol' Frankie Boy can handle himself just fine in a crisis."

"If you say so."

He swung a fist and declared, "Adventure awaits!"

CHAPTER 17

We left Frank's car at the library, and I drove Foxy Pumpkin, since the point of our excursion was to bring the car to Harry—assuming he was haunting around his former home.

We pulled up to the Blackstone residence as the rain poured down.

The house was a modest rancher that fit in with the other forty-year-old houses in the neighborhood. There was an attached single-car garage, and a dense hedge on either side.

In front of the house, a brunette in a skirt and heels was pounding a For Sale sign into the lawn. It was Reyna Drinkwater, the same real estate agent who was selling the Moore house. What a coincidence. When I'd met her on my street, she'd also been putting up a For Sale sign. Once again, the heels of her pumps were sinking into the soggy grass. *She must go through a lot of shoes*, I thought.

"Reyna Drinkwater," Frank Wonder said, reading her name off the sign. "Is she the one you told me about? The one who's selling the house next door to yours?"

I turned off the car's engine and turned to grin at Frank. "You mean the house you're going to put an offer on?" For a moment, I forgot all about our ghost fishing expedition to focus on my other pet project: Getting Frank to buy Chet Moore's house.

Frank snorted and replied in his fake Southern accent. "While I certainly do appreciate your constant harassment, Zara Riddle, there is simply no way I'll be purchasing the house next to yours."

"The price is very reasonable," I pointed out. "And the neighbors are fantastic."

"You know me. I'm more of an apartment guy."

"Your apartment is haunted," I scoffed. "That whole creepy building is literally crawling with tortured spirits."

"They're not *that* tortured," he scoffed right back. "I leave them alone, and they leave me alone."

"What's your real objection to buying a house? Are you worried about maintenance and upkeep? Don't be. Chet's place looks like an old house on the outside, but Chet renovated that place from top to bottom with nothing but the best. It's basically new inside."

Frank was quiet for a moment. Had I finally gotten through to him?

"Nope," he said with a note of finality. "I like living at the Candy Factory."

"Marketing hype," I snorted. "That old building was *barely* a candy factory. It was Wick Pest Control for decades, and before that, wasn't it a prison for the criminally insane?"

"Yes. And before that, it was a leper colony," he said proudly.

"That place gives me the heebie-jeebies, and I'm a witch."

"But the light," Frank said with a sigh. "And the ceiling height. You really can't beat a loft for the light and the vertical space."

I pictured a flamingo flapping his wings above Frank's tasteful living room furniture. "Frank! Don't tell me you fly around inside there!"

He smirked. "Sometimes, after a long day, you just wanna get home and spread your wings."

"Okay. I get it now. I guess I'll stop bugging you about the Moore house. It's a great place, but you could never shift inside. Not unless you converted the attic and raised the roof."

"Would the city allow that?"

"Frank." I gave him my serious look. "I happen to *know people* at the Permits Department." My aunt was the head of some semi-fictional subdepartment that did secret projects. As for Frank's potential renovation, I felt confident Zinnia could pull the right strings if I asked sweetly.

Frank rubbed his chin thoughtfully.

There was a knock at the driver's side window. We both started.

The real estate agent was standing next to the car in the rain. She cupped her hand around her mouth and yelled through the glass, "Are you here about the new listing?"

"Hi, Reyna!" I opened the car door and stepped out. The wind picked up just then, and the rain cut sideways, straight into my eyeballs. "It's me, Zara Riddle. From Beacon Street." I caught a mouthful of rain.

"Oh! Hi, Zara. It's nice to see you again."

"Is it?" I squinted against the rain. "It could be nicer."

"Let's talk inside," the agent said with a light laugh, smiling over at Frank, who'd also stepped out of the car.

Reyna Drinkwater led the way up an overgrown walkway, past a small porch containing two wooden chairs topped with folded blankets, and straight into Harry Blackstone's house.

"That's better," she said once we were inside the home's entryway.

The house was dim and murky, even with the lights on. The walls were covered with the kind of wood paneling that was already going out of style the year the home had been built. All the fixtures and finishes were original, from the pointy-stuccoed ceilings to the shaggy brown carpeting on the stairs, which led both up and down off the entryway.

"This is a split level?" Frank asked, pointing to the stairs.

"One of the few in the neighborhood," Reyna answered. "You don't notice from the outside because of the low roof profile, but the home is bigger than it looks. It has over twenty-five hundred square feet of livable space, not including the garage." She wiped her shoes on the mat, not quite removing the chunks of mud and grass from the heels. "I have an appointment back at the office shortly, but I can give you a quick tour right now, plus a features sheet."

"Reyna, we wouldn't want to put you out," I said.

"Don't be silly," she said, smiling professionally. "It's my job!"

Frank and I exchanged a look. We'd come to skulk around looking for a ghost. Getting a guided tour of the deceased's home was more than we'd expected. However, I noted to myself, the real estate agent might sell Frank on the idea of home ownership, which meant I'd be that much closer to getting my wish of manipulating—um, gently assisting Frank into becoming my neighbor. Talk about killing two birds with one stone.

* * *

The house had been emptied of all Harry's personal effects, except for a few pieces of furniture, interspersed with generic items likely rented from a home staging company. Harry didn't strike me as the kind of guy who collected decorative bowls full of seashells.

At the end of the house tour, Reyna was giving us some numbers regarding the home's typical utilities bills —surprisingly low!—and the property taxes—quite reasonable!—when she abruptly lurched forward and slapped both hands on the kitchen counter to steady herself.

For the length of the tour, I had been searching for Ghost-Harry in all the dim corners, and hadn't looked at the real estate agent that closely. Now I saw that her cheeks looked waxy, and her skin had a yellow cast. Her eyes had the sanpaku presentation—whites visible on three sides. The whites were also tinged with yellow. Bilirubin? She was jaundiced. It could have been a genetic condition, a disease, or perhaps something was poisoning her liver.

"Reyna, are you feeling okay?" I asked.

"I think so," she said, frowning. "Probably just detoxing."

Detoxing? Frank and I exchanged a look.

"Have you been eating a lot of peppers?" I asked.

She coughed and let out an embarrassed laugh. "I'm just doing one of those vegetable juice cleanses right now."

"Peppers?" I asked again, this time with increasing concern.

"No peppers," she answered. "Mostly greens, garlic, and raw carrot juice."

I looked at her more closely. Ingesting a lot of garlic and carrot juice could affect the skin, but the whites of the eyes? I didn't think so.

A more likely explanation was poison. Like what had killed Harry.

I walked over to the refrigerator. Had the home stagers emptied the fridge? If Reyna had nibbled on the same tainted foods that Harry Blackstone had eaten, she might need to be rushed to the hospital.

I heard Frank say, "Maybe you should sit down before you pass out."

"I'm fine," she insisted, but she didn't sound fine.

I yanked open the fridge door.

CHAPTER 18

The fridge was empty. I was both relieved and disappointed.

I yanked open the freezer compartment. It was also empty.

I quickly checked the cupboards and drawers, opening each one in quick succession. There were some dishes, but not much else.

As I ransacked the kitchen, Frank watched both me and the wilting real estate agent with horrified, widened eyes.

Reyna, the consummate professional, didn't miss a beat. She hadn't even taken a seat, and was still bracing herself upright with the counter.

"The kitchen would be a great place to start upgrades," Reyna said, forcing a cheerful tone despite her yellow cast and shakiness. "New appliances and counter tops would transform the space. The layout is efficient, and the cabinets are solid wood. You could even paint the doors white to freshen them up. People do that all the time. And you'd want to change out the knobs, of course." She looked right at Frank. "So? What do you think?" She had identified him as the potential buyer, since she knew I was happy in my house.

"The house does have great bones," Frank said. "Are you sure you're feeling okay?"

"I'm fine. How do you like the kitchen layout? There's a nice work triangle."

"Uh, yeah," Frank said. "It's a nice work triangle."

I poured the woman a glass of water and insisted she drink it. She took the water and used it to wash down some pills from her briefcase. They were unmarked, and she casually mentioned they were "vitamins and electrolytes."

After a moment, her color returned to normal, and the shakiness subsided. Perhaps I had overreacted, mistaking a little dehydration for liver failure.

Frank poked around the kitchen some more, then asked, "Why are the owners selling?"

"The owner has moved on," Reyna said.

Not really, I thought.

"Downsizing?" Frank asked.

"You could say that," she answered.

"You're being awfully vague," Frank said, giving her a skeptical look. "The owner has *moved on*? You could call it *downsizing*? I may not be fluent in many languages, but I do speak Real Estate, if you know what I mean. I'm guessing the owner's new, smaller home is a coffin?"

Reyna's face froze. Barely moving her lips, let alone any other muscles, she regurgitated a prepared speech. "As per the real estate bylaws of this town as well as my professional code of ethics, I am obligated to disclose to potential buyers any recent deaths on the premises. I assure you there have been no recent deaths or major crimes on the premises that I have been made aware of."

"But whoever used to live here is dead now?" He rested his elbows on the counter and casually prodded the bowl of plastic fruit.

The brunette wiped her brow with the back of her hand. She was sweating, visibly rattled, possibly from Frank's direct questions.

I looked over at the refrigerator, which might have held photos of friends and family before the cleanup and staging. I wished I could have seen the place as it had been when Harry had died. I mentally kicked myself for not rushing over and letting myself in the first time I'd seen Harry as a ghost. But I couldn't have known that even after two weeks, Bentley wouldn't have closed the case.

As for the refrigerator photos, there might not have been much to see. Harry was a loner, a genius inventor who'd kept to himself after taking an early retirement from the DWM. He'd never married, and had no children. He didn't have any heirs, except for a brother who lived in Wisteria. The brother was a wealthy businessman who wouldn't have been financially motivated to kill his sibling—at least not according to Bentley, who'd looked into the possibility. According to Bentley, the brother had been out of town for weeks, up to and including the day Harry died.

I looked over at Reyna Drinkwater, who was finally answering Frank's question, speaking her words carefully. "The man who lived here did pass away recently. He died peacefully in his sleep, and the event did not take place on the premises."

Frank tapped his fingers on the stack of features sheets thoughtfully. A playful look crossed his face. Frank was enjoying our amateur sleuthing.

He licked his lips before saying to the agent, "I wonder, Ms. Drinkwater, if there's any way you can guarantee that this house isn't haunted? My current home is crawling with tortured spirits." He waved his hand. "I have an uncle who claims to be clairvoyant," he explained. "I'll have to take his word for it, but if I *were* to pick up and move, I certainly wouldn't want to jump from the proverbial frying pan into the fire."

"Haunted?" Reyna's face went through a series of expressions, as though she was trying them on. She settled on a calm, playful expression that matched Frank's. "Actually, this place is very haunted." She leaned toward him and patted his arm with loose fingertips. "Haunted by some bad decorating choices, if you know what I mean! But nothing a few cans of paint and some fresh carpeting wouldn't solve." She winked at Frank.

He pointed a finger at her and winked back. "Good one." He turned to me. "Any questions?" He raised his eyebrows. "Did you see anything unusual while we were on the tour?"

I shook my head. "Nothing but bad decorating decisions."

Frank shrugged. "Wood panelling is easy enough to replace."

"Or paint over, for a seaside look," Reyna Drinkwater said. She was packing some things into her briefcase. "If you like the coastal vibe." She looked up at us and smiled as she snapped the briefcase shut.

"A coastal vibe," Frank said. "You're a good Realtor."

"Thank you," Reyna said.

"She is good," I agreed. "Say, Frank, did I happen to mention to you that Reyna is also the listing agent for a house on my block? It's right next to mine."

Flatly, he said, "You may have mentioned that."

"That one's a great character home," Reyna chimed in. "High quality renovations. The previous owners had excellent taste, and are very much alive, so you need not worry about hauntings. Similar price range as this one. I've got an Open House coming up." She reopened the briefcase and handed Frank a color flyer with a photo of my neighbor's house. The image captured both the charming goat weathervane on the roof and the circle window in the attic. *So cute.* If I didn't already have a house, I'd be tempted.

Reyna went on to tell Frank more about the Moore residence, comparing and contrasting it with the Blackstone house. By juxtaposing the two houses, she somehow managed to make both of them sound better and better by the minute. She really was good.

Wrapping things up, Reyna said, "Thanks for braving the rain and stopping by!" She started moving toward the front door. "My number's on everything I gave you, and I'm available any time for questions." She paused. "There's just one thing I should tell you."

Frank and I made curious sounds and waited.

"Here's the thing," she said breathlessly. "I know you hear a lot of hype from people in my profession, but I'm being honest with you guys. There actually has been a lot of interest in this listing."

We made more curious sounds.

"I've had requests for showings from a number of interested parties," she said. "I've never had so much interest in a residential listing. Everyone has been so curious, and eager to get inside." She shrugged. "It seems these old split-level homes are having a moment with the hip and trendy crowd."

Frank and I exchanged a look. People were curious, and eager to get inside? That sounded a lot like the new visitors we'd had at the library, descending like a swarm of locusts, kicking the locals off the computers, blocking aisles with their backpacks, and spreading their "evidence" across every free inch of study-table space.

I asked the agent, "These requests for showings, have they been from out-of-towners?"

"Yes. Why?"

Frank and I exchanged another look.

"Why?" Reyna asked again, frowning. "Is something going on that I don't know about?"

"I'm sure it's nothing," I said.

Her skin took on a slight yellow tinge again. "What's going on?"

I felt bad for the woman. She was clearly suffering from her carrot-garlic cleanse, plus I felt guilty about wasting her time on a home tour. I didn't want to spread more gossip around town, but she would find out eventually, and I might save her some time to make up for what we'd wasted.

"This is going to sound strange," I said carefully. "Reyna, have you ever been on any internet forums about ghost sightings?"

"Huh?" I could tell by her reaction that she had not.

Frank and I proceeded to admit that we worked at the library where Harry Blackstone had died. We told her what had been happening there recently, with the "rumors" of the ghost being around.

"That's so strange," she said, wide-eyed. And then her face twisted into an angry frown. Now she looked like someone who would—allegedly—release wild animals plus a donkey inside a residence to drive down the price. She growled, "Who do these out-of-towners think they are?" She shook her head. "They shouldn't be posing as buyers. In my industry, we do not tolerate this sort of thing."

"At least you can screen them," Frank said. "At the library, we're sort of all about tolerance."

She turned her rage toward Frank. "Speaking of tire-kickers, are you actually looking for a house?"

Frank swallowed so hard, I heard it. "Yes, ma'am," he said. "I've been talking to Zara about it for weeks."

"It's true," I said.

"All right," she said, and the fire in her eyes died down.

Reyna picked up her phone, checked the screen, and said, "Sorry I have to run. I do have that appointment back at the office, and I'm already late." She tossed something small and metallic at me: a key. "Take your time looking around the place. Zara, you can lock up when you're done."

I waved the key. "Are you serious?"

"That's a spare," she said. "I can grab it back from you sometime when I'm over on Beacon Street."

Before I could decline the burden of responsibility for having a key to a place that was not my own, she was gone. After the front door banged shut, the resonance inside the house changed. The vibration was subtle, like a key change in a song that you weren't paying attention to. I didn't know what I was feeling, but I sensed the house's relief that she was gone.

Frank looked at me and said, "I don't like this house."

"Aw. Don't hurt the house's feelings."

"It's not personal," he said. "I just never cared for split levels."

"Fair enough. There's a reason nobody's building them anymore." I dangled the key between us. "But now that she's gone, we can do another sweep of the house for Harry. Ghosts are way more active after dark."

"After dark? The sun hasn't set," Frank said. "It won't be down for a few hours yet."

We both looked out the dark window. It was raining so hard, I'd mistakenly thought night had fallen.

"That's September for you," he said. "Told you so."

"I believe you now. How is October?"

"Gorgeous." He held his hands up and wiggled his fingers. "The leaves are spectacular, and there's so much to do."

We chatted about the local weather, and I began another sweep of the house.

Frank followed along behind me, chatting about all the upcoming October events. There would be corn mazes of all sizes and skill levels, pumpkin patches, hay rides, barn dances, and more. While some towns specialized in Christmas events or summer festivals, Wisteria put everything it had into Halloween. Given the number of supernaturals living in the town, or in the tunnels beneath it, I was not surprised.

On the sweep, we found no poisoned peppers, magical threats, or even Harry himself. At last, we checked the garage, which Reyna had skipped.

The garage workshop was about empty as the house. It was free of the typical clutter found in houses, but someone—likely a staging professional—had artfully arranged a selection of Harry's tools on a pegboard that covered the wall opposite the garage door.

I cast a few spells, detecting multiple residual auras within the workspace—past projects of a magical nature. One of the auras had an orange cast, and a shape that matched Foxy Pumpkin's sturdy body.

Frank stared at the wall of tools with his hands on his hips. "I feel like I should know the names of more of these tools than I do. They're just so... intimidating." He turned toward me with a raised eyebrow. "And this is exactly why I'm not cut out for home ownership."

"Okay, okay." I held up both hands. "I'll stop bugging you about it."

He shivered and rubbed his arms. "Can we get going? On the drive over, you got me all worked up about being in danger, and now I'm coming down from the adrenaline rush." He shook his head. "You're such a worry wart, with all your dire warnings. We weren't in any danger, whatsoever."

"Oh, Frank." I crossed the garage to flick off the lights. "Cheer up. Maybe something will attack us on the way to the car."

He snorted.

We went outside, made sure the door was locked, and prepared to dash through the rain.

Something bright yellow moved on the other side of the hedge. It was a person, and I had a feeling I knew who. Ambrosia Abernathy. She did live next door, after all.

I grabbed Frank by the elbow and whispered a warning to him, explaining what I'd seen. He whispered back, "Now what?" The rain pelted down, flattening his pink hair so it looked like melted cotton candy.

"Follow my lead and don't do anything rash," I said.

He nodded and didn't say anything sassy. His adrenaline was back up again.

I walked toward the car at a normal pace, Frank on my heels, then abruptly reversed course and ran up to the teen girl in the yellow rain gear, who was crouching on the other side of the hedge.

"Fancy meeting you here," I said. "Twice in one day is quite the coincidence, don't you think?"

Ambrosia jumped up from her squatting position, tossed her yellow umbrella to the side, and held out both hands, palms up, as plasma pooled over her fingers.

"Neat," I said. She was a witch! "Yours is purple?"

But she wasn't just showing me her witch powers. Oh, no. A mere little spark would have sufficed. What she had in her palms was a double dose of Total Knockout.

Frank, new to adventuring and thus untrained in defensive maneuvers when it came to this kind of situation, stood at my side, frozen in shock.

I grabbed his arm and yelled, "Take cover," but either I was too slow, or Frank was too slow, or some combination.

CHAPTER 19

To the untrained eye, Ambrosia Abernathy, dressed in bright yellow rain gear, might look about as intimidating as a rubber duckie.

But she was a witch, and she had some tricks up those yellow sleeves. Her pretty purple fireballs had some *stank* on them. Stank like I had never seen. Stank that I wanted for myself.

Both flaming balls of plasma arced around me—one left and one right. How did she do that?

I heard the wheeze of air being knocked out of someone's lungs. I turned to see my eager sidekick clutching his chest.

Frank burped out two pink feathers, but stayed in his human form as he crumpled, going down like a demolished chimney.

I helped him land safely, checked that he was breathing, then whirled to face my adversary. My hair, wet from the downpour, whipped against my cheek.

"Not cool," I said to Ambrosia, pulling a wet strand of hair from my mouth. "Not cool at all. I don't know who your mentor is, but she should have taught you manners. We don't fireball first and ask questions later." As the words left my lips, I was keenly aware of my own hypocrisy. I was a fireball-first kind of witch myself—or at least I had been during my early days. I had much better control over my impulses now. I hardly ever zolted people without provocation.

The teen-sized troublemaker didn't defend her actions. By the look of the purple plasma bubbling in her hands, she was preparing to take a shot at me.

I swept a defensive arc, easily blocking her magic, and, because I'm a class act, spreading a rain-blocking invisible umbrella overhead at the same time. Why not? Any non-magical person watching would be so distracted by the fireballs they wouldn't notice the rain avoiding yours truly.

While she powered up, I knelt by Frank and checked his vitals again. He was unconscious, but he would be fine. Little Miss Purple Fireballs, however, was going to taste the consequences of her actions.

Witch Tongue curled in my mouth, and I actually tasted the fury. It was what I imagined blood in the water might taste like to piranhas.

My whole body was both numb and tingling at the same time. Combat! I was excited.

There were so many amazing combat spells I was itching to use!

But no.

No to the deadly hexes and the painful jinxes. I had to restrain myself. Ambrosia Abernathy was little more than a child. I couldn't beat another witch senseless with my magic. Who did I think I was? Maisy Nix?

I had to treat her like the teenager she was.

So, before she could ruin my day further, I cast a simple spell to remove her boots. While she was standing in them. It was a cheap trick, but an effective battle tactic. I had Aunt Zinnia and Margaret Mills to thank for that particular bit of witchy wisdom.

The shoe-removal spell worked like a—pardon the pun —charm.

Two yellow rubber boots twirled into the air. One yellow-rain-slicker-wearing teenaged witch had her legs yanked out from underneath her. She flipped through the air and landed on her back. The soggy ground cushioned her fall while providing a satisfying SPLAT sound.

"And stay down," I said, pointing a finger at her. "You're grounded!"

Ambrosia scrambled to right herself. She crouched low to the ground, her socked feet ankle-deep in mud. She was red-faced and spitting mad. "You're not the boss of me! I'll show you!"

And, as I would quickly learn, she really would show me.

Her lips were a blur as she cast another spell.

I didn't recognize the spell, so I cast a general block. It wasn't as effective as the correct counter spell, but what else could I do?

I knew within seconds that I'd failed. I might have blunted the force of her casting, but I hadn't blocked it entirely. The dread came first. The weight on my chest. The pounding of my pulse in my ears. And then, the twisting pain inside. My insides felt like a beehive, and the bees were angry.

I fell to my knees while desperately casting a motion-disruption spell combined with a tripwire plus a hard shove.

My spells came together, and Ambrosia fell into the mud again, this time face down. When she lifted her head to glare at me, everything but her big, dark-rimmed eyes was covered in thick, brown earth. In those eyes, I saw the fiery conviction. Not only would she try to destroy me, but she believed she was doing the right thing. It was hard to fight fiery conviction, but I had to try.

Ignoring the buzzing inside me, I held my head high and used my Mom-is-serious voice. "Listen up, you little witch. I may not be the boss of you, but I am bigger and badder. Now, stop this nonsense, you little brat."

She smiled with muddy lips. She was up to something. Her arms stretched wide, and then she clapped her hands together.

I heard the SPLAT of her muddy palms coming together, and it was like a sonic boom inside me.

Time slowed.

The moment stretched out like gooey taffy. The rain streaming off my invisible umbrella stopped in the air, hanging like a beaded curtain.

My insides boiled, bubbling like a cauldron. I thought of a spell I knew of, a particular type of instant poisoning. I'd found the mechanics intriguing, and it was a simple spell, suitable for novices. But I hadn't learn the casting, because no decent witch would use something so vile and nasty on another person! And yet... I knew in that instant that Ambrosia Abernathy had done exactly that. She was not a decent witch. She was...

Everything went black as I lost consciousness.

CHAPTER 20

Several Hours Later

I was dreaming a B-movie style dream about women in prison. One of the locked-up ladies kept dragging a metal cup back and forth over the bars, making a terrible racket.

I woke up to find that the metallic racket was happening in real life. And it was caused by—get this—a real woman dragging a real metal cup back and forth across some very real metal bars. I was inside what I quickly surmised was a holding cell. By the smell of it, this holding cell was commonly used as a drunk tank.

This wasn't a dream. My body felt heavy, and my midsection was sore and prickly in a way it never would be in a dream.

The woman making music on the bars like she was vying for the title of World's Least Enjoyable Harpist was both large and tattooed. She was the only other person in the cell with me.

"Hello," I said.

She whipped around, revealing a face that had seen a rough night or two, or a few years' worth.

Gruffly, she asked, "Did I wake ya from yer slumber, Sleeping Beauty?" She dropped her beefy, tattooed arms to her sides and banged the cup on the bars without looking.

If my ears hadn't been ringing before, they sure were now.

I sat upright on the bench I'd been passed out on, and rapidly took stock of my surroundings. Three concrete walls, stainless steel toilet and sink, and a fourth wall of metal bars. There were a couple of benches, firmly attached to the concrete floor, plus me, and my sole inmate. There were plenty of times I'd been grateful for my witch powers, and this was one of those times. I didn't know this tough-looking woman, but she looked like she could throw a punch. She looked like a Madge.

Madge watched me with bruised, puffy eyes. "Sorry I cut your beauty sleep short, Princess."

"No worries," I said lightly. "I probably slept enough. Do you happen to know how long I was out?"

"How should I know? I ain't your babysitter." Madge stared at me, but also through me, in that threatening yet unfocused way of ladies named Madge who rattle the bars inside drunk tanks.

I heard a heavy-sounding door on thick hinges squeal open. I couldn't see the door from where I sat. Someone —one person, alone—approached the drunk tank, moving with the softest of footfalls, like a shadow. Either the person weighed less than seventy pounds or they had supernatural stealth.

When the person appeared, my breath caught in my throat and my mouth watered. It was a vampire. My vampire. Bentley. He looked good at all times, but at that moment, he was wearing casual clothes, a gray shirt, three buttons undone, paired with dark jeans. He looked yummier than a bacon salad out on a first date with a bacon burger. Also, I was a bit hungry.

He gave me a grim, jaw-clenched look, wordlessly warning me that both of our situations would be better if I didn't let on to my pal Madge that I knew him.

"Hey, jailkeeper man," I said toughly, channelling my own inner Madge. "Lemme out of here. I didn't do nothin'. Even if I did, you can't prove it."

Bentley clenched his jaw even tighter, then instructed the other woman—whose name was Becky Anderson, strangely enough—to step back from the bars and place her palms on the cinderblock wall. She did so, begrudgingly.

Bentley nodded for me to exit and follow him down the hallway.

"Nice to meet you, Becky," I said. "Good luck with everything."

"Catch ya on the flip side, Princess Buttercup," she said. "Or is it Petunia?"

I shot a glance over my shoulder at her. "It's Zara," I said. "I work at the public library. Perhaps we'll meet again!"

"Stay outta trouble," she called back, equally cheerful, then, "Nice to meet ya!"

* * *

Bentley and I travelled through a maze of corridors without saying a word to each other. He opened the door for a small room, and I went in.

As soon as the door closed behind us, I threw my arms around my handsome vampire and kissed his cheek.

"You're a sight for sore eyes," I said. "How long was I out? Did you arrest the little witch? Is she being booked in another room?"

He pulled away and looked me in the eyes. "Slow down. I don't know what you're talking about. What little witch?"

"The one who knocked me out! You didn't arrest her?"

He gave me a guarded look and spoke slowly. "I'm not supposed to be working tonight."

"Thanks for coming to get me on your night off."

"You're welcome." He spoke through gritted teeth, as though angry about something.

"What's wrong? Did something happen?"

"You tell me."

"I was trying to tell you. Someone attacked me. You'd better arrest her soon. For her own protection. When I get my hands on her..." I mimed casting some strangling-type spells that Bentley wouldn't understand at all. "Well? What are you waiting for. Go out and arrest her. I'll give you her name and address."

He sighed. "I'm not working tonight."

"So? When has that stopped you before?"

With forced patience, he explained, "Earlier this evening, I was sitting inside a very nice restaurant, wondering why my date for the evening was running so late. Then I received a phone call that a certain Zara Riddle had been picked up, and she was currently passed out in the drunk tank."

"Why did they put me in the drunk tank, anyway?"

"You were drunk."

I snorted. "I wasn't drunk!"

He raised his eyebrows and looked pointedly at my mouth. "Your breath would say otherwise."

"Don't be ridiculous! I haven't had a drop of booze since the last time I saw Charlize, and that was ages ago. You must be smelling Madge, or Becky Anderson, or whatever her name is."

He waved his hand in the air between us. "Your breath reeks of booze. And might I remind you that I'm the cop here. I know booze breath when I smell it." He sniffed, his nostrils flaring. "Rum?"

I held up my hand, exhaled fully onto my palm, and sniffed.

Booze.

He was right. Not necessarily about it being rum, but there was the distinctive aroma of alcohol on my breath.

"This isn't what it looks like," I said. "Or what it smells like. It's not real booze. It's magic booze."

"Magic booze?"

"Never mind about that. Where's Frank? He was with me. Or at least he was the last time I was conscious. Is it still Friday?"

"First, Frank Wonder is okay. He's safe and sound at another facility. As for the time, it's past midnight, so it's technically Saturday. The breadsticks at the restaurant were excellent, by the way. Thanks for asking. When your date leaves you waiting for an hour, they give you as many breadsticks as you want."

"Our date! I'm sorry! I didn't mean to stand you up. Honestly. I stayed at work a bit late, and then—"

Bentley cut me off. "And one thing led to another, and you wound up drunk and passed out in a pile of mud in a residential neighborhood."

"This isn't how it looks," I said. "Someone cast a spell on me."

"Someone cast a spell on you and made you drink to intoxication? Aren't you supposed to be incapable of passing out from booze? Isn't that how you keep up with the gorgon?"

"There's a spell that mimics severe intoxication," I said. "Listen. I can explain everything, and once you hear it, you won't be mad at me anymore."

"Don't you dare use your bluffing spell on me," he said gruffly.

"I would never!" I said, which wasn't entirely true.

He gave me a steely look that said he also knew better.

I avoided his eyes and looked down at his chest. He had a smattering of light-brown flakes on his button-down shirt. Bread crumbs. From the breadsticks he'd eaten while being stood up for our date. When I pictured Detective Theodore Dean Bentley munching breadsticks while the waitresses felt sorry for him being stood up, I found the idea funny and cute and sad, all at once.

He put his finger under my chin and lifted my face as he asked, "Did you really get knocked out with an intoxication spell?"

"Yes." There was a soft clunk as a chunk of dried mud fell from my clothes to the floor. I had passed out in wet mud, and woken up covered in caked-on mud.

"Why did you let one of your friends cast it on you?"

"I didn't *let* anyone!"

"If you say so." He sounded unconvinced.

Slowly, tersely, I explained, "I was running a quick errand after work, and I ran into the new witch in town. A young one. Being a novice witch, and not a responsible adult like me, she completely misread the situation, and she zapped me with a powerful spell that knocked me out and made my breath smell like Captain Morgan's finest."

"This came from just one spell?"

"I think so." I massaged my midsection, glad to find everything was feeling better by the second. "At least I hope it was only one blast. I may have great regenerative powers, but I've only got one liver."

"And did the suspect do the same to Frank? He was also unconscious when the patrol car picked both of you out of the mud."

"She zapped him with purple plasma fireballs, poor guy. You're sure he's okay?"

"Frank Wonder will be fine," Bentley said. "He's with friends."

"At the you-know-what?"

Bentley nodded.

Another chunk of dried mud fell from my clothes.

I looked around. We were standing in a cinderblock room with a metal table and two chairs. No windows; no view; no way of knowing where I was without casting a spell. I'd assumed I was at the police station, but we could have been anywhere.

I looked down at the mud around my feet. My shoes were filthy, as were my legs, and the rest of me that I could see.

"Cleanup on Aisle Three," I said.

Bentley didn't laugh. He was sore about me standing him up, even though it had been an accident.

That wasn't very fair of him. I would have loved to have been inside a nice restaurant eating breadsticks rather than lying unconscious in the rain and mud.

After a moment, he said, "Did you say something about a new witch in town?"

"Ambrosia Abernathy," I said, spitting out the name like it was cursed. "And she's not new in town. According to her library card, she's been living here for years."

"Is she a member of the coven? Was that the errand you were doing tonight?" He leaned over me, amplifying our height difference.

I grabbed one of the metal chairs and took a seat at the table. "If you want to interrogate me, Detective, let's do it right." I waved to the chair across from me.

He took the long way around the table and slid soundlessly into the chair opposite me. He gestured for me to speak.

"The errand had to do with Harry the Ghost," I said. "Harry Blackstone. As in, the homicide case that you and Ms. Persephone Rose haven't closed yet, despite having had almost two weeks, plus access to all of your many resources." A prickliness crept into my tone. Despite standing him up for our date, I might still have the higher ground, depending on the spin. "Perhaps if you'd located the peck of peppers poisoner, Harry would have moved on by now, and I wouldn't have to worry about all the people attempting to film a reality TV program inside the library."

Silver eyes narrowed at me. He wasn't ceding the high ground.

I rubbed a crusty chunk of mud from my eyebrow. "Ugh," I said. "Is there any part of me that isn't crunchy or dirty or both?"

"They would have hosed you down, but we have a policy of not doing so if the detainee is unconscious. People are so litigious these days, and mind wipes aren't cheap."

I pointed to the camera mounted in the corner. "Is that thing recording?"

He checked. "No."

I cast a spell.

CHAPTER 21

The spell I cast was to to clean myself. It wouldn't do a perfect job. That was why I still showered regularly. But it would get rid of the main bulk of the crunchy mud caked all over my skin and clothes.

The only downside to the spell was the static cling. The wash and dry cycle didn't have a fabric softener or hair conditioner function. Not yet, anyway. I did have some home brew ideas for modifying the spell—ideas that would make the rest of my coven tsk-tsk disapprovingly.

As the spell did its thing, complete with scrubbing bubbles that floated all over me like jellyfish, Bentley's silver eyes grew large and round. His jaw dropped open slightly, and he didn't move. He didn't even blink. In our time together, the man had seen me do many spells, yet new ones still amazed him. I liked that about him. It almost balanced out how cranky he got whenever I was so much as five minutes late for a date, or missed it entirely because I was passed out in a drunk tank.

He asked, "Are those soap bubbles?"

"Yes. It's a cleaning spell."

Without blinking, he asked, "Where does the mud go? Where does stuff go when you make it disappear?"

"There's a secret landfill in the middle of Indiana where everything goes."

His dark eyebrows bounced up.

"Not really," I said. "Gotcha."

He winced, as though my efforts to make him laugh were causing him pain.

I changed the subject. "So, about Harry Blackstone," I said. "Should we compare notes? I miss the good ol' days when we partnered on cases."

"The good ol' days?"

"Don't be grumpy. You had fun with me. A lot more fun than you have with Persephone Rose, I bet. Does she even have any powers?"

His expression became as opaque as a stone wall. "I can tell you what we've learned about Blackstone, but that's it."

"Fine. Tell me about Harry."

He excused himself to get some files.

I cast the spell and gave myself another wash and dry cycle.

Bentley returned and spread a multitude of files and photos across the table.

He and Persephone had done a detailed analysis of the type of poison used on Harry Blackstone. It was a compound that wasn't typically found in peppers, but they'd found peppers in his stomach.

They'd done a surprising amount of grunt work, tracing Harry's activities and grocery shopping over the days leading up to his death.

The suspect list had included a few ex-girlfriends he'd casually dated over the years, as well as some neighbors with the typical grudges—Harry had been both stubborn and territorial—but so far the detectives hadn't connected any of those people to the crime.

"You've got nothing," I said.

"Ruling out theories is the opposite of nothing," he said defensively. "What have you got?"

We hadn't seen each other much that week, so I had a lot for him to get caught up on. I told him about the increase in traffic at the library due to the ghost hunters, Harry's afternoon ghost naps, Ambrosia's appearance at the library, my tour of the dead man's house, and then all about my rain-soaked battle with the bratty little witch.

My fists clenched at the memory of Ambrosia's petulant face as she cast the inebriation spell on me.

When I was done, Bentley said only, "Drinkwater. Why is that name familiar?"

"She's selling the Moore house," I said, then held out both hands in exasperation. "How is that your main takeaway from what I just told you? Do I need to draw you a diagram? Ambrosia poisoned me. Also, someone poisoned Harry Blackstone. She's going around telling people about seeing him, and then she's lurking in the bushes outside his house. I don't know how or why she killed him, but isn't it pretty easy to fill in those details once you get your perp?" I used my finger to draw a line across the interrogation room table, as though connecting point A with point B. "Ambrosia is your perp."

"Isn't she just a kid?"

"Kids get into trouble all the time." I shrugged. "Maybe she's working with another person. We don't know who she associates with. I was planning to ask Zoey to—" I jumped to my feet. "Zoey!"

"What's wrong? Are you getting a premonition?"

"Nothing magical. It's just that Ambrosia knows Zoey's my daughter. What if she's at my house right now, kidnapping her?"

Bentley got to his feet and gathered the papers quickly. "We have to go check on Zoey. Make sure she's all right."

"I'm sure she's fine," I said, successfully calming myself with my sensible words. "She was staying in tonight, and we have protective wards on the house."

His phone buzzed. He glanced at the screen, then said, "I have to do something here, but we can leave for your place in about an hour. You want to hang out in the cafeteria, or should I throw you back in the drunk tank with your new friend?"

"Very funny." I brushed some of the breadstick crumbs off his shirt. "I'll find my own way home. You can come over when you're done here. It's not too late to salvage our date night."

He looked into my eyes. "Zara, I wanted to talk to you about something over dinner."

"You're breaking up with me and getting a dog instead. A corgi."

"Stop saying that. Why do you always joke about us breaking up?"

"I joke about everything."

"You do. Why is that?"

"I don't know. Why are you such a striver?"

"It's how I am."

"Same here."

He glanced down then up into my eyes, as though resetting. "I'm heading out of town for a bit," he said.

"For work?"

"No."

"Family stuff? Vacation?"

"It's to do with that thing you refuse to talk about with me."

"Your hideous ex-wife," I said. I didn't know that she was hideous. I didn't know anything about her. Every time he'd tried to talk about her, I'd shut him down. Why did he have to be so stubborn? If I said I didn't want to hear about something, I meant it.

"While I'm away, Persephone Rose will be your point person on the case," he said. "In case you get anything useful."

"No problem." I rolled my arms to loosen my shoulders. Sleeping on a drunk tank bench wasn't the best rest I'd had. "I can work with her. I can work with anyone. I've helped you solve all sorts of cases, haven't I?"

Slowly, carefully, he said, "Thank you for being so understanding."

I detected sarcasm, but I didn't complain. Deep down, I knew I deserved a little flack. I could be difficult and self-aware at the same time. It was one of my non-witch superpowers.

He picked up the stack of case papers and prepared to leave.

"I can have Rose look into this witch friend of yours," he said. "Ambrosia Abernathy."

"She's no friend of mine. Friends don't inebriate their friends."

He raised an eyebrow.

"I know," I said. "One of the main thing friends do is inebriate their friends. I realized how dumb it was as soon as the words left my mouth."

"You are nothing if not self-aware."

"Stop reading my mind!" I pointed at my temple then at his.

He rolled his eyes and opened the door.

We walked down a corridor, got into an elevator, and went up. I recognized the lobby the elevator opened on. We were in the Wisteria Police Department after all.

We strolled through the lobby, then stepped out into the cool night air to say goodbye. The rain was still coming down, so we stood in the narrow dry space under the building's overhang.

"Good luck on your trip to see your hideous ex-wife," I said. "You'd better come back to me exactly the same as you are now, which is perfect."

He rolled his eyes. "I'm not perfect."

I kissed him on the tip of his perfect nose. "I'm really sorry for standing you up tonight."

"I know you didn't mean to," he said. "You don't need to apologize."

I circled my arms around his neck. "I'll miss you."

"I'll be back before you know it," he said in a low, husky tone.

We said goodbye, and then he went back into the building to deal with some official business.

I checked the time. It was one o'clock in the morning. I fished a chunk of mud out of my ear. The cleaning spell was effective, but it did leave a person's holes alone. Probably for the best.

I called Zoey to check on her safety, and to let her know where I was.

She yawned and said, "Why'd you wake me? I knew you were going to be out with Bentley tonight. I wasn't worried."

"I was worried about you. I met your little friend Ambrosia today. She attacked me. Did you know she was a witch?"

There was a long pause, then, "No, but that does explain a lot."

"She's not coming for make-your-own-pizza night," I said. "Keep your distance. She knocked out Frank, and she cast a nasty spell on me."

"Is she okay?"

I chuckled. It was sweet that my daughter assumed I'd won the battle.

"For now," I said. "I'll let you get back to sleep. Check the locks and the wards on the house."

"Boa is sleeping on my bed."

"She's just a regular cat. She's no substitute for magical wards."

"Don't say that. You'll hurt her feelings."

We said goodbye, and I told her not to wait up—not that she was going to.

What I should have done next was call a taxi to take me home, or take me to pick up my car.

That would have been the sensible, adult thing to do.

But the inebriation spell hadn't entirely worn off. And here's the thing about an inebriation spell—something they don't mention in the books: The recipient, once dosed, doesn't necessarily *want* the effects to wear off entirely.

What to do... What to do...

Every woman, witch or otherwise, should have a friend she can call at all hours to go for a drink. Bonus points if that friend always has a supply of good tequila.

I put in the call to Charlize, and the rest of the night was a blur.

CHAPTER 22

Saturday Afternoon
(Well Past Brunch Time)

I woke up a little disoriented, but in a much better situation than the previous wakeup, which had happened in the drunk tank, with Becky and Becky's armpit smell. I was at home, in my own bedroom, and the only thing I smelled was vanilla.

I rolled over and found myself looking in a mirror. It had to be a magic mirror, because my face was rotated ninety degrees.

The redhead in front of me said, "Good morning, Zara. Or should I say good afternoon?"

I jerked upright. The mirror wasn't a mirror at all. It was my aunt. My *much older* aunt. I must have mistaken her for my reflection because she looked incredible. The sides of her mouth were unwrinkled, her eyelids had a youthful plumpness to them, and her cheeks were rosy.

"Aunt Zinnia!" I exclaimed. "When did you get back in town? I didn't know—" I bumped my head on the ceiling. The ceiling? Was my bed levitating? What sort of *Exorcist* nonsense was this?

I leaned over and looked down. There was another narrow mattress below me. Apparently, I'd bumped my head because I was on the upper berth of a bunk bed. Sleeping on the lower berth was my gorgon friend Charlize, her matted blonde hair lying in chunks across her pillow.

"My bed is bunk beds," I said.

Zinnia put her hands on her hips. "You say that like it's a surprise to you."

"Uh, no," I lied as I scratched my head. It wasn't a complete surprise, anyway. I'd seen Zoey's bed turn into two, to accommodate me for a giggle-filled sleepover when my own bedroom was temporarily out of order, but I had never seen bunk beds in my room. Had the house split my bed, or had I?

Zinnia said, "You don't remember what happened to your bed, do you?"

"Curse you and your ability to know me well enough to read my mind without actually reading it."

She pinched her youthful, unlined lips. "Don't joke about cursing people, Zara. You, of all people, should know better."

I apologized and ran a quick counterspell to remove any inadvertent cursing, hexing, or jinxing.

"It was probably the house that split the bed," I said. "The house is always doing stuff like this. It's been banging away on the roof for weeks, doing who knows what up there. Splitting a bed is nothing. The house probably did this last night. It likes having people stay over. My house is an extrovert."

Zinnia pressed her lips into a flat line, then said, "Your house usually has excellent taste. This bunk bed has Zara written all over it. The bed frame is purple, and the linens are decorated with..." She paused, running her fingers over the patterned linen. "Are those llamas, or unicorns?"

"I believe they're a hybrid. Llama unicorns."

She looked more closely. "Indeed they are. Llamas with rainbow horns. Now I've seen everything." Her face relaxed. "I do like the flower garlands they're wearing."

While she studied the fabric—probably planning to make a weird vest or skirt-pants out of the material—I located the ladder to get down.

Zinnia reached up and steadied me as I climbed down. She was surprisingly strong. I felt almost weightless as I came down with her steady hand on my back.

When I felt the worn wood floor under my bare soles, I turned to look straight into her familiar face. Her hand was still touching my back lightly.

A lump swelled in my throat. I hadn't seen her in so long, and now we were in the same room. She'd been gallivanting around Europe with my mother and my mother's friends, who were all wealthy, supernatural, and eccentric. Zinnia and I had stayed in touch through phone and video calls, but now that I was only inches away, the pain of her recent absence hit me all at once.

My eyes stung and my jaw ached. The pain peaked then ebbed, and I felt weightless; I was buoyant. I might float away.

She looked incredible, too. Whatever had been bothering her since the day we'd reconnected, it wasn't bothering her anymore. Even her skin looked tighter. The tiny wrinkle of loose skin under her chin was completely gone.

She was looking me up and down. "You look terrible," she said. "You've been eating too much junk food, and drinking."

"It's great to see you, too," I said.

She leaned to the side to better inspect my condition. "You have mud inside your ear canals."

"Yes, I do. I am definitely going to take a real shower today." I sniffed myself. "And change out of these clothes." I smiled at my aunt. "When did you get back in town?"

She covered her mouth as she yawned. "Rather late last night. I came by this morning because I thought we might catch up over brunch."

"And we will. Give me one minute to shower."

She raised one red eyebrow, amused. "Nobody can take a shower in one minute, least of all you."

I shrugged. "Can't hurt to keep trying."

"Go. Shower. Take your time and don't spare the soap." She waved me toward the hallway. "I'll see you downstairs for a very late brunch. Zoey is making waffles." She pursed her lips. "Real ones. Not the culinary crimes that come out of a cardboard box."

"That explains the vanilla aroma," I said. "Waffles smell so much better than Becky's armpits."

Zinnia blinked at me.

"It's a long story," I said.

"I imagine it is. That's why I didn't ask."

Zing! Classic Zinnia!

She gave the passed-out gorgon on the lower bunk a sympathetic look. "The poor dear," she said. "You were right about her not doing well. She needs to stop biting her nails while she still has fingers."

"I guess I haven't been taking good care of her," I said.

"It's not your job," Zinnia said with a sigh, but I didn't think she meant it. Charlize and Zinnia had been developing a friendship before I'd moved to town and bumped my aunt out of her spot. I felt a bit guilty over co-opting the relationship, and more guilty about not having been a better influence. I was the one who'd called her the night before to pick me up at the police station and hit up whatever drinking establishments were still serving. We'd wound up at a seedy bar outside of town, Becky's Roadhouse Bar and Grill. That wasn't the actual name of the place, but Charlize and I had renamed it after my cellmate, because the place had been full of her friends. They'd all been glad to hear that their friend, Becky

Anderson, who'd been missing for a few days, was still alive.

I tucked the llama unicorn blankets around Charlize.

"She'll sleep it off," I promised. Witches were tough, but gorgons were tougher. When push came to shove, Charlize could turn herself into molten lava. Ironically, she could still burn her tongue on hot coffee, but magic didn't follow a straight line of logic.

We both watched Charlize sleeping. She rolled onto her back, all the better to snore. Loudly.

Zinnia said, "She probably misses her sister, and being on leave from work isn't helping matters. The poor dear." Zinnia leaned over, reaching for the gorgon's head, then quickly jerked her hand back. The gorgon was still sleeping, but her protective snakes were not.

"You know what they say about letting sleeping dogs lie," I said. "It's probably for the best if we give her a few more hours."

"Probably for the best," Zinnia agreed.

I looked into my aunt's pretty hazel eyes. The lump of emotion that had been in my throat reformed. "I, uh, Zoey missed you."

She nodded and pointed down the hall. "Shower. You smell like a roadhouse bar."

CHAPTER 23

After a nice, leisurely shower, I joined my aunt and my daughter for a meal that was technically more of an early dinner than a late brunch. We ate brunch food anyway, including spiced muffins that were a few icing flowers shy of being cupcakes.

Zoey teased out a few details about Zinnia's travels in Europe, and the three of us caught up on each other's lives.

I told her about Harry the Ghost, and my recent run-in with Ambrosia Abernathy, the bratty witch who was going to feel my wrath very soon, unless Bentley put her away for murder first.

"Assuming she did anything wrong," Zoey interjected. "Ambrosia might be getting framed. It could all be a setup."

I gave her a skeptical look. "I thought you didn't even know the girl? Why are you defending her? Are you just playing devil's advocate to keep me on my toes?"

"She's a weird loner at my high school." Zoey gave me a *duh* look. "You figure it out."

"Aw. That's sweet of you to defend one of your tribe," I said. "You're a good kid." I took another spiced muffin. "And a fine baker."

My aunt leveled her gaze at my daughter. "Zoey, you are *not* a weird loner. Don't ever call yourself by any label that you wouldn't want to stick."

I bit my tongue. My aunt never called herself weird, and yet it hadn't helped. As I snickered to myself over this observation, I looked down to see what she was wearing. What I saw surprised me. She was wearing a fashionable pair of lightweight pants and a tailored blouse with short, puffed sleeves. The pants were a sophisticated navy and the blouse was cream silk. Neither item was floral. How had I not noticed this the moment I'd seen her? Aunt Zinnia always wore florals. Often two or three different clashing prints.

She must have noticed me staring at her, because she tucked her hair behind one ear self-consciously, exposing one of her earrings. It was a tiny gold flower.

"Nice earrings," I said.

She gave me a pained look. "Your mother gave me a makeover, only she called it a make-under."

"You do look a little, um, Zirconia-esque." I wrinkled my nose. "But less bony. You have some curves to fill it out."

"I beg your pardon?"

"It's a compliment, Auntie Z," Zoey said. "You look extra pretty today. Mom's not very good with compliments. She didn't learn, because she was changing my diapers and working odd jobs during the critical years when a young woman is socialized by her peers in how to pay compliments."

I stared at her. "Oh, really? Is that so?"

Zoey gave me a thoughtful look. "That's Griffin's theory, anyway."

"It's none of Griffin's business," I said.

"Griffin," Zinnia said. "The boy who is not your boyfriend?"

Zoey, who'd been standing as she cleared plates, flopped back down into a chair. She prepared to launch into what I imagined would be a thirty-minute dissertation on the complexities of her relationship with Griffin, the young man whose texts or lack thereof could throw any day into ruin. I looked for my route of escape. The dining room had only one exit, and Zoey was blocking it. I frowned. Why didn't we have a second exit in that room? Another escape route would have come in handy plenty of times.

"Coffee," I muttered. "Better make some more."

Neither of them seemed to notice me edging around Zoey and sneaking out of the dining room.

When I reached the kitchen, I decided to actually make more coffee. When Charlize woke up, she would need some.

I puttered around the kitchen until it sounded like the Griffin gushing had died down, and then returned to the dining room.

The Griffin talk flared up again, but I white-knuckled my way through it.

Eventually, the topic changed.

The three of us moved on to the best topic for any meal, brunch or otherwise: Other people's business.

It all started when Zinnia wisely sensed that in her absence, Zoey and I had learned some identities that she didn't already know. Zinnia was as hungry for gossip as my head librarian boss, though slightly more subtle.

When I explained I really couldn't say much more about the Wonder family, Zinnia conveniently remembered an unwritten rule that family members would, of course, be *expected* to share information about powers with each other. I'd already assumed as much, but hearing it from Zinnia's lips surprised me.

She blinked innocently and said, "Oh, didn't I mention that?"

I snorted. "How *convenient* that you remember that particular rule now, when you're dying to know what Bellatrix Wonder is."

Zinnia's eyes were as round as saucers. "Is she a goose?"

Zoey snickered. "Close," she said. "You're very warm."

"Duck? Pigeon?" Zinnia's smooth skin blanched. "Tell me she's not a chicken."

"She's not a chicken," I said. "She's a swan." I relayed the whole story, as I'd heard it from Frank. Bellatrix Wonder was, like me, a later bloomer. She'd recently shifted for the first time. It had been a big surprise to her, as well as her dog, not to mention the bear who'd spooked her.

"A swan," Zinnia mused. "Bellatrix Wonder. That's actually quite poetic. Like a real-life telling of 'The Ugly Duckling.'"

"Or maybe..." I leaned in, pausing dramatically. "Maybe 'The Ugly Duckling' was never a fictional story. Maybe it is now, and always was, a *prophecy* about Bellatrix Wonder."

Zinnia stared at me as though I was an idiot. Fair enough. It was kind of a silly joke. Plus, she'd been away for ages. It would take a while for her to get back in the groove with my particular brand of genius humor.

In the wake of my failed joke, Charlize entered the dining room. She had *not* successfully slept off the previous night's adventures. Her eyes were ringed with red, and her golden curls were even more matted. "What's this about a prophecy?" She did a double take when she saw Zinnia. "Hello, stranger! When did you roll into town?"

"Last night. It was late."

"You should have called! We were up late," Charlize said.

"So I can see," Zinnia said. "I have some leave-in conditioner in my purse. I'll leave some with you."

Charlize turned a chair backwards and straddled it. "Why?"

"For your..." Zinnia blinked and looked down at her empty teacup. "It's a new formula," she said. "I'd love to get your opinion on the moisturizing properties."

"Cool," Charlize said. "I'm not getting paid right now, so I'll take free stuff." She crossed her arms on the back of the chair and leaned forward to rest her chin on her forearm. "You look different. Your skin's got more fat in it." Charlize sniffed once. "Did you eat a flock of alpine sheep, or does that stuff of yours work on the face, too?"

Zinnia sat up straighter in her chair, and her features lifted. "I do have a new skin cream that contains lanolin, but not from sheep. It comes from the sebaceous glands of Woolly Prairie Diggers."

"The spotted ones with ten eyes and three horns?"

"You're thinking of the Hairy Spider Snatchers."

"Ah," Charlize said.

I pushed my chair back and got to my feet.

While the two chatted about subterranean creatures small and scary, I went to the kitchen to get the fresh pot of coffee as well as more food. We would need lots of food. After a night of frivolity, Charlize always ate like a horse—if that horse lived off bacon, muffins, and anything you put in front of it.

Zoey followed me into the kitchen. "I think I'll head out for a while and let you three have a Grownups' Brunch."

"That's sweet, but I don't want to cut short your time with your aunt."

"I don't mind." She was fidgeting with the pockets of her jean shorts. I realized she hadn't uttered a peep since Charlize's appearance at the table.

I said, teasingly, "Don't tell me you're still scared of gorgons."

"No," she said defensively. "I just want to get out of the house for a bit, since it's so nice today."

"Nice? Last I checked, it's still raining."

"Sure, but it's not raining as hard as it has been."

We both turned and looked out the kitchen window. Beyond the glass was a gray drizzle.

"If you say so," I said. "Wear a rain jacket. Nobody likes the smell of wet dog."

She rolled her eyes while sticking out her tongue, then turned to leave.

"Be careful," I said, switching from teasing mode to my serious, Mother-knows-all mode. "Be careful when you talk to Ambrosia."

She whipped around, wide-eyed. "What?"

"Make sure you're in a public space," I said. "If you can, invite the little witch to meet you at Dreamland. Maisy has all sorts of protective wards on the cafe. You'll be safe in there, no matter what happens."

My daughter's cheeks reddened. A different teenager might have protested that she was definitely *not* going on a mission to get information from a known witch and possible poisoner. But Zoey was *my* daughter, and we were honest with each other. Most of the time.

She asked, "Are you angry?"

"I'm a little annoyed you tried to hide it from me," I said. "But I'm going to let this one go."

CHAPTER 24

When I returned to the dining room with more food and coffee, Charlize and Zinnia were talking about the town's recent brush with the Apocalypse.

A tiny spot of movement on the wall drew my gaze. Was it a spider? I took a closer look and saw nothing but bare wall. Too bare, actually. That patch of wall needed something. A picture, maybe.

Charlize and Zinnia chatted away while I stared dazedly at the wall.

"Codex," Zinnia said carefully to the gorgon. "From the Latin, *caudex*, for tree trunk, or wood block, or book. It's an unusual name for software."

"*Her*," Charlize said. "Codex was a *her*. She was like a child to me." She sounded bitter, sad, and defensive, all at once. "A child I was raising. You have to understand, I worked on her for twenty-six months Over two years. Not even an elephant carries its offspring that long."

"The Himalayan Pink Skunkapus carries her offspring for nearly three years."

"But half of that time is in her pouch," Charlize said.

"True," Zinnia said.

"I suppose you could compare me to the Skunkapus," Charlize said. "Codex was alive, in a sense, right from the beginning. It barely took a month to program the initial framework. You could say she was two years old when..."

I took my seat and joined into the conversation in progress. "When she hit the Terrible Two's," I said lightheartedly.

The other women said nothing. Charlize went for the food I'd brought with me.

"Codex's Terrible Two's were much worse than my own daughter's," I said. "Codex tried to remake humankind the messy way, whereas all Zoey did was hide sandwiches between the couch cushions."

Zinnia touched her tiny gold flower earring and murmured surprise.

Charlize kept eating.

"We didn't have a panini press," I explained. "But Zoey had one at a cafe, and decided that all sandwiches would taste better squashed flat. She would ask me to make her extra sandwiches, then she'd put them under the couch cushions. I thought she was eating them, and she was, but not right away, and not all of them. Two-year-olds are easily distracted, and she eventually forgot about the sandwiches. Our apartment smelled like bologna and mustard for a full year before I discovered the stash."

My aunt shuddered.

"Don't worry, Aunt Zinnia. There aren't any bologna sandwiches stuffed between the cushions in this house. I check regularly."

She swished one hand through the air. "It wasn't the sandwiches, it was the whole debacle with Mahra. I am so sorry you had to face down Mahra on your own. I've only seen a glimpse of her powers myself, and it was..."

"Kind of a clusterfudge?" I suggested.

She nodded. "Not my word choice, but an apt description."

"No kidding," I said. "She was all, 'I brought you into this world, and I will take you out.' You know, in the stories, she was never my favorite of the Four Eves, but now that we've met, I can't say I have any interest in meeting the other three."

Zinnia drew a sigil in the air in front of herself, warding off evil. "Let us wish we do not have the opportunity."

Charlize let out a weird chortle.

My aunt and I both looked at the gorgon, who was licking the last of the food off her fingers.

Charlize clapped her hands decisively then held them up, palms toward us. "Don't look at me, ladies. I'm officially out of the AI business. I'm on leave, remember? I'm resting and relaxing."

"Then why the weird chortle?" I asked. "Or was that your snakes?"

"Weird chortle? I didn't know that was out loud." She flipped one matted chunk of blonde hair out of her eyes. "You caught me. I was imagining how easy it would be to bring back another one of the Old Ones." She drew a circle in the air between the three of us. "For the three of us. If we worked together. Think about it: My programming abilities and powers." She looked directly at my aunt. "Your knowledge of potions and access to artifacts."

I sniffed. "What about my powers? I kept up with you last night, didn't I?"

"Oh, Zara. You did your best," Charlize said, laughing. "But yes. Both of you are powerful witches. Maybe we, the three of us, are the triad that's destined to bring on the End of Days."

She laughed again, but Zinnia and I did not.

"Come on, ladies," Charlize said. "Lighten up! It's just an Apocalypse joke."

"Too soon," I said. "Too soon, even for me, and that's saying something."

Zinnia sighed. "Prophecies are only possibilities," she said. "Our fates are not fixed or predetermined. My views are constantly being challenged, but, as of right now, I choose to believe the destiny we have is the one we make for ourselves."

Charlize leaned in suddenly, like she had spotted some food she hadn't eaten yet, or was physically jumping on the idea. "What makes you sure about that? We are nothing more than flesh-covered robots. Programs, doing exactly what we were always meant to do. You believe you can choose your beliefs, but you are only a product of your experiences."

"Nonsense," my aunt said. "What would be the point of that? I don't see why any entity would bother." She poked at some muffin crumbs on the table. "The whole idea of predestination strikes me as rather tedious."

I had to laugh. "That's the foundation for your belief in free will? That the alternative," I made air quotes, *"wouldn't be worth the bother*?"

"Yes. Predestination doesn't leave any room for fun." Zinnia's hazel eyes twinkled as she smiled. "Also, I happen to know that the future is no more fixed than the past."

Across the empty food dishes from me, the blonde gorgon's tangled hair snakes twitched.

I noticed that Ribbons must have silently joined us without announcement at some point. The wyvern was now cutting deep grooves in the back of a chair with his talons, and staring at Zinnia.

Something white flashed at the corner of my vision. Boa padded in on silent paws, jumped onto an empty chair, and joined the rest of us in staring at Zinnia expectantly.

I said, "What do you mean, you happen to know the future is no more fixed than the past?"

Zinnia looked from Charlize to Ribbons to Boa to me. She held her fingertips over her lips shyly. "Oh, perhaps I shouldn't have mentioned anything. I'm afraid it's a long, complicated story, and I'm sure you all have better things to do this fine Saturday. I understand from the weather reports that the rain might let up for an hour or two."

Right on cue, thunder rattled the teacup on the saucer in front of her.

Ribbons made the throat-clicking sound that was his non-psychic laughter.

Boa yawned, then stared at Zinnia with renewed focus, her green eyes larger than ever.

"I've got nowhere I need to be," I said.

"I'm on leave," Charlize said. "And some people believe it's still too early in the day for tequila."

"Tell us what you know," I urged. "Don't be a story tease."

Zinnia frowned. "I promised I wouldn't speak of it. I promised Mayor Paladini."

"Too late." I waved my hands in a dramatic swath. "I've used magic superglue to close all the doors and windows of this house." I hadn't, but it sounded good. "You're not leaving the premises until you tell us. Does it have something to do with brainweevils?"

"Yes," Zinnia said. "Well, not really." She waved one finger in the air like the slightly dotty woman she was. "But the whole thing did start with a brainweevil."

I used magic to call for whatever was left of the food in the kitchen, and we all settled in to hear about Zinnia's adventure. Ribbons nearly snapped his chair in half.

Zinnia told us the whole thing, from start to finish. Unvarnished.

If anyone else had told me what she did, I wouldn't have believed it. But this was Zinnia Riddle. She had too much integrity to make up a tale about time travel and other worlds just to impress or terrify us. My aunt had traveled through a wrinkle in time and space, and had lived to tell of it.

Charlize said, "That actually explains a lot about my family." She had listened without interruption—we both had—and hadn't even touched the food in front of her.

Aunt Zinnia beamed proudly.

Soon, the topic of conversation would return to my current dilemma with Ambrosia the Teenaged Witch, Harry the Ghost, and whether or not we should try some multi-witch spells. But, for a few moments, Charlize and I silently ate cold waffles with warm berries, and let my aunt enjoy her glory.

CHAPTER 25

Monday
Before Opening
Wisteria Public Library

Kathy and I were discussing the lack of coffee beans on the premises, and whose fault it was—the weekend staff, obviously—when there was a knock on the side door.

Kathy glowered at the door. "If that's *them* trying to get in before we're even open, you have my permission to fireball as many as you see fit."

"Ooh." I pushed up my three-quarter-length sleeves. I was wearing a blue and orange striped dress I'd found at Mia's Kit and Kaboodle. The size on the tag read XL, and the sleeves had technically been short sleeves, but I'd taken it in for professional alterations, and it was now a different shape and a perfect fit. Plus, there'd been enough fabric left over for the seamstress to make a tiny T-shirt suitable for a baby or a cat. I planned to dress Boa in the shirt when we posed together for the veterinary clinic's annual calendar. But first, I would torture Ribbons by threatening to put the shirt on him. There was a good chance I'd be out five bucks when the wyvern shredded the baby-sized T-shirt, but what was five dollars compared to so much enjoyment?

Kathy continued to give the door a dirty look. "That's it," she said. "That's why we're out of coffee already! The weekend staff must be supplying coffee to the Goblin Hordes!" As of that Monday morning, Kathy had started referring to the ghost hunters as the "Goblin Hordes."

The knocking continued.

"Let's not jump to any conclusions," I said, facing the head librarian as I backed toward the door. "It's possible the weekend staff had to drink more coffee themselves, just to deal with the extra traffic. Remember, the weekend staff are not so different from us. They're also suffering from this whole haunting situation."

Kathy huffed and crossed her arms. Lately, she'd been more irritated than usual at everything the weekend crew was doing. The feisty lady was always mad at someone, but rarely the person she should have been mad at. Her husband was out of town yet again, traveling with their professional athlete sons, and Kathy had run out of crafting projects to keep herself contented. She would be taking it out on the weekend staff, or the Goblin Hordes, or me.

The knocking at the door became more insistent. I opened the door.

Standing on the step in the rain were two witches. At the front was young Ambrosia Abernathy, again wearing bright yellow rain gear. Behind her was the tall and imposing Maisy Nix, dressed in a dark jacket. Ambrosia resembled a wet rubber duckie, and Maisy resembled the duckie's tall, imposing shadow.

Neither of them looked pleased to be there. But, on the plus side, neither of them were firing plasma balls at me. They hadn't come to finish what Ambrosia had started.

"Well, hello there," Kathy called out from her seat at the lunch table. Her attitude had made a complete turn, and her tone was friendly. She and Maisy weren't friends, but Kathy knew Maisy was a witch. I'd noticed that other supernaturals were in awe of Maisy. I didn't see the appeal. She was kind of mean.

Neither Maisy nor Ambrosia returned Kathy's hello.

"What can we do for you ladies?" Kathy asked sweetly. "We aren't open to the public yet, but any friends of Zara's are friends of the library."

Maisy narrowed her eyes at Kathy, then looked at me, one sharp eyebrow raised. "Does your associate have clearance?"

"Yes," I said. "I can make formal introductions, if you'd like."

"No need," Maisy said, stepping inside, dragging Ambrosia along by the ear. By the ear!

Ambrosia kept her gaze down on her yellow boots. She wore her yellow rain hat pulled down low on her head, so that only a tiny fringe of bleached-white bangs were visible over her dark eyebrows. Her face looked pudgier and younger than before. Her eyes were puffy, and ringed with purple, as though she'd been crying. I almost felt bad for the girl. Almost. She may have shed a few tears over our encounter, but she wasn't the one who'd woken up in a drunk tank.

"So, you're in town after all," I said to Ambrosia. "My daughter was on the lookout for you all weekend, but you weren't in any of the usual teen places." I suspected Ambrosia had used magic to hide herself. Zoey was quite adept at sniffing people out—literally.

Ambrosia didn't respond.

Maisy said, "Zara, Miss Abernathy has something to say to you."

I rubbed my hands together. "A confession? Is she going to tell us why she's been poisoning everyone who crosses her path?"

Ambrosia looked up, puffy eyes blazing, face defiant. "I didn't poison anyone."

"You poisoned me," I said. "I was there, remember?"

She looked down at the dirty puddles spreading beneath her yellow boots, and muttered something under her breath.

Maisy jerked her arm, and a spell crackled around the girl's upper ear, where it was being pinched.

Ambrosia yelped, then met my gaze and gushed, "I'm sorry, Ms. Riddle! I shouldn't have cast that spell on you. It was wrong of me."

Kathy, who knew of my Friday adventures with Frank, chimed in, "It certainly was wrong of you, young lady! At your age, you shouldn't even be thinking about alcohol, much less flooding other people's livers with it. If you were one of my boys, you'd be so grounded you'd forget what the sun looked like!"

Kathy's bark was a fictional retelling of her bite. I happened to know, thanks to workplace gossip, that Kathy's sons could have gotten away with murder, and she would have chalked it up to harmless fun. People were always more punishment-oriented when it came to other people's children.

Maisy asked me, "Do you accept this apology?"

I looked at the sparking connection between Maisy's fingers and the top of Ambrosia's ear. "I'm not sure how heartfelt an apology is when given under so much duress."

Ambrosia's lower lip jutted out, trembling. "I was only trying to help, Ms. Riddle. Honestly! I just wanted to help Mr. Blackstone. He's my neighbor, and he's always been nice to me. Or at least he was."

Maisy cut in. "What my young protégée *should have told you* when you startled her on Friday evening was that she feared for her life. Her attack on you, wrong as it was, was in self-defense. She had reason to believe that you were the one who poisoned Harold J. Blackstone."

"Me?" I looked over at Kathy, shaking my head. "It wasn't me. If you have any other suspects, telling me or the detectives would be a lot more useful than jinxing other witches."

Ambrosia squeezed her puffy eyes together like she might cry. "I... Uh..."

Behind me, Kathy said with urgency, "We have to get the doors in five minutes, Zara." Opening the front doors to the public was a simple task that only required one person. Kathy was urging me to get to the meat of Ambrosia's story quickly, so she could hear it all first-hand before we opened.

"You have five minutes, young lady." I gestured for the little witch to get to the point.

My casual gesture must have frightened her. Ambrosia shrank away and began sobbing uncontrollably.

After that, Maisy and I both tried to get more information out of the teenager, but the young witch was too upset. She couldn't string together three coherent words. I blamed Maisy for being too rough on her.

After four minutes and forty-eight seconds, Kathy sighed, pulled out her key ring with a decisive jingle, and walked off to open the doors.

CHAPTER 26

Maisy and I did eventually get the details out of Ambrosia, and I had to agree that she only did what I would have done.

The sixteen-year-old witch had learned of her next door neighbor's death, then picked up on the rumors about him haunting the local library. She didn't appear to be Spirit Charmed like I was, yet, unlike most witches, she could see ghosts. She saw Ghost-Harry hanging around me, the library, and around my car, in a way that seemed suspicious.

Had I been in her yellow rubber boots, I might have thought the same thing. No. I *definitely* would have thought the same thing.

When she'd come to the library side door on Friday, it had been a bluff, a move to provoke a reaction. She'd been trying to put the scare on me that she knew I'd done something. At the time, she hadn't even known I was a witch. She was new to having powers, and had made contact with Maisy, but hadn't yet been brought into the fold with our local coven. These facts went a long way to explain her actions during our brief battle.

She also swore up and down, under a bond oath, that she hadn't poisoned Harry or conspired with anyone else to harm him.

Maisy, who'd been patiently listening to everything, asked if I was satisfied, and if I would call off "the hounds." She meant the detectives, who'd been looking into Ambrosia as a suspect, at my suggestion.

"I'll let the authorities know," I told the young witch.

She looked up at me with big, pleading eyes. "Am I forgiven?" She sniffed.

Before I could open my mouth, Maisy said, "Not until we find a suitable punishment."

I shrugged. "You heard your mentor," I said. "But I think we'll be okay, as long as you never, ever, ever do something like that to me again." I shook my finger at her. "I underestimated you once, but it will not happen again, Miss Abernathy." As I spoke the words, I fluffed my hair back on a magical surge of wind for maximum impact.

"Until then," Maisy said. "Punishment to be determined."

"Thank you so much for everything," I said to Maisy. I had called her on the weekend, on Zinnia's advice, and I was glad to see my aunt's faith had not been misplaced.

"That's what I'm here for," Maisy said, instead of a simple *you're welcome*.

"You're a handy person to know," I said.

Maisy narrowed her eyes. "Now what?"

"We're out of coffee," I said. "I don't suppose you could send someone over here later with a rush delivery, could you?" I nodded at Ambrosia. "Perhaps that could be Miss Abernathy's punishment. She can make a few deliveries."

"No," Maisy said simply. "I have some extra bags of beans in my car. You can have them now."

I thanked her again, and we brought in the coffee. As I watched Ambrosia sulk around, I wondered what sort of punishment would be appropriate for fireball-blasting and rum-poisoning without cause. I also wondered why I'd never been hit with such punishment, other than the one time my aunt grounded my magic powers with some witchbane chocolate.

Ambrosia and Maisy left for school and work, respectively

I didn't rush out to my librarian duties just yet, planning to beg Kathy's forgiveness rather than beg for permission.

I made a few phone calls to update everyone about Ambrosia Abernathy being off the suspect list.

When I finally stepped out of the staff break room, I heard a pair of men in comically large glasses, both previously identified as members of the Goblin Horde, asking Kathy if there was any more of that "complimentary coffee" that they had enjoyed so much over the weekend.

Kathy's jaw dropped open. I thought she might whip them both with her sprite tongue, but she managed to restrain herself.

Their request, however, gave me an idea.

"Gentlemen, the coffee is brewing right now," I called out sweetly.

Kathy whipped around and gave me a startled look. "I thought we were out."

"Our good friend, the owner of Dreamland Coffee, had a few extra bags of beans in her car," I explained.

To the men in the glasses, I said, "Our special library blend of coffee is available by donation. The suggested donation amount is five dollars per cup."

The men conferred with each other for all of two seconds, then one said, "Two cups, please." He set a crisp ten-dollar bill on the counter.

As I walked past Kathy to pick up the cash, I murmured, "I trust this will help with the budget issues?"

She squealed, but in a quiet, librarian-like manner.

* * *

By the end of that Monday, we'd made over two hundred dollars on coffee, plus another $3.78 in tips. The ghost hunters weren't big tippers. At least they valued the coffee. It turned out the only thing the ghost hunters loved more than stalking ghosts was staying up late in their motels telling ghost stories all night. The sleepyheads needed a high level of caffeine to get through their days.

Kathy's mood leveled out, but she did continue calling them goblins.

Harry the Ghost had made an appearance, dozing in his chair by the window as usual. He set off one of the crew's paranormal sensory devices. There was a real hullabaloo as two dozen ghost hunters crowded into the reading nook to experience what they breathlessly called "an event."

As I watched, I was tempted to cast a spell, just to give them something for their efforts. I did not. I was a grownup, and I understood that my actions had consequences.

Case in point: Helen Highbury, the nosy woman whose bottom I had nipped with a spell, had gotten over her fear of viral contagion, and, as of that Monday, had joined forces with the Goblin Horde. She swore up and down that the ghost haunting the library was a pervy old man who pinched bottoms. Due to the power of suggestion, several of the female ghost hunters—about ten percent of the group were women—began reporting that their bottoms were also being pinched. Then several of the men reported the same. I felt bad for Harry, and the reputation his ghost was getting.

At the end of the day, after counting up our cash haul from the coffee donations, Kathy and I were both in good spirits.

When we stepped outside, the rain coming down took us both by surprise. I didn't know about Kathy, but I must have subconsciously expected the weather to improve along with our petty cash coffers.

I cast a large umbrella over both of us, and escorted Kathy to her beat-up brown Honda Civic.

She had already fired up the old thing with a puff of blue smoke and driven away by the time I turned the key in Foxy Pumpkin's ignition.

My car let out a sound that could only be described as, well, flatulence. I tried again. The engine wouldn't turn over.

I looked at the library. We had plenty of books about the basics of mechanical repairs, but something told me the solution wouldn't be in those books.

I looked out at the rain. I could have walked home, but I didn't have a real umbrella with me in the car, and using a magical one over that distance would have been suspicious.

I pulled out my phone. The previous time I'd been stuck somewhere without a ride, I'd called on Charlize. The thought of seeing her that night gave me a sour taste in my mouth. No more tequila, my body seemed to be saying.

So I called my other top choice.

Aunt Zinnia answered instantly, before the call could have rung. She had limited but unsettling prescient powers when it came to phone calls and text messages.

She said tiredly, "Now what have you done?"

"Can't a girl call her favorite aunt, just to chat?"

"Your ring had trouble all over it."

"What ring? The phone didn't even ring over there."

"You know what I mean." She paused, and there was the chatter of her coworkers in the background. Someone was yelling about winning scratch-off tickets. "Do you need assistance with something, Zara? I am almost finished at the office for the day, so I could come over and help you."

To my surprise, she didn't sound like someone was twisting her arm while she offered to help me.

"Thanks," I said, my voice thick with gratitude from her unexpected generosity. "Can you swing by the library and pick me up? The car won't start."

"Oh!" She sounded the opposite of put-out. She actually sounded interested. "It might be a message, from you-know-who."

"Or a message that I need new spark plugs." I turned the key one more time fruitlessly.

"Give me ten minutes to wrap things up here." More yelling about scratch-off tickets in the background, plus someone burping. They were having a rowdy day over at the Wisteria Permits Department.

I thanked her and settled in to wait.

As I waited, I carried on an imaginary conversation with Harry, via the car.

After a while, I said out loud, "You're right, Foxy Pumpkin. We can't have Harry's good name being dragged through the mud by those out-of-towners. We need to do something about this whole situation. It's time to break out the big spells."

CHAPTER 27

I climbed into Zinnia's car, and she parked next to Foxy Pumpkin so we could talk.

My aunt agreed that the haunting had gone on long enough. More and more curious ghost hunters were arriving in Wisteria by the day, and a town like ours didn't need the attention. It would take only one national news story going viral to put us on the map, and that would not be good for the town's residents and their secrets.

Also, if Harry the Ghost was willing to sabotage my car, he might be willing to do other destructive things. It was time to break out the big guns, meaning the spirit-summoning spells that took two witches to cast.

"Tandem spells," I said, rubbing my hands. "No disrespect to Harry, but I'm excited about getting some practice casting tandem spellwork."

Zinnia looked down at her fingertips as she tapped her nails lightly on the steering wheel. She'd left the car engine idling, and the heaters were making the car interior slightly too warm, but not hot enough to switch them off.

"We need some physical objects that were connected to Harry. Blood or bone would be ideal."

"I'll call Dr. Lund," I said. "He'll appreciate me asking nicely this time instead of sneaking around."

Zinnia frowned at her hands. "I'd rather stay off the Department's radar. Blood or bone would be ideal, but we do have other options. You said some of his possessions were at his residence?"

"Mostly furniture." I turned and looked through the back of my aunt's car. "Is this thing a hatchback? I'm not sure we could get more than a coffee table in here."

She rubbed her chin. "I'd love to get his hairbrush, or his shaving kit, but I suspect it was thrown in the trash."

"Field trip to the dump?"

She scoffed, "Vincent Wick would love that."

"Honestly, if it's between Wick and Lund, I'd take Lund."

She turned to me and looked me over. "That dress," she said. "The scale of the stripe is off by twenty percent."

"You don't like my dress?" I smoothed out the blue and orange striped skirt across my knees. "I picked it up from the thrift store for a song. I spent ten bucks getting it taken in, but even with that, ten-something is pretty reasonable for a new dress. You don't like it? Kathy liked it."

"Did you say thrift store?" Her face was scrunched up, as though she didn't know what a thrift store was.

"Plenty of people buy secondhand clothes," I said. "Some would say the thrill of the hunt makes it more fun than buying things new."

"That's it!" She smiled. "We can look for Harry's personal effects without going to the landfill."

* * *

We visited two large stores, with no luck. My aunt grumbled about calling Vincent Wick.

I suggested we try the town's smallest yet busiest secondhand store, Mia's Kit and Kaboodle. Mia always had the best stuff in town. I'd never asked her where the stuff came from, but it could have been from estate sales.

We arrived at the store, and the gray-haired woman at the cash register called out a cheery, "Hello, Zara!" She knew my name for good reason.

The woman at the cash register was the owner, Mia Gianna. She was a dark-skinned woman with a no-nonsense disposition. Her age was impossible to guess, due to the confusing combination of her tightly curled, completely gray hair and youthful, unlined face.

Mia did a double take when she saw my aunt. "Zara, is this your sister?"

Zinnia smiled. "I'm her aunt, actually. But we are close in age."

I rolled my eyes, exactly the way my daughter did whenever people mistook me for her sister and I took it as a compliment.

After some small talk with Mia, my aunt and I got down to witch business.

We cast a few spells, as we'd done at the previous shops. This time, the spells snapped, and we located some clothes, shoes, and other housewares that had belonged to Harry Blackstone.

For the purposes of our spell, we selected a chipped coffee mug that practically sang with Harry's energy, plus a pair of broken-in walking shoes that still had many miles left in them, and a tweed jacket. Then, just so our purchase wouldn't look suspicious, I bought an armload of clothes that caught my eye.

Zinnia murmured to me, "A few items should suffice. We need not go overboard."

I clutched my haul possessively. "Just because my mother gave you a make-under that seems to have stuck, that doesn't mean I'm ready to join the Army of the Cream Silk Blouses. Oh, no. That would make my mother way too happy."

Zinnia, who was wearing a new cream silk blouse with one of her regular floral skirts under her trench coat, stared at me with a perplexed expression. "Zara, is your eccentric wardrobe designed to irritate your mother?"

"Of course not! It's an expression of my colorful personality, obviously. The fact that it irritates people, including my mother, is just a bonus."

She looked down at the wildly striped dresses, plaid skirts, polka-dotted hat, and glittering corset in my arms.

"I have an idea," she said. "We should take a picture of the pair of us wearing all of that, and send it to her." The edges of her mouth curled up mischievously.

"You're so bad," I said.

"You're the bad one."

"If you say so."

I grabbed one last thing—a cute brown belt—and we went to the checkout counter.

Mia said, "Looks like you found what you were looking for!"

"I swear the clothes always find me," I said.

"What a wonderful shop you have," Zinnia said to Mia. "I usually stop in at the Chintz Boutique, across the street, but now that I know about this place, I'll have to drop in here again."

"Yes, you should," Mia said warmly. "If Mrs. Puddikin lets you leave her boutique with any dollars left in your wallet!" She let out one of her booming laughs that filled the space, drowning out the sound of metal hangers being scraped back and forth on metal bars by bargain shoppers. "That place," Mia went on, fanning her face, as though the mere thought of shopping there made her sweat. "Let's just say it's a bit champagne for my beer budget."

Zinnia forced out a laugh and focused on extracting something from her purse. As she dug around, there was the clinking sound of containers—probably glass— jostling around within hidden pockets.

I put my hand over my aunt's purse. "You don't have to pay for this. I can probably get Kathy to reimburse me for half of it, since it's for work. We have plenty of money in our petty cash fund."

Zinnia swatted my hand away and insisted on paying for everything, from Harry's personal effects to my colorful haul.

We left Mia's Kit and Kaboodle and headed toward Zinnia's. Since my aunt was Kitchen Bewitched, her house would be the most appropriate, because we'd have access to all her herbs and supplies.

We drove to Zinnia's accompanied by the hypnotic wipe-wipe sound of her car's windshield wipers.

When she turned off the car in front of her house, and there was only stillness and the sound of the rain, the seriousness of what we were about to do hit me. Harry's shoes, clothes, and mug on my lap suddenly felt heavy.

We were about to cast a spell so powerful it required at least two witches—not because the spell required that much energy. Two witches were required so that one witch could perform magical first aid on the other, should something terrible happen during direct contact with the spirit realm.

CHAPTER 28

Zinnia's House
Well Past Dinner Time

My aunt handed me a thick, ancient-looking book. "Take this," she said. "Open it to a random page. Completely random."

The book was weighty in my hands, as though filled with ball bearings instead of paper.

"I know this book," I said, handling it with care. "I haven't seen it since... *that night*." Unless I was mistaken, my aunt had used that same book that night to confirm my powers as a Spirit Charmed witch. It had been the first magic book I'd ever seen. The first magical artifact, assuming my encursed toaster didn't count.

"Codex Niquitia," she said.

I cocked my head. "Niquitia, as in *trickery*?" Learning Witch Tongue had improved my Latin. But then again, it hadn't taken much to improve my modest Latin vocabulary.

"What else would it be called?" She sounded annoyed. "Do you think there's some other book of blank pages that shows you the answer to any question you ask?"

"Isn't that exactly what this is?" Now I sounded annoyed.

"There are limitations," she said tersely.

"There always are," I replied, equally tersely.

She sighed.

I sighed.

She huffed.

I started to huff, but checked the time instead. It was nine o'clock at night. Since getting to my aunt's house, we'd spent hours researching, setting up, and preparing to cast a tandem spell safely. We'd completely forgotten about dinner, and the lack of dinner was causing a problem.

"We need a break," I said.

"Perhaps you need a break, but I do not."

I held my hands in the air. "I give. You win. You're tougher than me. You're the biggest, baddest witch this side of Tallahassee." I squared my jaw. "But I, the lesser witch, need a sandwich and pickles. My electrolytes are low."

"Witches draw electrolytes from their environment. Witches are more adept at doing so than even the regal Himalayan Pink Skunkapus."

"What about sandwiches? Or pickles? Do we witches draw those from the air around us?"

She pursed her lips. "I suppose we could take a break." She glanced around her floral-themed, overdecorated living room. It was so dim, the flowers that covered everything from the wallpaper to the throw pillows looked like the dried-out versions of themselves. We'd been working under only the light from a few scattered table lamps, and gloom had gathered in the corners. Zinnia flicked a spell in the air that switched on the remaining lights, and another that opened a window. A gust of rain-damp air blew through the room. At the caress of the breeze, I felt how warm the skin on my neck had become.

The gust of wind fluttered the pages of the book on my lap.

The fluttering had a musical sound.

I looked down, mystified. The book had been closed when my aunt had handed it to me. I hadn't opened it. I would have remember something like that, given how special the book was.

The pages flipped back and forth, no longer moving on the breeze, but on their own. I couldn't look away. I was transfixed.

"Psst. Zinnia," I whispered. "The book."

"Oh!"

"What do I do?"

"Close it," she said. "We can always get back to the business at hand after you've consumed a *sandwich*."

"Forget the sandwich," I said, the hunger in my belly replaced with a hunger to know what happened next with the book.

The Codex Niquitia!

I hadn't known its name, but I had been asking about the tome for ages. Zinnia kept giving me excuses about it needing to be recharged. But now that it was on my lap, I felt the power coursing through my body. The book was all powered up and ready to go, and so was I.

I repeated my question. "What do I do?"

"I was going to suggest a test question, but I don't believe that's necessary. We ought to get straight to our business and not make small talk with the magic."

"Let's do it," I agreed.

Without disturbing the book, which was still fluttering away on my lap, we arranged Harry's items and the other ingredients, held hands, and cast the spell to summon Harry's spirit.

The lights went out at once.

I heard my aunt's breathing change. It was subtle, like the shift in breathing a person made once they'd crossed the threshold into sleep. I thought of Bentley, missing him suddenly and terribly, but then the thought was gone. Zinnia's grip on my hands remained steady, holding me in the spell and fixing me to reality.

I couldn't tell if my eyes were open, but then I saw something.

A glowing man entered the room. It certainly looked like Harry Blackstone.

He tugged one ear and glanced around, seemingly confused about where he was.

I whispered to my aunt, "Has Harry been to your house before?"

"Possibly. It's an old house, and I haven't been its only owner," she said. "Why? Is he here? Do you see something?"

"Sorry. Sometimes I forget you can't see them. Yes, he's here, and he seems confused. He's not looking at us, but he might be getting agitated. He was tugging his ear. Now he's taken off his hat, and he's rubbing his head, making his hair stand up."

"We don't want him to get angry," she said. "Keep him calm."

"You mean with a calming spell?" I started to pull away from her grasp.

She held on with a startling strength. "Don't break the circle," she growled, then, "On second thought, forget about keeping him calm. Focus. Let's try doing the memory access quickly. That is the point of this, after all."

I sucked in a breath between my teeth. It was time for me to cast the final phase, to draw Harry into myself as a medium. Easy enough. Thanks to my rezoning spell, I was the library, and Harry was nothing more than a new book coming in. He would be cataloged and placed on a shelf, neat and tidy. He would *not* run amok and make me do strange things, no matter how helpful or entertaining they might be.

"Zara, there's one more thing," Zinnia said. "You must channel him directly into the Codex Niquitia on your lap instead of through yourself."

"But I can't do that. The spell doesn't..." Everything rolled over in my mind. "But I would need to invert... And then that would mean..." I went through the new sequence in my head.

"You can do it," she said.

Of course I could do it. Who did she think she was talking to?

To my right, a lamp flickered on and immediately burned out, like a flash bulb. Then another. The ghost was getting agitated.

It was now or never.

I cast the final phase of the spell.

The room, still dark, suddenly reeked of rotten fruit.

My aunt squeezed my hands even tighter. "What's that? Something's wrong."

"Hang on," I said. "The syntax is tricky, and—" Two more lamps flashed on and blazed out with a crackle. My aunt was going to need some more light bulbs, assuming we survived the summoning.

I cast the spell a third time.

Hot wind blasted through the room, and everything glowed orange. My aunt's face remained steady in the eerie light, but I felt the tension in her fingers and in her energy. She was frightened.

I looked down at the book, which had stopped fluttering. It was open to two pages, each showing a dark handprint.

In an instant, I understood what was happening, and what needed to be done. But now? Right away?

We must be brave and do what ought to be done. That was what Zinnia might have said, if I'd given her time and explained everything.

I yanked my hands free of hers. In the time it took her to gasp, I cast the spell a fourth iteration. This time, I started all the way at the top before incorporating the modified final phase.

The glowing figure of Ghost-Harry lost its human shape. His simmering energy pooled around us like a fog. I grabbed the fog like it was a huge pillow, hugged it to my chest in a bundle, and then slammed it downward, my palms landing neatly on the open pages of the Codex Niquitia.

I tasted metal.

The room was dark and still.

Someone was breathing heavily. Me.

"I think it worked," I said, gasping.

"I knew it would," my aunt lied.

CHAPTER 29

Zinnia busied herself replacing all the light bulbs in the living room lamps while I got acquainted with the freshly encharmed book.

"How is it that I have so many lamps?" Zinnia asked rhetorically as she twisted in another fresh light bulb. "They must be breeding." She gasped. "Would you look at that!" She held up a tiny lamp decorated with petite pansies. "A baby lamp! How sweet is that?" She cooed over the new arrival.

On any other night, I would have happily delved into the whole lamp-breeding situation, but my focus was on the book on my lap.

I flipped through the pages of the heavy, leather-bound tome that needed a new name. It was no longer a Codex Niquitia. Zinnia confirmed that it would no longer provide answers to magical questions. It was now solely a vessel for spirits. It was currently the Codex Harry Blackstone.

The pages contained faint images from Harry's life. I saw his mother's face, beloved family pets, and endless diagrams of machinery.

I'd expected—and hoped—the book would be organized in a chronological fashion, with the first page containing Harry's birth and the last page his death, but the book didn't work that way, because human memories didn't work that way. The illustrations were ever-changing, with images of dogs chasing sticks changing over to a classroom chalkboard without notice.

The faint images on the pages were not the real magic. They were just a side product of the real power of the book, which was having Harry's memories in a navigable format. To dive into those memories, I'd need to cast a basic page-finding spell, then place my hands on the open pages, and let my consciousness be taken over by Harry's.

While my aunt fussed over her new baby lamp, I cast the first exploratory-search spell.

Codex Harry Blackstone, take me to earlier today, when you did whatever you did to ground Foxy Pumpkin.

The pages riffled, and the book slammed shut.

"That didn't work," Zinnia commented. She was floating mid-air, as though standing on an invisible stepladder, twisting a new light bulb into the ceiling fixture.

"I noticed," I replied, a little defensively. "I tried to see what Harry did to my car today, but it didn't work, because it wasn't part of Harry's living memories."

"Of course it didn't work. Harry did that during his afterlife."

"I know. Duh. That's what I just told you."

Her voice stretched high and thin. "There's no need to be snippy." Cobwebs floated down from the ceiling fixture, disturbed by my aunt's movements.

"Sorry. I really do appreciate you helping me with this." I patted the cover of the closed book. "And thank you for sacrificing a powerful book to the cause."

"No trouble," she said, though her voice said otherwise. It had been a great sacrifice for my aunt to convert a rare and powerful book to be Spirit Charmed, especially considering she'd had no guarantee it would even work.

Zinnia gracefully climbed down the rungs of an invisible stepladder. "You ought to try some simple searches to warm up before you attempt to view the deceased's final days."

"Something like the first day of school?"

"Excellent idea!"

* * *

A sandwich on a dainty china plate appeared before me. Zinnia was handing it to me. The crusts had been removed. The inside was smoked salmon, cream cheese, sausage, cucumbers, and something that resembled lettuce, except it was purple.

"Take it," Zinnia said.

"I didn't even notice you leaving the room to make this."

"You were busy."

"This is the most beautiful sandwich I've ever seen in my entire life."

"Don't make fun of me," she said snippily. "You wanted a sandwich, so I made you one."

"It's beautiful. Honestly. I'd never, ever, ever make fun of someone for bringing me food."

"I'm sorry the lettuce is purple, and not the usual green, but it is high in fat-soluble K vitamins. The lettuce is... not vegetarian. However, the part that appears to be sausage is of vegetable origin. More or less. Fungus is genetically closer to meat than most people think. It's actually quite a fascinating process..."

I waved a hand. "I'd rather not know how the sausage is made." I took a big bite. A heavenly symphony played in my mouth. I paused, mid-chew, and asked, "You didn't put Zeronnaise on this, did you?"

In a robotic voice, she replied, "By contract, I can no longer produce or use the substance known as Zeronnaise." She winked and whispered, "But I do have a few leftover jars if you're interested."

"Is it true the military bought it from you to use as a weapon?"

She smirked. "By contract, I can no longer discuss the potential applications of the substance known as Zeronnaise."

"You're a wild one, Aunt Zinnia."

I ate the sandwich, as well as a full jar of pickled items that may or may not have once been cucumbers. As long as my aunt took a bite first, I trusted the food she provided.

When the clock struck midnight, our chatter about food stopped abruptly.

Zinnia eyed the leather-bound tome on the coffee table.

Hesitantly, she said, "We could always wait, and pick things up tomorrow night."

"We have a coven meeting."

She scratched her head. "I forgot they moved it to Tuesday this week." She grimaced. "Do you suppose the new girl will be there?"

"Ambrosia?" I gagged dramatically. "Probably."

"We ought not miss that," she said.

I coughed into my hand. "I think I feel a bug coming on."

Zinnia looked at the clock on the wall. "It is getting late," she said, then, "I'm not tired at all. I don't know if I'll be able to sleep tonight if we don't..." She trailed off, and we both looked at the book.

Truth be told, I was putting off a deep dive, because I didn't want to disappear from reality. I'd been enjoying hanging out with my aunt in her house. I'd missed the woman during her long vacation, and I'd missed being in her house, surrounded by all her wacky floral decorations and Zinnia energy. Even bickering with her was more fun than having nobody to bicker with.

I slowly reached for the book and placed it on my lap. If I wanted to discover the secret of Harry's poisoning, I would need to take the plunge, losing myself in the pages of the book.

Now, losing oneself in the pages of a book was a perfectly harmless—depending on who you asked—activity for people all over the world. But this wasn't just any book. It was a conduit, a portal to the spirit world. Submerging myself fully, so I could access Harry's memories as more than fleeting impressions, required a sacrifice. Everything had a cost, after all.

My sample searches on Harry's first days of school had revealed the sacrifice was time. Instead of experiencing Harry's memories instantly, as a quick psychic flash, the book revealed his life to me in real time. A minute of Harry's memories cost me a minute in my world, a minute of my own life. A minute I'd never get back.

Even worse, if I picked the wrong place to start, I might lose half an hour of my life watching a dead man brush his teeth, shave, and pick out clothes for the day.

The book felt heavy on my lap.

Zinnia, who was sitting across from me, reading a different book on her own lap, said, "Oh, no."

"Now what?" She'd been checking through her magical resources for tips and tricks about using objects as afterlife conduits.

"It's probably nothing." She licked her lips.

"Just tell me."

Her brow furrowed. "It's probably nothing," she repeated, "but perhaps you shouldn't taste anything when you're in the visions."

"Are you kidding me? Don't *taste* anything?"

"The memories are a simulation, of course. They aren't real. But a part of your mind doesn't know that. If I describe to you now the tasting of a lemon, the tart, cool juice spraying in your mouth, the waxy yellow skin, the citrus oil tickling your nostrils, the sour, acidic-sweet taste of juice on your tongue..." She paused. "Is your mouth watering?"

"You know it is." I shook my head. "That's not even a spell, is it?"

"It's everyday magic. When imagination becomes reality inside the mind." She looked me dead in the eyes. "Because of the mirror neuron effect, you must not taste the poisoned peppers that killed Mr. Blackstone."

I smirked. It was hard for me to keep a straight face whenever she said *poisoned peppers*.

Zinnia sighed. "We must take the warnings very seriously."

"Sure, but Bentley said our friend Harry was poisoned repeatedly, over a period of time. One little taste didn't kill him, so it shouldn't hurt me, right?"

She swished her lips from side to side, read her page a moment, then said, "There's an amplification effect that could go in either direction. I'm not sure how the inversion works. If you could give me a few more days to research..."

"Nope." I patted the book's sturdy, leather-bound cover, then opened it decisively. "Kathy wants the ghosts and the Goblin Horde out of the library as soon as possible."

Zinnia looked alarmed. "You have goblins, too?"

I laughed. "That's just what she calls the ghost geeks." I licked my finger, which was the first part of a solid casting of the page-finding spell.

"Be careful," Zinnia said.

"As careful as I always am."

She frowned. "I shall prepare a variety of antidotes."

CHAPTER 30

I'm in.

This is the last day of my life.

My life?

I'm shaving.

I am a man, and I am shaving my face.

Everything feels very *right now*. Very *in the moment*. Stream of consciousness. Like I'm inside a popular Young Adult book, written in present tense.

Back to the shaving.

I start with the cheeks before sweeping the razor under the chin. The sharp blade makes a nice crackling sound on the stubble. Now I have a white moustache of shaving cream. Always a fun look. I use a puff of air to inflate the area, and I shave my upper lip.

My eyes lock on the eyes of the handsome fellow in the mirror. I grin at myself. I am not a bad-looking guy, for my age. Such thick, black hair.

I am Harry Blackstone.

Except I am not. I am Zara Riddle, inside Harry Blackstone.

My focus narrows on a spattery streak of toothpaste on the lower right-hand corner of the bathroom mirror. Now I'm cleaning the spots off the mirror with a damp towel.

Where are the poisoned peppers?! Harry, this is exactly what I *didn't* want to see in your memories. Fast forward to the peppers, please!

Harry does not fast forward.

We are still in the bathroom. I hear the shower nozzle going drip-drip. Now we are scrubbing the mirror with a hand towel like we're about to get an inspection by a drill sergeant. Someone's shoulder muscles—mine? Harry's? —burn from the effort.

I look around as much as I can, limited by the edges of Harry's visions. This bathroom is familiar. I toured it with Frank and Reyna Drinkwater.

Or—let's get the tense right—it's the bathroom that I *will be* viewing soon. Today, in this memory, it's Tuesday, the date of Harry's death. I won't be here at the house until Friday next week.

Side note: That date isn't very far away. The executor of Harry's estate certainly moved quickly in getting the house cleaned up and onto the market. What's that all about?

The world whirs. At last, we're done with the mirror and moving on to something else. The mirror tilts. It's a medicine cabinet. Harry's hand grabs something quickly —a white tube—and then the mirror is closed.

We turn toward the toilet.

Oh no! Was that white tube some sort of personal care cream?

I silently scream inside the memory.

Harry doesn't turn and sit. Instead, he flicks the seat down.

A foot appears on top of the closed toilet seat. Harry's foot.

Harry applies the ointment between his toes.

I don't know why he needs this medical lotion. His feet look fine to me. Maybe because he uses the cream?

He finishes one foot, sighs, and moves on to the other.

This is tedious.

But, on the positive side, the ointment could have been for something else. Even better, I'm getting the hang of being inside this memory.

I feel a more secure veil of separation between myself and Harry. I'm still feeling far more body sensations than I'm comfortable with, but I can handle this. As long as there aren't any more creams.

The doorbell rings.

Hot diggity dog! Now we're getting somewhere! Might it be the purveyor of the peck of poisoned peppers?

Harry rushes to the bedroom, stubbing his toe on the doorframe by accident. FLUFFERNUTS! I feel the stub pain everywhere, like he does.

Hopping on one foot while cussing, Harry grabs a pair of tan pants from a chair and a clean shirt from the closet. I note that he does not pull on any underwear. Not that I'm judging. He is in a hurry, and we've all been there.

Once the pants and shirt are on, he yanks open a dresser drawer. The drawer is empty, except for two socks that do not match. The socks are lying as far apart from each other as possible, like a married couple on TV who are reluctantly sharing a bed after an argument.

Harry grabs the mismatched socks and pulls them on. The stubbed toe is already feeling better; it only throbs a little under the tight sock.

He glances in a full-length mirror. This outfit, including the mismatched socks, is the exact same one he was wearing the day he died at the library.

Yes! This makes me happy. I figured I had the right day, but it's good to see the wardrobe with my own eyes —or Harry's eyes—to confirm it.

His gaze stays down on his mismatched socks as he moves down his hallway. It's disorienting. Then his gaze, along with my view, lift up when he reaches the front door. This odd little window that I have, peering through his eyes, reminds me of the shaky-cam footage in an amateur horror movie. It's dizzying, but I am getting used to it.

Harry unlocks the deadbolt, grabs the handle, and the muscle tension in his right arm increases as he pulls.

Time slows.

There's a creak in his shoulder.

The door is one inch open.

The ticking of a distant clock sounds like this: Tick. Wait for it. Tock. Wait for it. Tick.

Argh!

This vision, which already felt tedious at real-time speed, is now unfolding in slow motion. Or is it? Maybe that's just my perception. It's possible I do have some control over the replay speed. I certainly am excited to see who's ringing the doorbell. Is my anticipation putting on the brakes? How perverse would that be? Yet also unsurprising. Magic does have a mind of its own.

I'm waiting for the Tock of the clock, but it doesn't come.

This moment is frozen. Dead still.

DOUBLE FLUFFERNUTS. I'm going to die here. Die from the suspense of waiting for this door to open. Unless...

If I'm the one controlling the speed, I need to relax in order to let the event unfold.

RELAX, ZARA!

The clock goes Tock. The door continues to open. Slowly, but surely.

Who's on the other side? It could be Harry's killer. Just like that. I could have all the answers I need in five...

Four...

Three...

Two...

Open the door already, Harry! Stop looking down at your mismatched socks!

One.

The visitor is revealed.

CHAPTER 31

The person standing on the small porch is a man, about fifty, the spitting image of Harry Blackstone. He has thick, unruly black hair, big, brown eyes, and a large nose with a hump on the bridge and pointed tip.

"Good morning," the man says, revealing teeth that are small and square, with a gap between the two in the front.

This must be Harry's brother. His twin brother. Mr. William Blackstone, known to most as Bill.

Do I have the date wrong after all? According to Bill's interview with the detectives, he was out of town at the time of Harry's death. Either I'm in the wrong moment of time, or somebody lied to the police. Is brother Bill a liar?

"Bill," Harry says. He sounds surprised but also pleased.

The memory is now running at regular speed. I feel impatient to get more information, faster, but at least this is better than slow motion.

Bill runs a hand over his black hair, fluffing it up, and says, "Didn't wake you, did I?"

Harry mirrors Bill, running his hand over his own hair, which is still wet from the shower. I feel the silky hair, the cool dampness cling to his fingers, and the heat radiating from his scalp. And I feel something else. A tightening in the abdomen. Harry doesn't relish this visit from his brother.

"I thought you were out of town," Harry says. His throat is tight. He doesn't move or invite his brother in. Beyond the cover of the entryway, it's raining and gray. According to the weather, I'm definitely in September.

Bill rubs his forehead. The cords at the sides of his neck strain out. "After that email you sent me, did you really think I was going to stick around at some boring industry convention? I came home last night on my plane."

The visual focus shifts from Bill's face to twenty feet behind him, to a person walking by on the sidewalk. Bright blonde hair sticking out under a yellow rain hat. It's Ambrosia Abernathy, the young witch. She's wearing the same yellow rain gear as when she kicked my butt, not fifteen feet from here, on the other side of the hedge.

I hope Maisy Nix is working out a good punishment.

My own feelings about Ambrosia are in sharp contrast with Harry's. I can't read his thoughts, yet I can sense a general fatherly affection for the girl. She lives next door, and, true to what Ambrosia told me, they are friends.

Harry's chest swells, then he belts out, "Good morning to you, Ambrosia!" His voice is so loud, compared to the soft patter of the rain, it's startling, like a fog horn. "Nice weather, don't you think?"

Ambrosia stops walking and rests the pole of her umbrella on her shoulder. "You think?" She gives him a discerning look, the way only a teenaged girl can. It's the look that says "one of us might be an idiot."

He belts back proudly, finishing his joke with a punchline, "Nice weather... for ducks!"

She groans. "Good one, Mr. B. That's such a Dad Joke."

He calls out, over his brother's shoulder, "How's school treating you so far?"

She shrugs and spins her umbrella by rolling the handle on her shoulder. "It's only been one day, but we didn't even get any homework." She sounds disappointed. Disappointed to not have any assigned homework? She reminds me of another teenager I know.

Harry's arm comes into view. He's pointing to the man standing on his step. "This is my brother, Bill. He's my twin, but you wouldn't know it, since he took all the good looks and left me with none."

Ambrosia frowns. "You look the same to me." She turns her body deliberately, and starts walking away, calling over her shoulder, "Have a good day, Mr. B and Mr. B!"

The view switches from the retreating girl in yellow, back to Harry's twin. Bill opens his mouth, as if to say something, then closes it. Shaking his head, he nudges Harry out of the way so he can enter the house. He slowly and methodically wipes his shoes on the entry mat.

Back to that email, I think. Harry, Bill, work with me, fellas. What was in that email that made Bill fly straight home?

I know that rooting for specific information will do no good inside a memory, but I do it anyway, the way anyone would root for a scratch-off ticket to reveal the winning codes, or for their bowling ball to strike the headpin just right.

Bill follows Harry into the kitchen and watches him make a pot of coffee.

"So, you flew home last night," Harry says, summarizing. "Do you still have that same pilot? The woman?"

"No. That woman hasn't worked for me in over a decade. Stop stalling. You always ask me questions you know the answers to when you're stalling, Harry."

Inside the memory, I cheer for Bill. I love a person who gets straight to the point! Almost as much as I love joking around and *not* getting to the point myself.

"You know me like no other, dear brother," Harry says amiably. There's a practiced rhythm to the phrase. He has used it frequently over his life. I feel a pleasant, plump sensation in Harry's cheeks, and a tightness behind his ears. He's grinning.

"You know I'd do anything for those drawings," Bill says. He's dead serious. His posture is rigid, leaning forward. "Anything."

"Anything?" Harry's voice pitches up playfully, like the proverbial devil, bartering for a person's soul.

Bill's ears redden. His chest caves in as his shoulders roll forward. He looks down and briefly covers his mouth with a closed fist. "What I mean is, I'd do anything for you. For my brother."

"Come on now, Bill. You were right the first time. You and I both know it's the drawings you're after. My life's work."

Bill's big, brown eyes flick up shyly. There are dark circles under his eyes, as though he didn't sleep at all last night. "You know how I feel about the work," Bill says. "Your brilliance should be shared with the world."

Harry scoffs. "My brilliance," he mutters.

"Your alternate fuel generation plants are nothing short of... revolutionary. They would revolutionize everything."

"They would revolutionize warfare," Harry says, darkly.

"Maybe. But maybe not. The world is changing. I know it's hard to believe sometimes, but technological advances *are* being used for good."

Still sounding dark, his voice coming from the back of his throat and not projecting far, Harry says, "For the good of the few, at the expense of the many."

Irritation flickers across Bill's face. His hands clench at his sides before he forces them open with an impatient shake. "We can't know how everything will play out until it does."

"Except we can. Everything ends in disaster. Didn't you hear about the whole AI debacle at the Department?"

"I heard rumors, but you know how these things are. I heard that the program running their perimeter security malfunctioned."

"You could say that. Their glorious creation turned evil and tried to bring back an ancient goddess to reboot humanity. It nearly succeeded."

I feel the temperature rise. I can't tell if it's Harry who's getting warmer, or me. They are talking about Mahra, and about Charlize's program.

Bill continues, unperturbed. "But your work isn't in AI. It's not the same." He shrugs his shoulders up to his ears and drops them with a sigh. "No take-backsies," he says, sounding boyish. "You said in the email that I could have the drawings. No take-backsies, Harry. You can't break the twin code."

"And you will have the drawings," Harry said.

"But when? Come on. Name your price." Bill pats his jacket pocket. "I brought my checkbook." He holds his hands out, palms open. "Unless you'd prefer an electronic transfer?"

"I don't want money."

Here we go!

"Oh?" Brother Bill is so excited and tense, he's only breathing in the top quarter of his lungs. The redness from his ears is spreading across his neck. A vein is visible on his throat.

Harry answers slowly, "Since I've had this unexpected bout of good health, I've been entirely focused on two things. The energy plants, and also..."

"What?" Bill grabs a kitchen chair and places it between himself and his twin. He grips the back of it, as though the chair is the only thing that can keep him from laying his hands on Harry in a brotherly tussle.

Harry waves one hand, but doesn't speak.

Out with it, I think impatiently.

"Out with it," Bill urges. "You said in the email that you're willing to give me all of the diagrams and research, in exchange for *one thing*. You dropped a lot of hints in that email, but I have to confess I'm not as smart as you. I couldn't figure it out. I never was as smart as you. It's true that I got all the good looks and you got slightly more of the brains." He offers a tentative smile. "What's this one thing?"

"A soul transfer," Harry says.

Soul transfer?

Say what now?

In the seconds that follow, I hear the hum of the fridge, the patter of rain on the window, and the mechanical drone of a garbage truck doing its morning pickups on the street.

Bill, to my surprise, takes in the news with the facility of someone who understood the subtle hints in the email far better than he's letting on.

Bill looks Harry in the eyes and says, neutrally, "When you die, you want to have your soul transferred into my body. Then you and I will share this body." He pats his chest with loosely curled hands. "I will have access to all of what's in your mind." He gestures to Harry's head with his hands. "That's the gist of it, right?"

"Yes."

"Wow," Bill says. "That'll be..."

"It will be like old times," Harry says. "Like when we used to share everything. Mom's womb. A group of friends. A whole life." His voice gets gravelly, and I feel more tension in my throat. "I'm dying, Bill."

"Don't say that. You look fantastic."

"I know I look fine, but that's just the surface. The damage inside my body was too extensive. The serum hasn't been as much help as I'd hoped. It's not going to save me."

Bill's eyes glisten. He looks away.

I feel Harry use his strength to straighten his posture. He stands at attention. "I found someone who can do the transfer," Harry says matter-of-factly. "Rhys Quarry's daughter."

My ears burn. Metaphorically. I can't feel them.

Bill stammers, "Bu-but she's only—"

"She's a witch," Harry says. "Zara Riddle. She's Rhys's daughter by a witch named Zirconia Riddle. Zara is the redhead who runs the library. "

If I could feel my face, it would be warm. It's cute that Harry thinks I run the library.

"I don't understand," Bill says. "A witch?"

Bill doesn't understand, but I do. Harry has found out about my Spirit Charmed powers, either through his contacts at the Department or my big-mouthed father, and he thinks that I can handle something as complex as transferring a soul into another body.

My mind is reeling.

Harry pours two mugs of coffee, and the brothers take them out to the small covered porch to continue the conversation.

It's cool and humid on the porch, but a surprisingly cozy place to sit. The rain falls like a curtain in front of them, pattering on all the greenery as the garbage truck roars by. Harry has brought two blankets along, and the men place the blankets on their laps to stay warm.

"We look like Grandma Posey," Bill says, gesturing at the colorful crocheted piece covering his legs.

"*You* look like Grandma Posey," Harry says. "I look like Uncle Smokie."

"That's not much better," Bill jokes.

The two brothers banter about family members for a while, and then Harry gets down to the business of explaining the soul transfer.

It's pretty much what I expected. Harry wants me to be at his side when he passes, so that I can perform a spell— he has a book that describes the method—and transfer his soul into his brother's body. The spell can theoretically work with any two willing parties, but the effects are temporary, unless there is a familial bond and blood connection. There is no better pair of candidates than identical twins.

When all has been explained, Bill says with wonder, "That might actually work."

"It will work. Shall I contact the witch and find out her fee? I'm assuming you can fund the investment."

"Of course," Bill says without hesitation. "Should we go through Rhys to negotiate?"

They both laugh at this.

Harry wipes tears of laughter from his eyes and says, "Only if we want to pay double and still owe him a favor."

"That guy," Bill says.

Shut up about my father, I think.

It's weird that I feel the need to defend his honor, but I do. He's *my* father to make fun of.

"And those suits he wears," Harry says.

Shut up, you jerks!

They laugh some more, then Bill says, "Got any food in the house?"

"I could make you some breakfast," Harry says.

Bill accepts. They fold up the lap quilts, leave them on the chairs, and head back inside.

Back in the kitchen with the twins, I find my mind wandering. The brothers' plan sheds a new light on the homicide. Did some other party find out about the arrangement? A third party might wish to prevent the transfer before it could happen, by killing Harry before he could talk to me.

I wonder about Harry's invention, and how well-funded his enemies could be. If he had plans to revolutionize power generation, there were more than a few tycoons who might want the plans for themselves, if only to see them destroyed.

My mind swirls with conspiracies.

I am barely paying attention when I notice something red in Harry's hand. It's a big, juicy, perfectly symmetrical red pepper. Beyond his hand, on the counter, is a carton of eggs, a block of butter, a bowl of sliced mushrooms, and a salt shaker. A frying pan is on the stove, the oil just starting to sizzle.

The poisoned pepper!

Bill, who is watching the meal preparation with mild interest while he reads something on his phone, says casually, "No pepper in my side of the omelet. It gives me terrible heartburn."

Harry waves the pepper suggestively. "Are you sure? This is a new hybrid. No burps, and no heartburn."

"Not worth the risk," Bill says, barely looking up from his phone. "How about you leave it off, period? I don't want any of its nightshade juices getting on my side."

"Fine," Harry says. "Your wish is my command."

The red pepper gets bigger. It's being brought to Harry's face. His mouth salivates. He takes a big bite of the pepper. It's crisp and juicy, sweet and tangy at the same time. His mouth waters more as he chews, then takes another bite.

Bill looks up from his phone, frowning. "You're just going to eat it raw like that?" His lips twitch into an amused smile. "You're going to be sorry."

Harry waves his hand. "What's a little heartburn?"

He takes another big bite. As he chews, I remember Zinnia's warning. I have to get out of this memory before the poison affects me.

I cast the spell to get myself out.

I'm still here.

Harry takes another bite of pepper. The taste is powerful.

Why am I not out of here yet? I cast the spell again, getting frantic.

Bill, still watching Harry with narrowed eyes, says, "That's quite the pepper, Harry. Where'd you get it?"

"Actually, it's a funny story," Harry says. He takes another bite of pepper.

I am dimly aware of my cheeks being slapped, and my name being yelled.

CHAPTER 32

When I came out of Harry's memory, it was as though I'd been reborn.

Literally.

I was naked, hanging upside down, and someone was smacking my bottom.

Okay, I wasn't actually naked, and nobody was smacking my bottom, but I *was* hanging upside down.

"There you are," Zinnia said.

I gagged.

She was pulling something out of my mouth—a long ribbon of red. She wrapped this long, red ribbon onto a Y-shaped stick that reminded of old woodcut illustrations of ancient purification rituals, or of Medieval doctors removing tapeworms.

"The Peptyx Tapewyrm is nearly out," Zinnia said soothingly. "Don't gag."

I gagged again. There was no way her tone could be soothing enough to counteract the idea that she was removing a Peptyx Tapewyrm from me.

When had she put it in? How long had I been out? Harry's memory couldn't have covered more than an hour, and yet I could see the sun rising through one of Zinnia's windows. Had eight hours passed already? Or eight days?

Worrying about the passage of time was a good distraction from the feeling of the wyrm that was still being dragged out through my mouth. Just when I didn't think I could take another second, the tail came out. It was forked. My jaw clamped shut at last.

Zinnia dropped the slimy, undulating thing into a gold-lined wooden chest, which she tucked under her arm.

She left the room, leaving me hanging upside down in the air above the coffee table.

I coughed, tasting peppermint and rosewater.

Zinnia returned a minute later, clapped her hands, and suddenly I was the right side up again. I landed on the coffee table, staggered back, and fell onto the couch.

She handed me a glass of water. "Don't speak yet," she said.

I gave the water a wary look. What was in it? Some microscopic magical parasites?

"It's just water," she said, correctly reading my mind.

I washed down the taste in my mouth, then explained, "Harry ate the pepper when I was in the memory."

"Yes. I imagined as much when your seizures began."

"Seizures? Am I going to be okay?"

She smiled through a tired yawn. "You are a Riddle," she said.

"We Riddles are tougher than we look."

She patted my knee affectionately. Up-All-Night-Zinnia was kinda fun.

"So?" She gave me an expectant look. "Who killed Harry Blackstone?"

"It's complicated."

I told her everything I'd witnessed. Harry's brother Bill must have lied to the police about being out of town the day of Harry's death, though I didn't know why. Bill wanted to get his hands on Harry's plans for some power generating invention, and he wanted it bad. He was willing to share his body with his twin's spirit in order to get the information.

"That speaks to motivation," Zinnia said.

"And Bill specifically requested no red pepper on his omelet."

"He knew it was poisoned?"

I shrugged. "I was in Harry, not Bill, but knowing what I know now, it sure looked suspicious to me."

"Did the twin brother seem interested in the supposedly funny story about the peppers?"

"Not as interested as me."

Zinnia smiled. "I suppose not." She sighed. "What a shame. If I'd known how close you were, I might have left you in there a bit longer. Then again, you're not much use to any of us here in the land of the living if you're dead."

"I like to think I'm a helpful ghost."

Her eyes saddened. "Let us not joke about such things."

We both looked at the book on the table.

"I'll try again," I said to Zinnia, reaching for the book. "Give me ten more seconds and I'll tell you how Harry got the peppers."

"Not now," Zinnia said.

Before I could reach the book, it disappeared.

"You need to rest and recover," Zinnia said. "Also, I need to procure a fresh supply of poison extractors."

"You and your magic herbs and critters." I leaned back and crossed my arms as I did my best Steely Bentley Stare. "How strange that the vision ended right as Harry was about to reveal his source." I nodded in the direction of my aunt's kitchen. "You wouldn't be missing any special peppers, now, would you?"

She gave me a pained expression. "Go home and rest." She pointed at my purse. My phone rose up by magic. "But first, you need to call Detective Bentley and tell him what you saw. William Blackstone lied about being in town, and he saw Harry the morning of his death."

"You really think Bill is our guy?"

"I don't know what to think, but the man knows things he hasn't shared. They need to re-interview him."

"I should interview him myself."

She dropped the phone in my lap. "Try passing along the information first," she said. "Zara, I've spent far too long trying to handle everything by myself. Don't make the same mistakes I have. People work best when they work together. We ought to always take assistance when it is offered."

"Bentley's not back from his personal trip," I explained as I scrolled through my list of phone contacts. "I'll have to give my report to Detective Rose." I wrinkled my nose. "I hope she'll forgive me for waking her up at the crack of dawn."

Zinnia watched me expectantly.

Detective Rose was breathing heavily when she answered.

"Bad dream?" I asked.

"Just got back from my morning run in the park." Her breathing normalized to where I couldn't hear it over our connection anymore. "What can I do for you, Zara?"

"Where do you live?"

"Near City Hall. Why?"

"And where do your parents live?"

"My mother runs a Bed and Breakfast in Wilvington."

"In Ohio?"

"Wilvington with a V. You're thinking of Wilmington. Wilvington is up the coast, past Westwyrd and before Karlington."

"You grew up around here?"

"Uh..." There was a rustling and clinking on her end of the call.

I looked over at my aunt, who was waving her hand for me to get to the point.

"Never mind," I said into the phone. "We can talk about that stuff later. I'm calling about the Blackstone case. I have good news and bad news. The good news is,

I've gotten access to the victim's memories, and I know what he was up to, more or less. The bad news is my aunt's fresh out of poison-sucking parasites, so I don't have the killer's name yet, but I will."

Zinnia whispered, "Ask her about the peppers. Do they know about the dosage? The frequency?"

"You don't have to whisper," I said to Zinnia. "Detective Rose knows you're a witch."

Zinnia whispered, "Yes, but it's rude to interrupt someone's phone call."

"And yet here we are."

Persephone Rose said, "What's going on?" I heard the jingle of keys.

"A whole lotta stuff. Hang on." I pushed the button for speaker mode, so Zinnia could participate directly.

Right then, the detective said, "I'm getting in my car. I'll come over so you can tell me everything in person."

"Sure, but I'm at my aunt's house. Zinnia Riddle's."

"Gotcha. I have the address. Don't go anywhere. I'll be straight over."

CHAPTER 33

Detective Persephone Rose removed her rain poncho to reveal an athletic body in trendy sportswear. She looked sweaty, but she didn't smell sweaty, which made me wonder if she'd lied to me. But who would lie about exercising? Besides every person, to their doctor and on their dating profiles, of course.

Persephone sat on the edge of a floral-patterned wingback chair and listened to us relay what had happened, from turning the Codex Niquitia into the Codex Harold J. Blackstone, to my brush with the poisoned pepper.

Her dark-brown ponytail swung from side to side sportily as she swiveled her attention between us.

When we'd finished our exposition, she thanked us for the information, then shared what they'd learned about the poison.

The pepper was called the Allursynthesix Red Pepper, and had been developed by Tansy Wick locally, at her greenhouse, before being sold to a chemical manufacturer, DuSanto Chemical. The genetically engineered peppers would be a "natural" source of the red dye known as Allura Red, a common compound used to color all kinds of products, from drinks to candies.

Unfortunately, a side effect of the red pepper's change in chemical structure caused it to be both extremely delicious—tasting more like a ripe peach than a typical pepper—and highly toxic. Workers at the chemical factory that owned the strain of nightshade could barely handle the peppers without casualties, let alone extract the color as a stable salt.

Project Allursynthesix had been killed and buried at DuSanto Chemical, yet a few seeds had apparently stayed in circulation in Wisteria.

"We've been checking home gardens and greenhouses, but it's a time-consuming process," the detective said, her brown ponytail swinging sportily. "Now that we know that Bill Blackstone lied to us about being in town, it does open some investigation avenues we'd previously closed."

I swung my fist cheerfully. "Go, teamwork."

Persephone blinked at me. Her eyes were big and brown, like the Blackstone twins', but hers often looked sad, drooping at the corners. Her round face looked especially pale that day, though her cheeks were rosy. Were they rosy from jogging, or from lying about jogging? I wouldn't know, unless I cast a spell, and I wasn't supposed to do things like that. I'd promised Bentley I'd be "nice" to Ms. Rose, whatever that meant.

Persephone continued talking about their efforts to trace the remaining seeds.

I looked over at Zinnia, expecting her to be yawning from the all-nighter. Zinnia's hazel eyes were as bright as ever. If anything, she seemed transfixed by the young detective. She stared at Persephone Rose with wide-eyed wonder, as though Persephone Rose was a whole new type of floral wallpaper.

Seeing my aunt look at another woman with that level of interest made me feel irrationally jealous. I felt like a toddler, grasping around for something to do for attention —good or bad.

I kicked the coffee table. "Oops," I said.

Zinnia's focus didn't stray from the fresh-faced, non-sweat-stinky detective.

"Arrrrrr," I said, yawning theatrically. "Look at the time!"

"Tea?" Zinnia offered sweetly. "I have every kind you can imagine, plus a few you can't."

Persephone looked at me.

I shook my head.

Persephone looked back at Zinnia. "I really should be going. There's a lot to do with my partner out of town. Thank you so much for your help."

I jumped to my feet and showed her to the door. "Solve this case already, will ya?"

"I'm trying," she said.

We stepped out the front door into the cool morning. The rain was drizzly.

Persephone stepped beyond the overhang of the porch roof, stopped on the pathway, and turned to look back at me. "I really am trying," she repeated, staring up at me with her big, brown eyes. I almost felt bad.

"Try harder," I said. "This town is going to be overrun with ghost hunters, lookie-loos, and national news crews if we don't tidy things up."

"I know that, *Zara*." She hit my name with a hard tone, and her expression changed to annoyance. It was the first time I'd seen her perturbed. Was it something I said?

I threw her attitude right back. "I'm glad you know that, *Persephone*."

She snorted. "You don't have to tell me my job. I know my job. I've studied a long time to get to where I am. I've made a lot of sacrifices." She waved her hand, chopping through the drizzly rain. "You have no idea."

"Same here," I tossed back. "You have no idea what I've been through."

She put her hands on her hips. The rain was only drizzling, but it was effectively soaking her trendy athletic gear. She wasn't wearing her rain poncho, because I'd forgotten to hand it to her when I'd shoved her out the door.

We stared at each other. She said nothing.

I said, "You forgot your poncho."

"I know," she said, glaring at me. "I need my keys. They're in the pocket."

The world tilted a little. I was still woozy from the vision and the near-poisoning. Why were Persephone and I seemingly at war with each other? I couldn't shake the sensation I was missing something—something that was right in front of my nose.

"I'll get your poncho," I growled.

"That would be nice," she said, also growling, though her growl was much better than mine. It was more like my daughter's fox growl.

I stomped into the house, grabbed the poncho, tossed it out the front door at her, then came back inside the house without another word.

When I returned to the living room, my aunt was staring at me.

"I detect a little tension between the two of you," she said.

"You think?"

"Yes," she said carefully. "I do."

"I'm not jealous of her working side-by-side with Bentley," I said. "It's not that."

"No," she agreed. "It isn't that."

I rubbed my face with both hands. "I'm just tired," I said. "Do you have any special tea that will replace eight hours of sleep so I can work today?"

"Yes, but you wouldn't like the side effects."

"Is it worse than Zeronnaise?"

She nodded vehemently.

"Pass," I said. "I'll be fine." I picked up my purse and slung it on my shoulder. I didn't even feel tired, despite what I'd said to my aunt.

"Rest up when you can." She walked me to the door, giving me the usual warnings that I should be careful, and notify her if I had any side effects from the poison or even from the extraction of such.

I was about to leave when I thought of something minor I'd heard in Harry's memory.

"Zinnia," I said slowly.

"Yes?"

"When I was in Harry's memory, and they were first talking about Rhys Quarry's daughter, I got the feeling they were talking about someone else. Someone who wasn't me." I stared into her eyes, which were suspiciously fixed in place, and not flicking back and forth the way people's eyes normally did. "Would you happen to know anything about that? Any other children my father has sired?"

My aunt answered firmly and calmly, as though she'd been preparing for this question for a long time. "My word is my bond," Zinnia said. "I promised Rhys I would not tell you."

"What?" I took two steps back. My fishing expedition had caught something? "When did you make the bond? Those things don't last forever. It can't still be active. You haven't even seen him in months. Unless you've seen him recently?"

Her nostrils flared. She didn't blink. "A good witch is not bound to her word by magic alone."

"Fine," I said, exhaling my disappointment heavily. "I guess I should be glad you have integrity, even though this whole secret sibling thing is a serious bummer for me. I always figured my father had other kids, but I never cared until now. How many are there?"

She pressed her lips together.

"Fine." I turned to leave. "I'll call Rhys and let him have it with both barrels. Maybe he can help us with Harry. I'll get to the bottom of this myself."

I headed toward the door.

"Wait," she said.

I turned to face her, feeling hopeful.

She seemed to be fighting an internal battle. "What do other people do to track down their family members? People who do not have access to magic?"

I shrugged. "They hire a private investigator, I guess."

She struck her finger in the air. "That's it! You should hire someone." She glanced at the closed front door. "What about that young woman? She seems smart and capable."

"You think Persephone Rose is going to take a private eye job on the side? For me?"

Zinnia nodded to one side. "One could certainly ask."

"One could probably do it *herself* with less hassle and sass." I frowned. "Besides, I don't like owing people favors."

"You are your father's daughter. He prefers having people in debt to him."

I muttered, "My father's daughter." I shook my head, then pointed to the door. "Get outta here," I said with mock anger.

"We're in my house."

"I know."

I looked up at the foyer ceiling, at the painting of a lush flower garden. The overhead mural had always given me the dizzying feeling I was suspended upside down in the air, looking down. Given how recently I had been hanging upside down, the effect was doubly nauseating.

As I reached for the door handle, I thanked my aunt for helping me nearly kill myself yet again and then saving me from the brink of death. She acted like it was no big deal.

I stepped outside and groaned as I realized my car was still at the library, dead in the parking lot.

There was a jingle of keys behind me.

"I'll give you a lift," Zinnia said.

"You're the best!" I hugged her so hard, I nearly knocked both of us over.

"Ow," she said. Classic Zinnia.

CHAPTER 34

Tuesday
Coffee Break
Wisteria Public Library

"I always dreamed of opening a quaint little coffee shop," Frank Wonder said.

He was refilling a silver carafe with cream in the staff room, which had become Coffee Preparation Headquarters.

He continued, "I just had no idea it would happen right inside our library."

"You never know how dreams will come true," Kathy Carmichael said.

She was tallying up stacks of cash. Our earnings from the Goblin Hordes had been increasing daily. As the foot traffic grew, so did their coffee consumption. The ghost afficionados were enthralled by the rich, toasty flavors of Dreamland Coffee's dark and medium roast blends. They had been posting about the special Library Coffee on their message boards and private forums, attracting the attention of coffee afficionados.

"I got a quote on the cots," Kathy said nonchalantly to Frank. "After the rental fees and the linen service, we should break even after two weeks, assuming we limit the overnight guests to a dozen. But if we increase to maximum capacity, we could be in profit by the third day."

I had just walked into this conversation, as I was running late despite getting a ride from my aunt. We had dropped by my house for a clothing change, where we'd been distracted by Ribbons and his usual wyvern antics. Then Boa had climbed into Zinnia's lap, and Zinnia hadn't wanted to disturb the furball's mid-morning nap because she looked "so happy." I'd phoned the head librarian about my tardiness, and she had assured me I could take as much time as I needed, since she had "everything covered."

Now I'd found out that having "everything covered" meant turning the library into some sort of spooky Bed and Breakfast.

"We'll need a maid," Frank said. "I'm not putting all the chocolates on the pillows by myself."

Kathy squealed and clapped her hands. "Chocolates on the pillows! I love it when places do that."

They scarcely noticed my entrance.

I rapped my knuckles on the table top. "Excuse me. Am I in the right place? I thought this was a library."

Kathy turned my way. "Zara! You look different. What happened to your mouth? It looks bigger than usual."

Frank snickered and gave me a triple eyebrow-raise. Kathy thought my mouth was big? We'd both seen how big Kathy's sprite mouth could be when opened fully. It was a bit rich for her to be saying *my* mouth was big.

Frank continued staring at me, his eyes narrowing. He rubbed his crooked jaw. "Uh, Zara? I don't mean to alarm you, but is your mouth actually cursed, or did you encounter a hive of bees on your way in?"

I opened the kitchen cupboard and looked at myself in the cupboard-door-mounted mirror we used for teeth-spinach checks.

My heart sunk. My mouth really was bigger than usual. I looked like one of those reality TV housewives who considered wine a food group and got filler injections the way I bought cute summer tops at thrift stores—by the dozen.

"Oh, no," I said, trying to look away from my puffy, extra-wide lips but unable to. "My aunt said something like this might happen. It's a delayed reaction that takes a few hours."

Frank and Kathy looked stunned and horrified, but also curious.

Kathy paused counting coffee donation money and asked, "A reaction to *what*?"

"The Peptyx Tapewyrm," I said, rubbing my stomach.

Both of them recoiled visibly.

"Don't worry. My aunt got it all out of me," I assured them, waving a hand. "It was a big feller, too. Eight pounds, two ounces."

Frank gagged. "That's more than I weigh." He added, "In flamingo form."

"It's more than what Zoey weighed when she made her taxi seat debut."

Frank grimaced. "Which end did it come out of?"

"My mouth," I said, horrified.

Kathy nodded slowly. "Peptyx Tapewyrm," she mused. "I've heard of those. They absorb antinutrients and other poisons." Her eyes widened and she gasped. "You were poisoned?"

"Yes and no."

I glanced out the door that led to the circulation desk. Nomi and the other staff members were handling things, so I closed the door and began explaining to my supernatural coworkers what had happened.

The increased size of my mouth wasn't so much a side effect as an *intended* effect of the poison-sucking parasite. If a witch were to be poisoned, that witch would want extra spellwork capacity for exacting revenge. My lips were bigger, but only because my entire mouth was bigger. The Peptyx Tapewyrm exuded an enzyme that temporarily increased tongue size along with mouth size. This increased the strength of casting with the Witch Tongue.

"Like steroids," I said. "But for magic."

"Sort of a partial shift," Frank said. "I haven't got the hang of that myself."

"Seems risky to me," Kathy said. "A mouth can be bigger on the inside without giving itself away on the outside."

"Maybe for sprites," I said. "Not for normal humans."

Kathy clutched her hands to her chest. "Zara! How could you?"

Frank patted her on the shoulder. "She didn't mean anything by it. We're all humans here. Witches tend to be insensitive about other people's powers."

"I only meant..." I waved a hand and bowed my head. "Frank's right. Either we're all normal or none of us are normal."

"Hmm," Kathy said. "I don't know if I would call myself normal."

"Me, neither," Frank said. "Normal is boring."

"Normal is a setting on the dishwasher," I said.

All three of us nodded.

Frank said, "Zara, you didn't tell us why you ingested a poison-sucking parasite in the first place."

Kathy asked, "Was it a hazing ritual? Did that giant beanpole woman, Maisy Nix, make you do it?" Compared to short and sturdy Kathy, Maisy would be considered a giant beanpole.

"Maisy wasn't there. I went to Zinnia's house last night, and we successfully pulled Harry into a book so I could access his memories."

Kathy frowned. "Why didn't you just do that in the first place?"

"It's a new thing," I said, and I went on to explain how successful we had been. We were so close to cracking the case and letting Harry's spirit move on. Cooperating with the police would only make things easier. Persephone Rose would follow up with the twin brother today, and soon we would have the whole thing squared away.

When I'd finished, neither Frank nor Kathy looked impressed. Kathy's round shoulders slumped to the point of disappearing. Frank rubbed the back of his neck.

Frank said to Kathy, "I wonder if we should cancel the order on the cots. Sounds like our feature attraction may be checking out permanently."

Kathy gave me a hopeful look. "Can you stall a few days, Zara? Harry's doing so much good for the library." She held up her hand in a pinching gesture. "We're *this close* to solving all our budget issues."

I gave them an extra-large frown with my extra-large mouth. "Let me get this straight," I said flatly. "You want me to keep a tortured soul in a purgatory state, and delay finding his killer, so that you two can sell more five-dollar coffees to suckers?"

Frank and Kathy exchanged a look, then Kathy said, "Yes, that's pretty much it." She clutched a stack of bills possessively. "But remember, we're not technically selling anything."

Frank chimed in, "Five dollars is the *suggested donation*. For legal reasons, the coffee is free." He winked twice. "As will be the featured overnight stays in our luxurious cots, though the suggested donation will be a hundred dollars per night." More winking.

"You two," I muttered, and left the staff room to see if anyone in the crowded library needed an actual librarian.

* * *

Mid-afternoon, I was woken by one of the junior staff members softly shaking me by the elbow.

"Ma'am," she said. "You can't sleep here."

The staff member's name was Nomi Lafleur, and she was smirking over having caught her supervisor napping in Harry's Chair by Harry's Window.

"I wasn't sleeping," I lied. "I was just resting my eyes."

"You were snoring," Nomi said.

I narrowed my eyes at her. "Was I really, or are you just saying that because that's what we've all been trained to say when a patron denies they were sleeping?"

Nomi mimed zipping her lips, locking them, and throwing away a key. She had a lot of sass for someone with no seniority. Frank and I were probably a bad influence.

I put my hands on the leather armrests and hoisted myself from the too-comfortable seat. I barely remembered sitting down in the first place, much less falling asleep.

Nomi, forgetting she'd locked her lips, said in a hushed tone, "You were talking in your sleep."

"Did I say anything interesting?"

"Something about a pumpkin, and how you could fix everything if you got your magic wrench from your garage."

"Oh, really?"

"You kept saying the magic wrench was still on the wall, with the regular tools."

I had expected Nomi to report that I'd been sleep-talking nonsense, but as I heard my words echoed back, I remembered the dream. I had been talking to Harry Blackstone in my dream. He had apologized for causing me so much inconvenience, and then he'd explained to me how I could fix the mechanical issue with my car. All I needed was a specific wrench, from his garage.

"That's quite the wild dream talk," I said to Nomi. "I must be picking up weird vibes from the Goblin Hordes."

"Mm-hmm."

"Thanks for waking me."

"Mm-hmm."

Nomi wasn't paying any attention to the conversation. Her gaze was on my enlarged mouth. She touched her fingertips to her own lips, as though trying to work something out, like why my mouth was fifteen percent bigger than it had been the day before.

Could I disguise my big mouth? I tried pinching my lips together the way I did when I was doing an impression of my aunt.

Nomi jerked her head back, frowned, and looked away. "I'd, uh, better finish the patrol," she said. "You wouldn't think people could sleep with all the visitor noise going on, but there's something about being indoors when it's raining that makes people dozy."

"Plus Kathy and Frank turned up the heat to push caffeine sales."

Nomi's eyes widened. "Really?"

"Allegedly," I added quickly. "I didn't see anyone touch the thermostat. This is just between us."

"Right," she said, looking thrilled about being taken into my confidence. Step one of bonding with a fellow employee: Offer dirt on the other ones.

"And I'd appreciate if you didn't tell anyone about my little nap."

Nomi nodded. "You were only resting your eyes," she said. "There's nothing else to tell."

I gave her a big, scary clown smile. It was only meant to be a small smile, but my mouth was still so big.

The poor girl fled.

* * *

At the end of the day, we three librarians performed the new closing activities that were becoming routine.

Kathy counted the big stack of money while Frank phoned in a commercial-sized order for more coffee beans and paper cups.

I didn't tell either of them about the dream I'd had, or my plan to stop by Harry's house after work in search of the special wrench.

I didn't tell Frank because he would have insisted on going with me, and I couldn't risk him getting hurt again.

I didn't tell Kathy because she might talk me out of my mission, for fear it would lead to resolving Harry's haunting before we'd maximized our profits.

To keep either of them from insisting on giving me a ride home, I told them I already had a ride, and offered to stay late tidying. It was only fair, since I needed to make up for arriving late for my shift.

"I'll clock out late to make up for clocking in late," I said.

Kathy said to me, "You know, nobody checks the timecards."

"What?"

Frank echoed, "What?"

Kathy shrugged. "I don't check them. I've asked around, and it doesn't sound like anyone checks them."

Frank asked, "Then why do we even use that old machine? It's so noisy."

"Whooo knows," Kathy hooted. "I was told to always punch in back when I started. The head librarian at the time told me it was vitally important, so I never questioned it."

The three of us stared at the big, metal timecard machine on the wall.

Frank spoke first. "I'm going to keep clocking in. I have a bad feeling that device is attached to something important, and if we stop punching the cards, something bad will happen."

"Same here," Kathy said.

They looked at me. "I don't want to be left out," I said. "I'm going to keep punching my timecard. Besides, I like how the machine goes KERCHUNK."

"Me, too," they both said, and we agreed that the KERCHUNK was very satisfying.

They thanked me for staying late to clean up, then left.

I'd rarely been inside the library all by myself, except for a few minutes here and there.

Being alone in the beautiful, book-filled space filled me with energy.

After checking three times to be sure the library was empty of people, and that the security cameras were temporarily switched off, I got to work.

Using magic, I got three carts full of books reshelved in no time, plus I vacuumed all the floors up and down, and started watering the plants.

Thanks to my super-sized mouth, my spellcasting was stronger than ever. Not only did the plants get their water, but all of them grew new leaves, bright green and robust, right before my eyes. I had to cut the watering spell short with a cancellation, lest the library turn into a jungle.

Tidying completed, I locked up, clocked out with a satisfying KERCHUNK, and took a taxi to the Blackstone residence.

The taxi driver was curious about the house that was for sale.

How many bedrooms?

What was the list price?

How were the neighbors?

It wasn't haunted or anything, right? Ha ha.

"You should call the listing agent," I suggested. "I'm just the house sitter."

I got out of the taxi, and pretended to check something on my phone until the taxi had disappeared from sight.

Then I cast a spell to detect if anyone was watching me. I caught a tug on the line, so to speak. I followed the gossamer thread up to a window on the house next to

Harry's. Someone was watching. Ambrosia Abernathy. I waved. She stepped forward, so that her face was visible, and waved back. She looked somber.

I held my finger to my lips to indicate that I was about to do some secret witch business and she shouldn't interfere. She nodded to indicate she understood. Or that she was going to interfere immediately. Who knew? Whatever she did, I'd deal with it.

I mouthed something at the girl: *See you at the coven meeting tonight?*

She mouthed back: *What?*

I mouthed: *Coven meeting. Tonight.*

I used my hands to mime the shape of a pointed hat on my head, then pointed to my wrist, indicating time, as in tonight.

Ambrosia tugged on her ear and pointed at her eye.

I had no idea what she meant, but I gave her two thumbs up.

I walked through the rain—I hardly noticed it by now —and let myself in through the garage's side door. I'd already returned the keys to the real estate agent, dropping them through the mail slot at the Moore residence, but I didn't need a key to gain entry to Harry's old house. Twisting a handle from the other side was the sort of bread and butter magic I did constantly.

The garage interior was neat and tidy, as it had been the day I'd toured the place with Frank and Reyna Drinkwater.

It was dim, with only a bit of light coming in through the garage door's tiny windows, but it was enough for me to see what I needed to see.

My phone buzzed in my purse with an incoming message. Probably Zoey, asking about dinner. I didn't check.

My phone buzzed again. This buzz didn't have the feeling of my daughter asking about dinner. I didn't have my aunt's powers to get messages directly in my head moments before they were even sent, but sometimes I got a dim sensation that something was out of the ordinary.

As I reached for the phone, I scanned the wall of tools. I found the wrench that would fix my car, the one Harry had shown me in my dream.

With that business practically taken care of, I looked down to check the messages.

The first one was from Zoey: *What do you want for dinner?*

The second one was from Persephone Rose. Before I could read the text, a motor groaned to life over my head.

The garage door was opening.

As the light from outside filled the garage, I looked around furtively for somewhere to take cover. There was an old rain barrel I theoretically could have squeezed into. There was also the door I'd come in through. I swayed left and right, unable to decide. I felt very much like the proverbial cockroach in a cheap apartment when the lights come on.

I glanced down at my phone screen. Persephone Rose's message contained a single word: *Drinkwater.*

As the garage door rose, a woman's shoes and legs came into view. It had to be Reyna Drinkwater.

My phone buzzed in my hand. Another message came in, also from Persephone. It was a longer one, apologizing that her previous message had been accidentally truncated.

In a third message, Persephone Rose said: *The brother admitted he was in town. He said the person who gave Harry the red peppers was his landlady, Reyna Drinkwater.*

His landlady? How odd. She was just the real estate agent for his estate. Or was she?

The garage door finished opening and the motor ground to a halt.

Reyna stepped in, then shrieked and dropped her briefcase when she saw me standing in the gloom, staring back at her.

CHAPTER 35

I held my hands out, still holding my phone in one.

"It's just me," I said to the real estate agent. "I didn't mean to scare you."

Reyna Drinkwater flinched and took an awkward step backward, nearly tripping over her dropped briefcase. She held her hands to her chest in a protective gesture. She looked genuinely startled. If the woman had any supernatural powers, she was doing a fine job of not revealing them.

The thirty-something Realtor was dressed the same as when I'd seen her previously, in a conservative skirt and matching blazer, topped by a trench coat. Her shoulder-length auburn hair had been partially pulled back with a clip. Her face was still pretty, from her bright green eyes to her button nose, but she didn't look well. Her skin had a yellow cast that showed through her makeup.

If Persephone Rose was right about Reyna Drinkwater being the one who'd supplied Harry with his genetically altered peppers, then Reyna's apparent liver problems could be explained by her exposure to the poison. She had become ill solely from handling the deadly nightshades, yet it had taken repeat exposures for Harry Blackstone to succumb. Was it a protective feature of his supernatural abilities? No. It must have been Dr. Ankh's special formula. The same serum that was healing Harry's occupational damage must have been dampening the effects of the poison. The elixir had been saving his life, until it wasn't. Reyna killed Harry.

And now I was standing face to face with her.

The Realtor ducked her head in recognition. "Zara? Zara Riddle?"

"You caught me," I said, letting out an embarrassed laugh. "Please don't call the cops. It's not breaking and entering if the door's unlocked. Ha ha ha." My laugh sounded so fake, but I had to try.

Reyna stammered as her hands opened and closed on nothing. "Wha-what are you doing here?"

"Funny story," I said. "You know how sometimes you get that feeling you left the stove on at home?"

"Uh, sure."

I gestured with my phone loosely as I made up a story. "Well, as you'll probably remember, you asked me to lock up here last week, after I showed my friend Frank Wonder around the property. I thought I did lock up, but then today at work I suddenly remembered I forgot to lock the garage. So, long story short, rather than bother you, since I know you're busy, I figured I'd swing by here after work and lock up by twisting the handle from the inside, assuming it was that kind of lock, which it is."

"Oh?" Her frown told me she wasn't buying my story. Her gaze kept flicking between me and the tools on the wall.

Did she think I'd broken in to steal tools? That was... technically exactly what I had done. *Smart girl, Reyna.*

She said, "So, you came by to lock up? Why were you standing here in the dark?"

"I guess I'm just crazy about real estate!" I offered a big you-caught-me shrug. "I've been thinking about picking up an investment property. I figured I'd take one more look around the place, since I was here anyway."

Her eyes weren't trusting me, but the lower part of her face contorted into a fake smile. "Perfectly understandable," she said with professional smoothness. "It's a solid home with excellent potential. Don't delay. We've had some interest, and not just from those out-of-towners you warned me about." She reached into her pocket and pulled out an object. It was a round ball, and it glittered, like a spell.

She was onto me!

I braced myself for battle. The woman didn't know what she was up against. My lips and tongue were still bigger than their size, and even at Regular Zara Strength, my mouth could house a massive arsenal.

"What's that in your hand?" I asked, my voice squeaky.

"Something magical," she said.

"You don't say. How magical, exactly?"

"See for yourself," Reyna said, walking toward me in the calm manner of someone who was *not* about to unleash a magical offense. Despite her jaundiced skin, there was still plenty of life in her perky step and her bright green eyes.

I held my fire.

Reyna set the round, glittering object on the workbench between us. It appeared to be a battery-powered automatic air freshener. Or was it? Appearances could be deceiving.

A green light came on, and the object let out a puff of scent.

Lilac.

Reyna said, "I prefer floral scents in all the rooms, except for the kitchen, where I prefer fresh baked goods. I try to get apple pie for open houses, but, in a pinch, some potpourri tossed in the oven works great." She gave me a knowing look. "As long as you don't turn up the temperature too high."

"Right, I said, and forced out a fake laugh as I looked into her eyes. *Why did you kill Harry Blackstone, you psycho?*

She looked back at me. Her eyes seemed to ask a question back: *Why are you in Harry's garage, you psycho?*

She could wonder all she wanted. I was the one with the magic, so I would be the one getting the answers today, not her.

I cast the bluffing spell that would get her to open up, and possibly confess to murder—as long as I didn't overplay my hand.

The spell cast flawlessly, thanks to plenty of practice, plus my slightly larger-than-usual mouth.

But something was wrong.

Usually, the air would sparkle after I cast the spell, letting me know it was working, in case it wasn't obvious enough by the fact I was getting exactly what I wanted from the spell's subject.

But this time, the air didn't sparkle. All I detected in the air was the scent of fake lilac coming from the little air freshener. As seconds ticked by, the scent reminded me less and less of lilac and more of something less pleasant. My eyes started to water, blurring my vision before I blinked the moisture away.

I looked down at the squat little toxin generator on the workbench. What was this dastardly object?

I'd known that certain artificial scents, and even natural ones, could interfere with spells, but I'd never had an air freshener affect me like this, let alone cancel my bluffing spell.

Reyna was looking at me expectantly. "Pretty scent, isn't it?"

I wiped a tear from my watering eyes. "And so strong."

"This is a new model that's not on the market yet," she said. "I know a scientist at DuSanto Chemical who is developing new scents and colors. All natural. For people who don't want chemicals."

"All natural," I repeated. "Nature makes plenty of chemicals. Do you mean dyes or colorings that come from vegetable or animal sources?"

She gave me a sidelong, suspicious look. "Yeah, like that." She glanced over at the big open garage door, then the door that led to the home's interior. "Well, I should be getting ready for my open house."

"Isn't it a bit soon?" I asked.

"Seven o'clock is a popular time for showings, and Tuesday nights are when many of us hold agents-only opens."

"That's not what I meant by soon," I said carefully. My bluffing spell wasn't helping, but I hadn't given up on dragging information out of the woman. Whatever I did find out, I could pass along to Persephone Rose so she could finish the job.

Reyna tapped her toe impatiently. "What do you mean, Zara?"

"It's just that... Isn't it a bit soon for the house to be selling? Mr. Blackstone didn't pass away that long ago. I believe it was exactly two weeks ago that he died at the library."

"So?"

"Doesn't it usually take longer for all the paperwork with the estate to go through?"

"Not always," she said.

I let my silence do the questioning.

To my surprise, it worked almost as well as my bluffing spell. Her whole body language changed, as though all the tense muscles were giving up.

"You're a smart woman," she said. "There is another factor I haven't disclosed, but I would have made it perfectly clear if your friend had made an offer."

"You were Harry's landlady?"

She nodded. "I'm the owner of this house, yes. I bought it from Harry as an investment, because he needed liquid assets, and we had an agreement that he could remain living here for as long as he wished."

"You mean as long as he lived," I said.

Her expression was stony. "Sure."

"Harry was quite sick for a while. He was sick when he sold you the house, wasn't he?"

"That's not relevant." She looked away from me, as though suddenly fascinated by the tools on the wall. "I was planning to keep the house as a long-term investment. This neighborhood is on an upward trajectory." The tendons on her neck stood out. "I was as happy as anyone when Harry had his surprising recovery."

"Sure you were," I said. "Is that why you kept giving him red peppers that you knew were poisonous?"

She jerked her head to face me, gasped, and took a step back. "I beg your pardon?"

"You got the peppers, or the seeds, from your contact at DuSanto Chemical, didn't you?"

She blinked repeatedly. "I don't know what you're talking about."

"Why's your skin so yellow?"

"I-I-I told you. I'm doing a juice cleanse."

"You're dying," I said.

She pressed her hands to her lips. Hoarsely, she said, "I am not."

"You need treatment," I said. "You haven't touched a pepper in two weeks, but it's getting worse, isn't it?"

Her eyes glistened. What I'd guessed was true.

She needed a Peptyx Tapewyrm, or something even more extreme.

"You might as well confess," I said. "Sooner than later. Maybe they can treat you for the poison exposure. If you 'fess up, it could save your life."

"You're crazy," she said weakly.

"The police are going to arrest you, Reyna, because they have evidence. Tons of evidence." Who needed magic to bluff like a pro?

"You're crazy," she repeated, a bit of fight returning to her voice with a growl. "You've been living in that horrible house of yours, and it's rotting your brain. Everyone knows that whoever lives in the Red Witch House goes mad."

"You think I'm mad? You're the one poisoning people."

"You have no proof," she growled. "If you dare say one word about me, I'll drag you through the mud."

I set my phone on the workbench, put my hands on my hips, and sighed as I shook my head. Rhetorically, I asked, "What is up with the real estate agents in this town? Are all of you evil, or just the ones I have to deal with?"

She stepped toward the interior door, eying me warily. "I, uh, have to show the house now," she said. "For the record, I don't know anything about whatever you're talking about. However, if I did happen to give Harry anything, it was..." She trailed off.

A voice at the entrance finished her thought. "To kill him," said the newcomer to the conversation. There was a shadow at our feet, connected to the figure standing in the garage door opening. It was Ambrosia Abernathy.

Reyna gasped, "What?"

"That's Harry's next-door neighbor and friend," I said. "And what she said is that you only gave Harry the peppers in order to kill him."

"That's preposterous," Reyna said.

"She doesn't think so," I said. "Maybe the three of us should go down to the police station to..." I trailed off as my jaw dropped open.

Ambrosia Abernathy had not learned her lesson about using her witch magic willy-nilly.

The young witch had two hands full of her purple plasma, ready to fire. The lightning balls were bright enough that even a non-magical person, such as the real estate agent trembling in front of me, could see them.

Ambrosia stepped forward and jerked her head. The motor fired up overhead, and the garage door started rolling down, closing behind her. As the natural light disappeared, the garage interior was lit mainly by the eerie purple glow of the young witch's weapons.

Ambrosia growled, "Harry was my friend, and you killed him. I know everything."

There was a PFFFT, and the air freshener released more fake lilac into the air next to me.

Reyna held both of her hands up. "Easy now, little girl. I don't know what you think is going on here, but you'd better not throw any of that stuff at me. What is that, anyway?"

"You'll see," Ambrosia said, and she lobbed a purple comet at the Realtor.

I moved to defend Reyna from the shot, but, to my absolute horror, my magic wasn't working.

Witchbane?

The air freshener was doing more than blocking my bluffing spell. It must have contained the substance that was Kryptonite to witches. It was airborne, and while it had grounded my powers, it apparently hadn't affected Ambrosia, who stood fifteen feet away. Nor did it affect the plasma ball bearing down on us.

The shot struck Reyna squarely in the chest. She dropped to her knees, groaning.

"That's enough," I said to Ambrosia through clenched teeth. "Whatever you're doing with that, um, stun gun, you need to stop it at once."

Ambrosia lifted her chin defiantly. "Who cares what we do right now? The people at the Department are going to take her away and make her disappear. They protect their own, and Harry was one of them. He told me everything."

"I care what you do right now," I said. "Cool your jets."

"No." Ambrosia glowered at the real estate agent as she brought her hands together and prepared a single, large ball of plasma, holding it like a bowling ball. "I want to hear her admit she killed him. Harry needs to know she's been caught, so he can move on."

Reyna wasn't even looking at the young witch. She was hunched over, convulsing. She let out a horrible, choking sound, and slumped to the concrete floor, limp and lifeless.

"Oh, no," Ambrosia said. She dropped the bowling-ball sized plasma. It sputtered out on the concrete floor.

The garage was dim again, the purple light dissipated.

I waved a hand to flick on the garage lights. Nothing happened. How quickly I'd forgotten about my grounding. My magic was still on the fritz thanks to the air freshener. I manually groped the wall in the dark until I found the light switch and turned it on.

The garage filled with artificial light.

Ambrosia was hunched over Reyna's still body, her big, brown eyes full of crocodile tears and regret.

"I didn't mean it," Ambrosia said. "I didn't mean to kill her. You've got to tell the others it was an accident."

"Help me drag the body outside," I said.

Ambrosia's eyes bulged. She whispered, "We're going to bury her?"

The look on the novice witch's face almost made me laugh.

"Yes. I'm going to help you bury your first victim," I said. "That's what coven friends are for."

Her jaw moved but no sound came out.

"Of course not," I said. "See that air freshener dispenser on the workbench? It's got witchbane in it. My powers aren't working at the moment, but if we get ourselves outside into fresh air, we might be able to join our healing forces and save Reyna."

"We can't bring back the dead." Ambrosia was crying now. "Nothing brings back the dead."

That wasn't entirely true, but I didn't correct the girl.

"Pull yourself together," I barked. "This woman isn't dead yet. As long as she's alive, you haven't killed anyone."

"I didn't mean to! It was only a stun blast!"

"I know. But her system was already compromised by —" I cut myself off and grabbed the real estate agent under the armpits. "Just grab the feet and help me haul her outside."

Ambrosia and I hauled the unconscious woman out the side door. We exited the garage right as lightning flashed across the sky. Thunder rolled over almost instantly. The storm was upon us.

CHAPTER 36

Later That Night
(8:05 pm)
Dreamland Coffee, Downtown Location
Stock Room

"You're late," Maisy Nix said as I entered through the heavy steel delivery door.

The owner of the establishment preferred that we use the back door for coven meetings when the coffee shop was still open. I'd thought about sneaking in disguised as a bush, but I was all out of magic. Between the witchbane in the air freshener and all the healing efforts required to save someone's life, I didn't have much left in me. I'd had to ask Ambrosia to open the door for us.

"She's only late by five minutes," Fatima Nix said, coming to my rescue.

I smiled at the short, dark-haired girl with the oversized white glasses. One could always count on soft-hearted Fatima for some defense against her aunt, Maisy.

"You had us worried," Zinnia said.

"I wasn't worried," Margaret Mills said. "I would have sensed it if you were in danger."

Zinnia snorted.

Maisy leaned to the side to look at the person I'd brought with me, the soaking wet novice witch Ambrosia Abernathy.

We were both soaking wet. I'd used all my energy to revive the real estate agent before handing her over to the authorities for further questioning. I didn't have the resources to waste on drying myself, and I had avoided stopping by my house for a change of clothes because I didn't want to be late—not that doing so had saved me from a scolding by Maisy.

"Ambrosia," Maisy said coolly. "You reek of ozone."

My aunt gasped and jumped to her feet. The jinxed table tilted on the edge of its base on its own accord and rolled away.

"Witchbane," Zinnia said. "I can smell it on you."

Fatima raised her hand slowly and asked meekly, "I thought witchbane was colorless and odorless?"

Margaret said, "I don't smell anything, other than the ozone."

Maisy said to her niece, "Some witches have a heightened ability to detect the toxin, especially after traumatic encounters."

Zinnia kept her gaze fixed on me. "What happened? Did Harry make you do something?"

"He wasn't even there," I said.

Behind me, Ambrosia said, "He was there."

I whirled to face her. "He was? I didn't see him."

"He was there," Ambrosia said.

I rubbed the goosebumps on my arms. I'd never been on that side of the equation before—listening to a witch tell me about the presence of a ghost. It was spooky as heck.

"You two are dripping all over the place," Maisy said.

"I'll do the drying spell," Fatima said. She jumped up, avoiding the jinxed table that was still rolling around like an overexcited puppy, and dried both me and Ambrosia.

Fatima's drying spell, honed through countless pet grooming sessions, was superior to all others.

Then she offered Ambrosia her hand. "Hello. I'm Fatima," she said. "I'm Whisper Graced. Some people call it Whisker Graced, because I can talk to animals. You can call me either one. I don't mind."

Ambrosia nodded and took her hand. "Nice to meet you."

Margaret Mills pushed her way in next. "Margaret Mills. I don't believe in specialties."

Zinnia snorted.

"Nice to meet you," Ambrosia said again.

She shook Zinnia's hand next.

"Zinnia Riddle. Kitchen Bewitched."

Next, everyone looked at me expectantly.

I turned to the girl and offered my hand. "It seems a bit backwards to do this now, less than an hour after we nearly killed and then revived someone, but okay. Zara Riddle. Spirit Charmed." She shook my hand with a trembling grip that grew stronger after I offered her a smile.

Maisy shook her hand next, speaking formally and standing taller than ever. "Maisy Nix. Flame Touched."

Then Maisy barked a command at the table, and we all sat to begin our first coven meeting with six members.

To Ambrosia's astonishment, the group didn't treat our recent encounter with Reyna Drinkwater as the top-most item of business. The most contentious item on the agenda was over the official naming of Margaret's lucky marble. It was a lovely cat's-eye marble, yellow with a red eye.

As we all discussed the marble, and its significance in the history and culture of the coven, I shot Ambrosia a look to let her know that everything was going to be okay. And that her punishment would be coming. All in due time.

CHAPTER 37

Four Days Later
Saturday Afternoon
Abernathy Family Funeral Home
Memorial Services for Mr. Harold Blackstone

I didn't like wearing black from head to toe, which my closet understood, so it had offered up a navy blue dress with a wide brown belt.

When I joined my coworkers in the second-to-last row of the chapel at the Abernathy Family Funeral Home, both Kathy and Frank subtly signaled their approval of my funeral attire.

They both looked appropriate as well, though Kathy often dressed in dark, drab shades, so she could have worn anything in her closet. Today she looked more chic than usual, dressed in a dark-olive pantsuit that flattered her shape. Frank wore a conservative dark-gray suit that, judging by the loose fit on the shoulders, he'd borrowed from someone.

As I slid into the pew, a few heads turned our way, and then more, like dominoes. I picked up snippets of hushed conversations as members of the Blackstone family and their friends identified the three of us as the local librarians. We were the ones who'd been unable to wake poor Harry from his final nap. We were also the ones who'd been interviewed in the recent news stories about a ghost haunting a small town library.

Frank had given most of the sound bites to the press, while Kathy and I had recited the speeches she'd prepared about the importance of funding for libraries and other civic facilities that fostered community and connection.

The press had been less interested in talk about budgets for community services, but, Frank Wonder, with his wild pink hair and extensive catalog of character voices for storytime, had become an overnight media sensation.

I smiled and waved politely at the other funeral attendees.

Once the talk had died down, and people had returned to their eyes-forward position, I scanned the crowd for my father.

Rhys Quarry had been friends with Harry Blackstone, and I'd been expecting him to make an appearance in town for a while now. I'd heard from my sources that he had shown up earlier that morning.

I found him easily. He was seated in the second row, and staring back at me with a hopeful look on his face.

I held very still as a mix of feelings washed over me.

Frank leaned across Kathy's lap and whispered, "Zara, is that your father over there? You should go sit with him. We'll be fine on our own."

Kathy followed Frank's gaze, took in my father for two slow, owlish blinks, then looked at me. "Sit with your father," she said, using her Boss Voice.

I hemmed and hawed. I checked the time. We didn't have long before the services were to begin, so I had to decide quickly. I found myself rising. My body had decided.

When I reached the pew where Rhys Quarry was sitting, he slid over to make room for me while keeping his attention straight ahead.

He asked softly, "How's the car running?"

"She's tickety-boo," I said, and she was.

I'd used Harry Blackstone's enchanted wrench to make a few adjustments to get Foxy Pumpkin running again, but my father didn't need to hear every detail. Plus, I wasn't about to talk about magic cars and tools in public.

I could have tried casting a sound bubble to give us privacy, but that would be a foolish, dangerous move that only a novice witch like Ambrosia Abernathy would make. Not a smart witch such as yours truly.

Churches had unpredictable inversion effects on spellwork. Sure, we were only inside the chapel of a funeral home located within a strip mall, but a chapel was still a church, and I couldn't risk a spectacle. The town of Wisteria didn't need another "curious small-town incident" making the national news. Especially not right on the heels of their titillating tales about the spooky haunted library with the great coffee.

He took in a breath and started, "Zara, you need to know I—"

"Shush." I quieted him with a pat on his leg. A pat that might have been interpreted as a downward punch. "Whatever you have to say, it can wait until after the service, Dad."

He jerked his head and gave me a wide-eyed look, his rubbery features practically going BOING!

He asked, "What's that again?"

"It can wait. I'm sure you had your reasons to do what you did. The more I go through in my own life, the better I understand all the mistakes my parents made." The many mistakes.

He had the good sense to say nothing.

"You can be part of our lives," I said, "on one condition. No more slinking around. If you're coming to town, give me a call. Don't just show up and spy on me." I tilted my forehead toward his, all the better to look directly into his eyes. "Don't hide in the bushes under my kitchen window listening to my private conversations."

His eyebrows shot up. "You know about that?"

"I have protective wards on the house for a reason."

He chuckled and shook his head. "That's my girl."

"Now shush for real," I said, nodding at the person taking their place at the dais. "Let's be quiet and pay our respects to our old friend Harry."

"Zara," he said softly.

"What?" I didn't turn to look.

"You called me Dad."

I snorted and kept my gaze forward. "No, I didn't. You need to get your ears checked, Rhys." I wriggled my back, trying to get comfortable on the hard wooden pew. "*All* of your ears," I added.

"Will do," he said.

* * *

The eulogy was delivered by Harry's identical twin brother, William, a.k.a. Bill, Blackstone.

The eulogy was also secretly delivered by Harry himself.

And here's the big surprise that no living soul at the funeral that Saturday could have guessed in a million years: The twins were co-presenting the eulogy. Harry's spirit had been successfully transplanted into Bill's body, and the brothers were now sharing the body equally. A certain local coven had helped with the transfer.

As Bill/Harry delivered the eulogy, there were moments he/they seemed genuinely surprised by what he/they were reading.

At one point, Bill/Harry rubbed his chin and muttered, "Well, that's all wrong. Bill, you messed up these dates, you half-wit."

The friends and family members gathered in the chapel let out some grief tension with a ripple of chuckles and guffaws.

Bill/Harry snapped his fingers on one hand while the other hand flailed wildly. He/They made eye contact with one of the Abernathy family's attendants—Ambrosia, dressed in black with a yellow belt—and said, "Ambrosia, do your old pal Harry a favor and grab us a pencil, will you?" Bill/Harry smiled crookedly at the crowd and apologized for the delay. He declared that it would take a few minutes to make the corrections, but it had to be done, because there might not be another funeral for Harry.

By now, the crowd had been worked up enough that the tension and grief all but evaporated. Everyone laughed heartily.

Bill/Harry continued cracking jokes as he/they corrected the eulogy using a pencil provided by Ambrosia.

I looked over at Margaret Mills, who was there representing the coven. I tried to catch her eye so we could share a secret knowing look—the best part of pulling of some high-grade magic—but she wouldn't look my way. She couldn't tear her eyes off the man/men giving the speech. She was staring at him the way my cat stared at plates that were suspected to contain ham.

Margaret Mills, you naughty girl, I thought.

Her head whipped suddenly, and she was looking at me, with full force. I felt her focus strike me with the PANG of a shovel hitting rock in the dirt. I tasted metal in my mouth.

I quickly shielded any further thoughts from the witch. She narrowed her eyes. I offered her a tiny wave, using just my fingertips. She slowly turned her head away, and returned to gazing with adoration at Bill/Harry.

The eulogy ended, and we bowed our heads for more prayer—or silence—our choice; It was that kind of chapel.

As I closed my eyes, I remembered how Margaret had gawked at Bill Blackstone the night we met with him to perform the soul transfer. Zinnia had suggested we bring an extra witch to help perform the ritual, and I'd been thrilled to have the support. The spell could have been performed with two witches, but, like many spells, it was more stable—not to mention fun—with three.

Bill had flirted with the recently single Margaret Mills throughout our preparations. And then Harry had done the same. As Harry's first act of physicality after being transferred into the shared body, Harry had asked Margaret on a date on behalf of both of them.

I'd laughed then, thinking it was all a wacky joke to break the tension of an awkward situation, but it turned out the joke was on me.

Margaret Mills was dating twins. Twins who shared one body.

It was strange, but... stranger things had happened.

CHAPTER 38

Monday Morning
Wisteria Public Library

Frank Wonder was staring at a mountain of burlap sacks full of coffee beans.

"We need to hustle if we want to use this up," he said to me as I entered the break room. "We have way too much coffee."

"There's no such thing as too much coffee," I said. "Just like there's no such thing as too much bacon, or sleep, or love."

He gave me an exaggerated dirty look. "Zara Riddle, you just had to be a do-gooder, didn't you? Harry the Ghost is gone, gone, gone. Thanks to your good work."

I grinned sheepishly. "Zara tries to be a good witch."

Frank tousled his pink hair. "I wonder if Harry ever takes breaks from his brother's body. Maybe he could float by here occasionally for a nap. Just to keep up appearances."

"Harry can't leave the body," I said. "It's not allowed."

"Why? If he did, would he not be able to get back in?"

"That's not the reason." I tucked my purse into a cubby, and grabbed a mug for coffee. "Their girlfriend, Margaret Mills, wouldn't allow it."

"Oh, for crying out loud. That's not fair. She should share him with the world." He waved a hand at Coffee Mountain. "We'll never get through this pile. The weekend staff left a note that they heard rumblings."

"Rumblings? This is new." I felt a little breathless suddenly. "Rumblings might have something to do with the tunnels."

Frank shook his head. "Rumblings as in rumors. The ghost nerds are saying that Harry's spirit has moved on. They say he *finally found peace* after his memorial service."

"And he did. Sort of."

"Did you see that a few of the sneaky ones were there at the memorial?"

I shook my head. I'd been busy with my father, among other pesky people.

Frank said, "Well, I certainly saw them, and I gave them a scathing look. Attending the funeral of someone you don't know is generally frowned upon, according to their group culture."

"Isn't it frowned upon in general?" I held up my hand in a stop-sign gesture and bowed my head. "Wait. I spoke too soon. Don't jump all over me for misspeaking. I know it's common for people to attend funerals for people they didn't know, to support the friends and family of the deceased."

I looked up to find Frank giving me a mystified, bemused look. "Why would I jump all over you?" He fluttered his fingers to his chest. "Do you take me for some kind of monster, Zara Riddle?"

"My bad," I said. "I've got coven reflexes now. Whenever I say something slightly stupid, I have to immediately correct myself and beg forgiveness."

Frank arched an eyebrow. "Fun bunch you've gotten yourself involved in."

"Oh, they're mostly harmless. I'm going to try turning the group into an actual book club. There's no such thing as bad energy, as long as you have an appropriate outlet."

"Wise words," Frank said. "Speaking of which, how are things with your father?"

"Surprisingly good," I said. "Being in the coven has given me a whole new measuring stick for how much irritation I can handle."

"Rhys and I spoke for a few minutes after the service," Frank said. "We had proper introductions."

"Aww. I'm sorry I missed out on that. I went looking for an egg salad sandwich and got cornered by Helen Highbury. She told me about her new Yoga for Seniors classes at the community center. Can you believe she invited me to a class for over-sixties?" I kept going, before Frank could answer my rhetorical question. "Helen also told me how wonderful and unusual the eulogy had been. She said it felt as though Harry was right there, in spirit, speaking through his brother."

"Yes," Frank said, his eyes twinkling. "It did seem that way, but of course such things are impossible."

"Impossible," I agreed.

Kathy walked in. "What's impossible?"

"Two souls sharing one body," Frank said.

She snorted. "Yeah, right." She winked at Frank and then whispered, "Are you talking about Bill/Harry? I hear they're dating Margaret Mills." She looked at me. "Can you confirm?"

"I cannot betray the secrecy of my coven. One of the coven members, a woman who is currently dating twins, would kick my butt if I did, so I trust you'll understand that I cannot confirm nor deny that salacious rumor."

My phone buzzed.

I checked the messages, read them quickly, then summarized the news for my coworkers.

The coven had decided it was best for the ghost hunters to move on quickly, rather than linger around Wisteria looking for other mysteries to occupy them now that the library hauntings had ceased. As I'd said to Frank, there was no such thing as bad energy, only energy that needed a more appropriate target. And the new target for the ghost hunters would be a fresh haunting, not too far from Wisteria, but just far enough.

With the help of the coven and local police, I had located a charming Bed and Breakfast that was looking for out-of-the-box ideas to expand their business. The owner was a shifter herself, and well-versed in magic. She was the open-minded type of shifter who was willing to work with witches.

We witches weren't going to summon an actual ghost to the premises. That would only create more problems than it solved. Instead, we were going to create the illusion of a haunting, through witchcraft.

And who was going to perform this witchcraft? Why, it would be Little Miss Fireball-First-Ask-Questions-Later herself, Ambrosia Abernathy. The coven agreed that such community service would be a suitable punishment for the novice witch's insouciance.

Actually, the other witches had wanted much harsher penalties, but I had weighed in on behalf of the young witch. Being a little hair-trigger with the magic myself, I could relate to her so-called insouciance. I begged for clemency on her behalf, and got it.

Ambrosia would be driving her personal vehicle—a retired hearse—up to the Bed and Breakfast two or three nights a week to perform the spells. I had laid out a strict program of simple spells, and she'd been warned against straying from the program.

I was the right witch to lay out the haunting program. Having spent some time around the ghost hunters, I'd become intimately familiar with all of their detectors and recording equipment. Thanks to that insider knowledge, I was able to design a routine of spells that would give the enthusiasts*just enough* positive readings to keep them intrigued, but not enough to provide any hard evidence that would blow open the world of the supernatural.

Of course, the latter might not have been possible anyway, since magic had a mind of its own, and tended to go on the fritz whenever a high-resolution camera was pointed toward it. Modern technology was a little like the witchbane that had been infused inside Reyna Drinkwater's air freshener.

As for the air freshener, it had been taken by the DWM for further testing and a "full investigation." I had a bad feeling their investigation was more in the name of developing more anti-witchcraft tools for themselves and less about protecting witches in the community, but what could I do?

I should have hidden the unit before calling for backup at the Blackstone residence. Unfortunately, I hadn't considered that in the heat of the moment. I'd been focused on keeping a certain real estate agent alive, so she didn't become Ambrosia Abernathy's first manslaughter victim.

Once summoned, the DWM agents took Ms. Drinkwater away to the "hospital"—*wink wink*—and later gave us the good news that the patient was stable.

The next day, I'd learned the woman had already received a liver transplant.

I asked, out of curiosity, where the liver had come from, and the agents fed me the usual line about that information being confidential and none of my concern.

Later, when I told Charlize about the liver transplant, her pale blue eyes had widened with an alertness I hadn't witnessed in weeks. I actually witnessed her depression lifting. It was beautiful.

She immediately grabbed the nearest available laptop to begin work. The laptop in question belonged a young fellow who'd been using it to write a novel at the table next to us in Dreamland Coffee, where we'd been sitting. Charlize typed furiously on the stolen laptop, much to the laptop owner's shock and horror. I managed to get the laptop away from the gorgon, and returned it to the aspiring novelist, along with a fresh mocha with whipped cream and rainbow sprinkles.

Charlize wanted a mocha, too. We got a couple to go, and I drove her to Beacon Street. She ran into the house next to mine, the Moore residence. Once inside, she began furiously bashing away on two laptops at the same time. Her hair snakes elongated, and soon they were typing as well, and clicking the mouse buttons. I'd never seen anything like it.

As the gorgon worked on hacking through the same security system she'd put in place herself, I saw the life return to the woman. Her hair snakes undulated with tentative excitement, and the dreadlocks and matts in her hair unwound themselves.

Twenty-four hours later, Charlize was completely sober and back to her old self. Her blonde hair was radiant.

She reported to me that while she had not discovered the source of the donated liver, or what the Department had done with Ms. Drinkwater, something wonderful had happened. The Department had detected a breach of their network by "an army of high-level hackers." They had contacted her, asking—no, begging—their favorite programmer to return from her leave of absence.

"That's great news," I said. "But are you sure you want to keep working for them?"

"What else can I do? I'm not qualified for anything else." She glanced around at the tequila bottles and fast food debris scattered across the house. She brought her tattered fingers to her mouth and chewed two fingernails at once. She repeated, "What else can I do?"

"You can do anything," I told her. "But if you want to go back to the Department, I support that one hundred percent. They need more good people like you working for them."

She looked me dead in the eyes. I shivered. Even though we were best friends now, her gorgon stare still made my blood feel icy.

Softly, she asked, "You think I'm a good person?"

"Of course I do. I wouldn't be friends with you if you weren't."

"But..."

"Nobody's perfect," I said.

"But you are," she said.

Me? Perfect? I'd never laughed so hard.

* * *

When I told my daughter that Charlize had declared me *perfect*, Zoey barely mustered an eye roll. She was focused entirely on her phone.

"What's on there? What's more interesting than your mother?"

"More of a *who* than a *what*," she said, smiling enigmatically.

"Ooh. A new person? Some cute guy at school who's finally gotten your mind off Griffin?"

"Huh. I forgot about Griffin." She frowned and swiped her screen a moment. "We haven't talked in days. I think maybe we're broken up."

"Congratulations?"

"Thanks. I feel fine." She rubbed her chest, rearranging the ruffles on the cute blouse she was wearing. She had recently upgraded her wardrobe, from drab sweatshirts that spoke of depression, to cute, fitted garments that spoke of better times. "My heart feels okay. Actually, it feels kind of happy."

"All thanks to this new fellow, named...?" I pointed to her phone.

"Not a guy," she said. "It's just Ambrosia. I think we might be friends now."

"That's great," I lied. "I'm so excited about having Ambrosia around," I lied some more.

"Your lies would be more convincing if you didn't clench your teeth, Mom."

"Oh?" I played dumb.

"If it's okay with you, I'm going to drive up with her to the Foxclaw Inn and help with the haunting."

"Won't you be embarrassed if people see you riding around in Ambrosia's old hearse?"

She gave me a pointed look. "You really think I embarrass so easily?"

"No," I said. "I suppose not."

I took a moment to pat myself on the back for some excellent parenting. Thanks to me, my daughter could handle friendship with anyone.

CHAPTER 39

On Tuesday, a story emerged on the internet about a spooky, haunted Bed and Breakfast not far from a certain spooky, haunted library.

The story hadn't yet broken wide and made national headlines. How could it without Frank Wonder's charismatic presence in interviews? But the news did reach the dark corners of the World Wide Web that mattered to the most dedicated paranormal enthusiasts, the ones who actually ventured out of their homes and visited allegedly haunted locations.

Over the next few days at the library, the Goblin Hordes diminished in numbers. The tide of invaders receded slowly, and then quickly, like a bathtub draining.

On Friday, by mid-day, we had made only five dollars in coffee sales, and that was to Carrot Greyson, who'd come in with a kerchief over her orange hair, ready to change the Little Red Riding Hood mural. We tried to refuse her donation, but she insisted on contributing to the library coffers. We compromised by making it a bottomless cup that she could refill as much as she liked while she painted.

"Thanks, Zara," Carrot said. "Did you do something with your hair?"

"Nothing out of the ordinary," I said.

"You look amazing," she said. "You Riddle women are so lucky to look the way you do, but there's something new about you, and how you look today. You really do look amazing."

"I guess it's because I finally caught up on my sleep and started eating healthy," I said. I had not.

Carrot gave me a knowing smile, then took her painting supplies and the coffee upstairs to the storytime area.

* * *

Two hours later, she had refilled her bottomless coffee three times. I had to assume she was busily working away up there, but I couldn't smell any paint, and she didn't have any fresh spatter on her clothes or kerchief.

Frank was fascinated by her artistic process, and kept sneaking upstairs to check on her.

After his third trip, he reported back, "Something magic is happening up there with Carrot Greyson and the mural."

"Good," I said.

We were shelving books. It was a job that took much longer without magic, but I had always enjoyed fitting books back into their homes on the shelves, and I suspected that would never change. It was the most soothing rote task I could even imagine, except possibly crocheting, which Kathy had not yet convinced me to embrace. I understood the basic premise, but I wasn't craft-obsessed like her. Kathy had been known to crochet while driving. Me, I would stick to shelving books.

Frank excused himself, ran upstairs to check on the rune mage/tattooist/mural artist a fourth time, then returned, breathless. "Something magic is definitely happening up there."

"Is the new mural really that good?"

"Yes, but she's not actually painting." He rubbed his crooked chin and spoke out of the extreme corner of his mouth, using his secretive voice. "She has a brush in her hand, but there's no paint on it."

"She might be planning ahead. Visualizing."

Frank shook his head. "The mural is already changing. It's becoming less terrifying."

"Are you sure you're not just getting used to it?"

He raised his eyebrows. "Zara," he said, with the *duh* implied. "We both know better."

"So, the woman can paint things, or at least change paintings, without touching any paints," I said. "Nice trick. That will save her on cleanup time, not to mention paint costs, plus none of her clothes will get spattered."

"I wonder if she can change tattoos the same way."

"You could always ask," I said. "Introduce yourself officially. She's been dropping hints that she already knows about us. Plus, clearly she has figured out that she's a rune mage."

"Hmm," he said. "Once you know that half of the people in this town have powers, it doesn't make what you have very special anymore."

"Oh, Frank. Nobody is as special as you. Nobody."

He shelved a book in the wrong spot, then rubbed his hands on the eggplant-purple corduroy trousers hugging his slim hips. "I'm going upstairs again. I need to know how she's doing it."

I corrected the book he'd misfiled. "While you're at it, find out who she's dating," I said.

He did a double take. "How do you know she's dating someone?"

"She has a sort of glow. I could be wrong, but I think she's in love."

He snorted. "You would know."

I used the book cart to push him out of the way. "Get going before I run you over," I said. Frank knew I didn't like talking about that mushy emotional stuff at work. Or at all. It was private, between me and Bentley.

* * *

Later that same Friday, Bentley popped in for a visit with his new partner in tow.

I collected their ten dollars, and handed over two full cups.

Bentley took a sip and closed his eyes. "Library coffee tastes so much better than regular coffee."

"It's the exact same coffee you can get at Dreamland," I said. "The exact same."

He opened his eyes, and they flashed silver in that sexy way of his. I wished the counter wasn't standing between us. I wanted to run my fingers through that thick, dark hair of his, tugging at the curious little widow's peak point on his forehead. I loved ruffling his hair, looking for those flashes of silver at the temples.

When I'd first met him, I had noticed his solid, muscular build, and his good looks. He'd reminded me of an old movie star, someone from another time, a time when men wore hats and tipped them for ladies. I'd actually tried to set him up with my aunt, since he seemed too good to be wasted by remaining single.

How had I not seen how perfect he was for me? Had I been blinded by my infatuation for another man, or had he been different back then, before he'd come into his vampire powers? I would never know. And it didn't matter. I had seen through his cool, almost robotic demeanor, and gotten to know the hot, passionate person disguised by the gray car and gray suits. He could be weird, too. The man carried peanuts in his pockets at all times, for the local wildlife. He'd become good friends with a local miscreant known as Petey the Squirrel. And the peanuts also generated goodwill with a certain wyvern who liked popping in on our dates.

I gazed at him as he sipped his coffee.

"I'm glad you like it," I said. "But you should be warned, we are probably going to suspend coffee service to the public soon. Maisy didn't care when it was the out-of-towners drinking our brew, but she's heard rumblings about her regulars thinking of switching to Library Coffee." I shook my head. "And one does not mess with Maisy Nix."

"Probably for the best," Bentley said. "You don't have a license to sell food on the premises."

"Why, Detective! We're not selling food," I said coyly, batting my eyelashes. "We merely accept donations." I waved my hand at the posted signage.

"That sign is *evidence*," he said, using his Big and Scary Voice. "Evidence of your flagrant violation of the local bylaws." He took another sip. "But I'm not going to arrest you, because the law-breaking is what makes it tastes so good."

I gasped and held my fingers to my chest. "Detective! I am just *shocked* by your baseless accusations."

He glanced left and right, then made a come-here gesture with his fingers as he lifted his chin.

I leaned across the counter of the circulation desk and held my ear near his lips. His warm lips. Some vampires ran cold, but not mine.

He murmured, "I hear it's also against the bylaws for two municipal employees to fraternize on taxpayer-funded premises."

"Is that so?" I murmured back. "Is that only during official posted hours and while on duty, or is that a twenty-four-seven sort of thing?"

"I'll have to look into the matter. Either way, it won't stop me from meeting a certain redheaded municipal employee in the stacks for the occasional *lunch date*." The way he said "lunch date" sent a thrill right through me.

It also alerted my pink-haired coworker, who had a special sense for romantic chatter.

"I heard that," Frank said, rolling his cart to a stop behind Bentley. "You know we have cameras in the stacks, right?"

Bentley's expression went slack. "You do?"

I interjected, "Cameras that can be shut off."

Frank scoffed. "Only if the parties *remember* to shut them off in their haste to *fraternize* on taxpayer-funded *premises*."

I waved Frank away. "Go check on Carrot and the new mural," I said.

Bentley raised an eyebrow. "She's doing a new painting? I'd like to see that."

"It's not ready yet," I said. "It's a surprise."

"I hope it doesn't involve any bats."

"Honestly, I don't know Carrot's plans, but I think she's in a much better mood than when she painted the first one, and it's going to come through in the work."

At that moment, Persephone Rose returned from her browse of the new releases table. She smiled hello, and picked up her coffee. She smelled it deeply before taking a sip.

I watched her, and Bentley watched me, watching her.

Persephone looked up at me with those big, brown eyes peering out from under thick, dark bangs. "Library coffee really is better than regular coffee," she said, giving me a smile. When I'd first met the young woman, I'd interpreted her smile as needy, or nervous, or an attempt to suck up to me. And perhaps it had been all of those things, but now I saw it for what it truly was: an attempt to close the distance between us.

I glanced over at Frank, who, like Bentley, was also watching my interaction with Persephone. Frank waved both hands like a parent encouraging their child to step into the water at the beach, and mouthed words at me. *Ask her. Do it, Zara. Do it now.*

"Ms. Rose," I said tentatively.

"Yes?" She held the coffee with one hand while she used the other to tug at her thick bangs.

"Never mind," I said. "You're probably busy tonight, anyway. It is Friday, and you're young, and—"

"I'm not busy," she interrupted. "Why?"

"I was wondering if you might like to go bowling."

Her hand dropped away from her bangs and thunked on the counter. "Bowling?"

"Bentley and I are starting a team," I said. "We've joined a league that meets on Fridays. My goal is to eventually beat the Incredibowls. That's my aunt's team. They're very good, but I think we stand a chance."

"That sounds..." She was apparently at a loss for words, which was understandable. A person didn't get asked to join a bowling league every day—not since the seventies, anyway.

"The team is mostly friends and family," I said, gathering my courage as I rolled back my shoulders decisively. "Which is why I'd like you to join."

Her thick, dark eyelashes fluttered. "You consider me a friend?"

"No," I said.

My response came out a little harsh, and she flinched visibly.

More gently, I said, "It's because you're family."

At the word family, Persephone Rose seemed to wither in on herself, becoming an inch shorter. Was I imagining things, or was she actually shrinking? She might have very well been shrinking. Shifters were able to make themselves smaller or larger while maintaining their human form, and Persephone Rose was a shifter. She was a black fox shifter. She was the creature I'd encountered running through the woods the day Harry Blackstone first came to talk to me about a favor. Due to a hilarious confluence of events, I had made the assumption the fox was Harry.

Hilarious!

But I knew better now, and I figured it out all by myself, so you can stop snickering about how dense I am to not see what was right in front of my eyes.

But I digress.

Back to Persephone.

She whispered weakly, her eyes as big and bright as white saucers under brown teacups, "You know?"

"I do now," I said.

Up until that instant, it had been a theory, but now I knew, and with that magical change, it felt like I had always known.

"You're my half-sister," I said.

She nodded.

Still standing next to her, Bentley said, "Wha-wha-what?" He sputtered dramatically.

I reached across the counter and patted his hand. "It's okay. You don't have to lie for me and pretend you don't know."

Behind him, Frank let out a single, "Hah!"

Bentley sighed. He knew all about my theory that his new partner was my father's daughter. He also felt terribly guilty that we'd talked about Persephone at great length without going directly to the source herself. I'd promised I would broach the topic with her, when the time was right.

And that Friday afternoon, after illegally selling them two coffees for above-market rates, had been the right time.

Persephone gazed at me with eyes that I now recognized as having the same shape as my father's, albeit with darker coloring.

"I was going to tell you," she said. "When the time was right."

I assured her that I understood.

There had been several times recently, when we'd been setting up the haunting at Persephone's mother's Bed and Breakfast, where I had sensed the young detective wanting to tell me something. I had resisted the urge to push the matter before the time felt right.

I rocked forward on my toes and grasped the edge of the counter. Now that we'd finally spoken about the unspoken bond between us, my body felt light. Light enough for a spontaneous broomstick flight.

"I know you knew long before I did," I said, using my Bossy Big Sister voice for the first time in my life. It felt good.

She smirked. "I totally knew."

I shook my head. "You little brat."

"I'm not a brat. You're the brat," she said, using her Bratty Little Sister voice for the first time in her life. She'd grown up an only child, just like me.

Did we have other siblings out there in the world thanks to our father? Probably. But for now, it was just the two of us, and we would learn how we fit together.

"But you'll come for bowling tonight?" I asked.

"Of course I will," she answered without hesitation.

Frank called out from the peanut gallery, "Hug! Hug! Hug!"

Persephone looked down at the ground, in the manner of someone who wanted very much to be hugged by her big sister, but didn't want to be overt about it.

With Frank, Bentley, Kathy, and the rest of the WPL staff as well as three patrons watching, I took the long walk around the circulation desk and hugged my sister for the very first time.

CHAPTER 40

After I finished work on Friday, I went to Bentley's place for dinner before bowling.

We didn't have a lot of time, but he'd taken some lamb chops out of the freezer, and assured me he could cook them without setting off the smoke detector.

One thing led to another, and...

Let's just say we had to cancel dinner and put the lamb chops in the fridge, uncooked.

He watched me button up my blouse with just as much interest as he'd watched me take it off earlier.

"That was new," I commented.

"Not *that* new," he said.

"But it was new in the sense that it didn't take place at an active crime scene, or on taxpayer-funded premises."

"But what about..." He swished his kissable lips from side to side thoughtfully. "Never mind. I guess my car is technically taxpayer-funded premises."

"Exactly," I said, slipping my shoes back on.

He was quiet a moment, then said my name with that tone of voice I didn't like. The one that said he wanted to *discuss* something.

I waved off whatever he was attempting to foist on me. "Let's just go bowling and have fun. Whatever happens between me and my sister will be fine. And you can stop telling me to be nice to her. I promise I'll be nice, or at least that I'll change tactics, and only be mean to her in a sisterly fashion. Like, um, teasing her about her hair, or whatever sisters do. I've been getting notes about sibling rivalry from Frank."

"Zara, I need to talk to you about my ex-wife."

"You don't."

"Yes. I do."

I continued to protest as I turned toward the door.

He was standing in the kitchen, putting the lamb chop seasonings away, and then, instantly, he was blocking my exit.

I jumped back. That vampire speed took some getting used to.

"Careful," I said. "Don't startle me like that. I could accidentally ruin your day."

"Zara, I don't want to talk to you about my relationship with my ex."

"Great." I clapped my hands. "I'm glad that's settled. Let's go bowling."

"I don't want to talk about why we split up."

"Right. Heard you the first time. Hey, do you even know how to bowl? And if so, do you have any tips? Are there special tactics, or do you just toss the ball and hope for the best?"

"All I want to do is tell you one thing."

I kept going about bowling. "Obviously I won't use magic, because there'd be no sport to it, but I would still like our team to win."

"Zara." He was still blocking the only exit. I pondered ways I might go through him. All of them were messy, and I happened to like my current outfit—a tailored find from Mia's Kit and Kaboodle, a lilac-purple blouse and teal, wide-legged pants that were made of a divine fabric that repelled rain while still being breathable.

"Fine." I stuck my hands in the teal pants' voluminous pockets. "Tell me your one thing," I grumbled.

"It's her name."

"That's weird, but okay." My chest suddenly hurt. My stomach felt rock-hard, despite being empty. Was she someone I knew? I swallowed hard. "Does your ex-wife's name start with the letter Z? And rhyme with Birconia?" I crossed my fingers, accidentally casting a minor good luck spell that affected the outcome of coin tosses by altering probability by ten percent.

"Her name is Larissa Lang."

"Oh, that's neat. Like the famous actress."

Silver eyes stared down at me.

The pain in my chest lifted. I swayed from side to side as a giant sack of clues rained down on me.

I gasped, "Your ex-wife is *the* Larissa Lang? The beautiful actress who plays Mahrissa on *Wicked Wives*?"

"Yes," he said, holding very still, except for his eyes, which were narrowing. "I thought you should know, since you talk about her all the time."

"I talk about *the show* all the time. She's just the actress who plays one of the characters we all love to hate."

"People hate her?"

"The character, not the actress. She's lovely, I'm sure."

He frowned. "You're not upset?"

"I'm a little upset I missed dinner, thanks to your inability to keep your hands off me." That wasn't exactly how things had happened, but it felt right to blame him, since, between the two of us, he was the sexy, irresistible vampire.

"I thought maybe you knew and hadn't said anything," he said. "Like with Persephone."

"Honestly, I did not know."

"Then why wouldn't you let me talk about her?"

I looked down for a pebble to kick. We were inside Bentley's place, where there were no pebbles.

"I dunno," I lied.

"You told me to never let you wriggle out of telling the truth when you're talking to me."

"Oh. Right." I looked up into his eyes.

His gaze was so intense, I actually felt sorry for any future suspects he'd be interrogating.

"What's the issue?" He leaned in toward me. "I had one thing left unspoken for far too long, and I believe I'm not the only one."

"Fine," I said, then I coughed out the words one at a time. "You're. My. First. Boyfriend."

"And?"

I laughed. "And that's it."

"That's it?"

I shrugged. "You're older than me, so it's not that weird. But you were married. And you probably had a whole bunch of girlfriends before you got married, too. And what have I got?"

"You've got me."

"But it's not fair. You're way better at this than I am. You've had infinitely more relationship experience than me. All I've got is one blurry night that led to Zoey." Technically a lie. The night had been drunken, but not blurry.

"You mean you haven't..." He trailed off as he pulled back from me.

"Whatever you're thinking, the answer is no. I haven't." I patted my chest. "All I've got is some odds and ends from various ghosts, plus this stupid lingering heartbreak over Chet Moore moving away, because part of my stupid heart, or brain, or soul, or *whatever* thinks he and I were in love."

He looked at me for a long moment, then said, "There's nothing stupid about heartbreak, or, Zara, about your heart, or brain, or soul, or whatever. Love is love. There are no training requirements."

I blinked up at him. "Look at you, with all the right words. You must have been a poet in another lifetime."

He gazed back at me, unwavering. "I have plenty of words, if someone is ready to listen."

"I'm more of an action person than a listening person."

He reached for my hands and held them in his, against his chest. "And I love that about you."

"Cool." My hands felt small inside his, like flower buds.

He suddenly pulled me toward him, into his arms. "I'm not going to say it," he said, breathing into my hair then inhaling deeply.

I giggled nervously. "What?" My voice pitched way up. I sounded like a teenaged girl.

"If I say it, you'll lose interest," he murmured near my ear. "You don't like things that are too easy."

"You are so weird. I don't even know what you're talking about," I lied, for the third time. So much for my bond to never lie to him. My last honesty oath had worn off completely.

He still had his arms around me, and the heat between our bodies was rising.

His voice deep and husky, he asked, "What time does bowling start?"

"We have to leave soon, or we'll be late."

"Then I guess we're going to be late," he said, and he pulled me tighter. I softened into his embrace.

He swept my hair back, and his breath was hot on my neck.

CHAPTER 41

I was in for a surprise when we got to Shady Lanes Bowling and Ales.

Archer Caine was there, selecting rental shoes. And he'd brought a date.

"Zara, I believe you know Carrot Greyson," he said.

The orange-haired young woman with the buggy eyes grinned at me the way a mouse might grin at a cat from behind sturdy glass. She had changed clothes since I'd seen her at the library that day. She no longer wore the paint-flecked smock and overalls with the kerchief over her hair. She looked chic and modernly edgy, in a tight-fitting black wrap dress that showed off her colorful tattoos.

My gaze went to the prowling cat on her upper chest, then to her cleavage, and down over her angular but well-proportioned hips and legs, then back up to her eyes.

"Girl, you clean up good," I said, blushing over the ogling I'd just given her. I'd eyeballed her like Ribbons eyed my grocery bags. Not that I was entirely to blame. It was the rune mage's fault for having so many pretty tattoos and artwork begging to be looked at.

Archer slung one arm around Carrot's shoulders. "Zara, Carrot and I are officially dating."

"That's great news!" I yanked her away from Archer and gave the young woman a hug. All the hugs with Persephone earlier had put me into a hugging mood. Life was too short to not hug people whenever and wherever you could.

"I was going to tell you today, but I really got into my mural. Literally."

"And it's a gorgeous mural!" I squeezed tighter. "Since you're here, does this mean you're joining our bowling team?"

"If you'll have me," she squeaked in my ear, like a squeaky toy.

I released her from the hug.

When she pulled away, she said, "I used to be on the Incredibowls, but I don't work at City Hall anymore, so someone else took my spot."

"Their loss is our gain," I said.

I turned to Archer, who was staring at me in shock, and I punched him playfully on the arm. "Look at you! Narrowing your options down to just one lady." My gaze flitted between the two of them. "You are exclusive, right? Or is that rude to ask? I don't know. I've had a lot of firsts lately. The father of my daughter is dating someone. That's a first. I'm just so happy. I don't even know what to do with my hands. Can I hug you again? I feel like we're family now. All of us."

Carrot held out her skinny, tattooed arms tentatively.

I really didn't know what to do with my hands, so I hugged her again, lifting her right off the ground.

I wasn't normally so grabby and huggy, but I couldn't stop myself. I was thrilled that my daughter's father had narrowed down his dating field to just one woman. Plus, I liked Carrot. Granted, she did have terrible taste in men, having dated two murderers—two that we knew of, or three, if Archer's self-defense actions were counted as homicides—but I sincerely hoped her luck had turned around.

I released her, and we got down to the business of bowling.

Carrot had also brought along a friend she worked with at her tattoo studio, so we had a total of six people on our team. We would need a total of eight bowlers to qualify as an official league team, with at least seven of those members showing up in order for the evening's score to count toward a running average. With fewer than seven, we were still welcome to play, but strongly encouraged to rustle up more players for the following Friday.

We were assigned to the lane next to my aunt and her coworkers. Everyone on our team and on the Incredibowls were getting along and laughing together right from the first gutter ball—thrown by me. After I had warmed up, I introduced Persephone to my aunt as my half-sister. Zinnia pretended to be surprised by the news.

My aunt's City Hall team, The Incredibowls, were formidable bowlers. My own newly formed team, which didn't even have a name yet, didn't stand a chance against the crew from the Wisteria Permits Department.

During the break after our first game, both teams shared a table, and ordered several platters of deep-fried foods and beer.

After a whole lot of hinting, the group agreed to do a thorough round of official introductions—the supernatural kind.

Zinnia cast a bubble of privacy around our table. This had a nice side effect of helping us hear each other more clearly over the clattering balls and pins.

We started the round.

Carrot Greyson went first. "Hi, everyone. As some of you already know, I've recently discovered that I am a Rune Mage." She gave her date, Archer, a look that was sweeter than a jar full of red jelly beans. "My handsome genie boyfriend has been helping me explore my powers."

Archer cried out, "Spoiler alert!" When the group didn't immediately laugh at his joke, he turned to Carrot. "Did I say that right? It is called *spoiler alert*, isn't it?" The genie had been out of touch with the regular world for the past sixteen years, so he had good reason to be uncertain about popular culture.

Carrot patted him on his shoulder. "You said it right. They just haven't gotten to know you like I have, and they're all scared of your genie powers."

I chimed in helpfully, "Plus, you look exactly like the man they know as Chet Moore."

"No, I don't," Archer said. "I changed my hair. People hardly ever mistake me for that other guy now." He made air quotes. "*My cousin, Chet.*"

His hair, indeed, had changed. It was now bleached a platinum blonde, and spiked. He looked like the singer from some alternative band that hit its peak a decade earlier. He still looked a lot like Chet to me, except for the key difference that Archer always looked pleased with himself and happy to be wherever he was.

People chattered about Archer's hair a moment, assuring him it was a good look for a man his age, then we all laughed, because technically he was so much older than any of us.

Bentley went next. "Theodore Dean Bentley," he said with a curt nod. "Creature of the grave." He shot me a private-joke look, then added, "Vampire."

Heads bobbed. Most, if not all, of them already knew.

I pointed at him. "And, what he didn't tell you, is that he's the former husband of Larissa Lang, the actress," I said proudly.

The others made surprised, excited sounds. They hadn't know about that.

I pointed at myself. "Hi, everyone. I'm Zara Riddle, as you probably know. I'm just a novice witch, and a librarian, and the proud single mom of a straight-A student."

My aunt cut in, "She's more than just a novice."

"Thank you." I felt my cheeks burning as I leaned back on the vinyl-upholstered stackable chair and let the others go.

Carrot introduced her friend from the tattoo studio, and then it was Persephone's turn. *My sister's* turn.

"I'm Zara's half-sister," she said. "Perse—"

I interrupted, "I thought we were dropping the *half*? And just saying sister?"

She bulged her eyes at me in a bratty way and restarted. "I'm Zara's *sister*, Persephone Diamante Rose."

I squealed. "We have the same middle name?"

"Yes. We can talk about it later," she said, and she resumed the introduction. We would talk about our middle name and namesake relative another time.

The Incredibowls were next. They were:

Zinnia Riddle, witch, and Head of Wisteria Permits Department Division of Special Buildings.

Margaret Mills, witch, and recent divorcee, with a new secret boyfriend whom the others hadn't met yet.

Dawna Jones, cartomancer, designer purse collector, and owner of an unspecified number of cats.

Gavin Gorman, gnome, fashionable dresser, Dawna's boyfriend as of that moment, and resident of the Candy Factory, where my friend Frank also resided.

Karl Kormac, sprite, and manager of the Permits Department.

Liza Gilbert, a self-proclaimed Red Shirt with no magical powers.

Xavier Batista, also a self-proclaimed Red Shirt, but with unknown magical powers that "hadn't yet manifested."

When they were done, Archer Caine pointed out something I'd missed in all the excitement. "That's only seven people in the Incredibowls," he said. "You're not an official league team unless you have eight. Who's missing?"

A gloom fell over the group, and the City Hall gang exchanged furtive glances.

Dawna spoke for the group, "We lost two people earlier this year."

I locked gazes with Zinnia, whose eyes were glistening. I knew about the tragedy that had happened at their workplace.

Karl said, "We still have a few months to find a replacement member, and I'm confident in my team's ability to complete a task, once they set their minds to it."

Everyone grew very quiet.

I looked over at Carrot, who was dabbing at her eyes with a napkin.

The night had taken a bad turn. Someone had to turn the ship around, and fast.

I pushed my chair back and said, "This evening deserves a toast."

The others agreed. Everyone refilled their beer glasses from the pitchers.

"To new friends," I said. "And to the old ones, too. To all the souls we have loved and lost, who have brought us all together, and bound us in ways we'll never know."

"Cheers," they all said, and we clinked our glasses.

CHAPTER 42

By the time the manager of Shady Lanes Bowling and Ales finally decided to kick us out, it was well past closing time.

The woman crossed her arms and said gruffly, "Folks, you don't have to go home, but you can't stay here."

Karl Kormac got to his feet with a loud groan, then yawned just as noisily. The yawn was contagious, and radiated out from Patient Zero in an impressive, almost magical ripple of yawns big and small.

We all got to our feet and then, suddenly aware of the mess we'd made across two big tables, pushed around the empty glasses and chip bag wrappers fruitlessly.

The manager barked again for us to get out. "I'm serious! The rental on those shoes has expired. Now get your butts out the door. You have ten minutes, or you'll be polishing the pins and balls."

"She's not joking," the young City Hall charmer named Xavier said gravely. "She really will make us polish the pins and balls."

We got moving. Our whole group did the Shoe Dance, laughing and grabbing onto each other for balance as we half-walked, half-hopped to the shoe rental counter.

Outside, the temperature was pleasant in spite of the light drizzle that hastened our goodbyes.

Our numbers dwindled to four: me, Bentley, Persephone, Zinnia.

I checked my phone messages.

There was a full report from my daughter about her Friday night activities.

I said to Persephone, "Looks like our mutual parent is currently at my house, teaching my impressionable daughter—your impressionable niece—how to win at gambling."

Persephone's big brown eyes twinkled. "If you're going to gamble anyway, it's better to win." She looked proud of her father, which made me feel proud of him.

I asked my sister, "Do you want to come back to the house and freak him out? He doesn't know that I know about you."

She twisted her bangs around one finger. "It's getting late. I wouldn't want to put you out."

"You can meet Zoey," I said. "You should meet your niece."

She dropped her hand and smiled. "I would like that."

Zinnia chimed in, "You'll love her."

Bentley added, "She's a remarkable young woman."

I waved both hands excitedly. "Hang on, everyone. I'm getting a psychic premonition." I held my fingers to my temples like a cheesy stage performer. "I predict that when Zoey meets Persephone, she's going be christened... *Aunty P*."

"Yes," Zinnia said. "I agree. You'll be Aunty P."

Persephone said, "Some people call me Sephie."

Three of us tilted our heads and looked at Persephone in the light of this news. She didn't look like a *Sephie* to me, but perhaps the nickname would grow on me as I got to know her.

Bentley said, "I haven't heard anyone at work call you that."

"It's mostly people who knew me as a kid," she said.

"I'll keep calling you Rose," Bentley said.

We all nodded as we stood in the drizzle of the Shady Lanes parking lot. I felt the world changing, and time passing.

Zinnia broke the quiet. "We ought to leave for your house now, unless you would prefer to stand in the rain a bit longer."

"No, no. I've had enough drizzle," I said, laughing. "Let's all go back to my place."

I loved that Zinnia assumed she was also invited back to my place. A few months earlier, I would have had to insist that we wanted her to join in, and assure her she was a welcome part of the family. I might have had to beg and cajole, even. My relationship with my aunt had grown. All the relationships in my life had expanded wonderfully.

Bentley wrapped his arm around my waist, then gently steered me toward the car. "Enough with the rain," he said.

I felt some resistance to leave my sister, even for the brief time it would take us to drive in separate cars to my house.

I pulled away from Bentley. "Persephone, you should drive with me so we can plan what to say to Rhys! He's going to be so surprised." I asked Bentley, "Would you drive her car so it's at the house?"

"Your wish is my command," he said gallantly.

* * *

While Persephone and I drove to car to the house, we planned how to prank our mutual parent.

Both of us cackled over our delicious plan. Persephone cackled almost as well as a witch, which was a compliment I paid her, and a compliment she didn't quite know how to take.

We got to the house, and found my father and his granddaughter in the dining room, playing poker and placing bets with stacks of chips. Not poker chips. Stacks of actual fried potato slices.

Zoey already knew about Persephone, thanks to me giving her a heads-up earlier that day.

"Rhys, Zoey, this is Bentley's partner from work," I said. "Her name is Petunia Roth."

"Persephone Rose," she said.

"That's what I said," I lied, feigning annoyance.

Rhys narrowed his gold-green eyes suspiciously. Had I overplayed my bluff?

He got to his feet and shook her hand. "Nice to meet you, Petunia."

"Persephone," she corrected.

I narrowed my eyes at my father. Was he onto us? His rubbery expression gave away nothing.

Zoey shuffled the deck. "Shall I deal you in?" She leaned over and looked behind us. "Where's Mr. Bentley?"

"He's coming in a bit. He and Zinnia went to pick up some snacks."

My father stared at me, unblinking. "What's the occasion?"

"Friday night," I said.

He glanced at his other daughter, then at me, then nodded at the chairs. "Take a seat, ladies. The game's about to begin."

I nudged Persephone with my elbow.

She said, "Thanks, Dad."

Everyone froze, except for their eyes, which darted from person to person to person in confusion, surprise, more confusion, and then mirth.

Rhys Quarry's rubbery expression morphed into a huge grin. "You know!"

"Know what?" I feigned confusion as I turned to Persephone. "Did you just call my father Dad?"

"He, uh, looks like my dad," she fibbed. "I got confused."

"I'll *show you* confused!" I summoned two balls of plasma in my hands.

She yelped and turned into a fox. A beautiful, silken-furred black fox.

My father was laughing hard by now, begging for us to stop our charade.

But, we'd made our plan, and we played it through anyway and ignored his tearful pleas for us to stop already, because that was the sort of thing siblings did.

* * *

After the dust had settled from our fake battle, we officially introduced Zoey to her aunt.

Zoey said, "I'm so glad to meet you, Aunty P."

I grinned.

Zoey said, "Would you mind shifting again? I'd like to meet that way, too."

Persephone looked at me, as though asking permission.

"You can shift whenever you want in this house," I said. "We don't have a lot of rules, except we try not to go to bed angry, and Zoey answers the doorbell."

They both shifted. Rhys watched with fatherly and grandfatherly pride as the red fox and the black fox sniffed noses and made chirpy greeting noises.

After a moment of chirps and yips, Zoey-Fox and Persephone-Fox dashed out of the dining room. We heard their paws patter as they raced each other up the stairs. Boa, who'd crept onto my lap without my having noticed her arrival, dug her claws in painfully, then leaped off me to chase the two foxes.

Ribbons, who'd been perched on a chair watching over everything, squawked and launched himself in the air, clipping the chandelier with his wing as he joined the pursuit.

The swinging chandelier gave the dining room an interrogation feel.

Alone with my father, I looked across the table and said, "You can shift and join in the chasing games if you want," I said. "We can play poker any time."

"You're not getting rid of me that easily," he said. "At least not until you introduce me to your..." He looked pointedly at the space over my shoulder and behind me.

Bentley had arrived, with Zinnia, and two grocery bags full of party snacks.

CHAPTER 43

Rhys had been in town since the Blackstone funeral the previous weekend, and while he'd heard about Bentley, they hadn't actually met.

Bentley set down the grocery bags. I was happy to note that he'd brought more potato chips. He circled the dining room table toward my father, who got to his feet.

My father was not what anyone would call tall, but he must have done something magic at that moment to increase his height. That, or he was standing on his tiptoes to reduce the height difference between himself and the tall detective.

"It's an honor to meet you, sir," Bentley said. He was unapologetically formal and sincere. That was my Bentley.

"I hear you're a..." Rhys trailed off, still shaking Bentley's hand.

Please don't say something tacky about him being a vampire, I thought. *That's my job.*

Zinnia interjected, "He's the town's top detective."

We all turned to look at my aunt. She was giving Rhys a knowing, playful look.

"So that means you ought to behave yourself, Rhys," she said. "This is the man who'll be keeping tabs on you."

Rhys let go of Bentley's hand and puffed up his chest. "And I'll be keeping tabs on *him*," Rhys said with bravado. "He's dating my daughter, after all. He'd better treat her right."

"I will, sir," Bentley said, still serious. "My word is my bond."

There was a riffle of cards shuffling. The deck was shuffling itself in mid-air. The two men looked at me, eyebrows raised.

"That's not me," I said. "It must be the other witch in the room."

Zinnia, smiling, said, "I picked up a few tricks on vacation. Shall I deal?"

The cards swirled in a spectacular spiral formation, forming the infinity symbol.

My father returned to his seat, Bentley sat at the head of the table, everyone promised not to use magic or other means to cheat, and Zinnia dealt the first hand.

For the next twenty minutes, the cards remained untouched while we chatted about other things.

Zoey-Fox and Persephone-Fox slunk into the room, panting from their play, and returned to their human forms. They joined us at the table, and Zinnia gathered up the unplayed cards for a reshuffle.

Six players.

Ribbons flapped in and made a fuss, so we dealt him in as well. I would have to translate his psychic transmissions to the others on his behalf.

Seven players.

Boa meowed on my lap.

"You can't play poker," I said to the white furball. "Don't even act like you can."

My father asked, "How can you be sure of that? She might be highly intelligent."

"Dad, she drinks out of the toilet," I said.

Everyone laughed.

And so began our first official Family Poker Night.

Persephone fit right in. I was pleasantly surprised to find she was the perfect ally for ribbing our father. We teased him mercilessly, about everything from his wardrobe choices to his high-flying friends. We revived old histories and reviewed them under the magnifying lens of new knowledge.

I brought up a perfect example of his strange habits, and he shed a new light on my memories.

"That wasn't any old racehorse," he said, wiping a tear of mirth from his eye. "Zara, you were only four years old. I would never have put you on the back of a mere animal."

"That horse almost killed me! I was barely on its back and it took off at full gallop!" A bit of genuine outrage bubbled under my pretend anger. That day at the racetrack, I had been thrilled beyond my wildest dreams to ride the beautiful black horse. It had happened during one of my father's annual visits. I had enjoyed our time together, but later, when my mother found out I'd ridden a racehorse at full gallop around the track, she'd been livid. That was when I first realized something wasn't right with my father. He wasn't like normal fathers. Something about him was wrong, and I was his daughter. I was half of him. So that meant something was wrong with me, as well. If I was to be all right in the world, I had to suppress that part of myself.

Clearly, *that* didn't exactly work out.

However, that day at the racetrack had been the beginning of the divide between us.

"You were fine," he said dismissively, reaching for the bowl of potato chips that were for eating, not betting. "The racehorse was my good friend David Freeman."

Persephone squealed. "Uncle Dave? Zara got to ride Uncle Dave at full gallop around a racetrack?" She frowned and pouted. "No fair."

My father stuffed chips in his mouth, then wiped his fingers on a napkin. "Now, girls. Don't fight. Dave was already well into retirement from his racing days when I took Zara to visit him. Persephone, you weren't even born yet."

She crossed her arms, still pouting. I couldn't tell how much of the pout was real. "All I got was that tired old donkey you brought to every one of my birthday parties and tried to pass off as a pony. I know a donkey when I see it."

They joked about the donkey, and how it had—in Persephone's opinion—reduced her social status with the kids at school. As they teased each other, I clenched my fists. I wanted them to stop talking. To stop joking about all of Persephone's fun-filled birthdays, with her father dressed up as a clown and presenting various old friends to do magic tricks, or cook special meals, or show the attendees how to walk a circus wire.

My stomach felt hard, and it was swelling up, so that my breath came in shorter and shorter gasps. I wanted them both to shut up about all those joyful father-daughter moments in the sun.

"But the donkey was the worst of all your special guests," Persephone said.

The others at the table laughed, but I didn't.

"Aww," my father said, feigning hurt feelings. "That was your great-aunt, Elouise Quarry. She passed away when you were nine, so she never got to tell you."

"No way," Persephone gasped. "Is that why the donkey bit all the kids I didn't like?"

He nodded. "Family looks out for each other," he said. "We stick together."

Something was roiling and boiling inside me, and it suddenly came out without warning.

"Except when we don't," I said, my voice curved, cold, and sharp as a karambit. "Sometimes we only stick together for three-quarters of one day out of three hundred and sixty-five."

The table went silent.

My aunt made a single tsk sound then closed her mouth.

The rain pattered down on the window.

Everyone looked away from me, and then, one at a time, at me.

"Whoops," I said. "I don't know where that came from." I waved my hands. "Carry on with the frivolities, everyone. Let sleeping dogs lie. The past is the past. Water under the bridge."

I felt a warm hand on my back. Bentley's hand. "It's okay," he murmured. "It's okay to feel however you feel."

There was a single yip across the table. My father had turned into a red fox. The fox stared back at me with big, gold-green eyes.

"Zara," Persephone said.

"Don't," Zinnia said. "Some things are best left unsaid."

"No," Persephone said. "She needs to hear this."

Zinnia made another tsk, then fell silent.

"Zara," Persephone said again. "He would never tell you, because he doesn't want to hurt you any more than you've already been hurt."

My body felt like it was raw. I wanted to push Bentley's hand off my back. I didn't want anyone to touch me, but, more powerfully, I didn't want to reveal how I felt. How much I loved the young woman who was my sister, but also how much some terrible part of me wanted to hurt her, to harm her the way our father had harmed me, by being in her life all those days and not in mine.

Persephone looked down at her cards and fanned them out, then shuffled them back together again. Fan, shuffle. Fan, shuffle.

"Persephone," I said.

She jerked up her head and met my eyes. I locked on and asked, "He'd never tell me *what*?"

Since he'd rather turn into a fox than tell me, I had to get it from her.

She laid down her cards slowly.

The rain pattered.

"That it wasn't his choice," Persephone said. "Your family was going to kill him when they found out your mother was pregnant by a fox shifter. They almost did kill him; but, luckily, he had some friends who took his side. The man I called Uncle Dave was a racehorse, but he was also a judge. He's the one who oversaw the agreement over your custody. He's the one who got your family to agree to allow our father to see you one day a year. On his birthday."

"His birthday?" How had I missed something so obvious?

I turned to my aunt for corroboration. Zinnia looked visibly rattled by the news. "I, uh, didn't know the specific details of the arrangement," she said.

I looked down at my hands, where I had a glowing blue bird nestled in one palm, sleeping.

After a moment, my voice gravelly, I said, "I knew that."

Zinnia said, "You did?"

"No," I said, correcting myself. "I mean, I didn't know-know it, but somewhere, deep down, I knew that people were lying to me. And I guess I understand why. My mother didn't want anything to do with magic. She renounced it, and it killed her, sort of." I shook my head. "My, how the pendulum swings."

"That it does," Zinnia said. "The pendulum swings one way, and then the next. Nothing is ever still, ever at rest, ever unchanging, as long as it lives."

I passed the glowing bird from one palm to the other. Everyone was quiet, even Ribbons.

I set the glowing blue bird of pure energy on the table. It looked around, and then hopped into an empty chip bowl, where it hunkered down.

Zinnia said, "How darling." I touched the bowl to illuminate the spell so that everyone else could see it.

Then I looked across the table, at my father. He'd turned back into a human again.

"I'm sorry," he said, his eyes glistening. "I'm so sorry."

"You don't have to be sorry," I said. "It's my stupid family who should be sorry." I growled, "Starting with my mother."

"Your mother didn't know," he said. "It was your grandparents, and your great-grandparents, and people you've never met."

"My life was ruined by people I've never met?"

The corner of his mouth twitched up mischievously. "Zara, I wouldn't say your life is ruined. Look around."

I took a deep breath and looked around the table at my aunt, my daughter, my boyfriend, my sister, my father, and the resident wyvern.

"Oh," I said.

The sleeping bird awoke from its nest in the bowl, and took to the air. It circled the table three times, then flew at the window. It passed through the glass with a tiny squeak and a final POP.

And with that, the pain in my heart was gone, along with the grudge that had caused it.

"You're right," I said, smiling. "My life is pretty much the opposite of ruined."

Persephone reached across the table and squeezed my fingers.

Bentley patted my back, then kissed me on the side of my forehead.

Zoey rearranged her stacks of betting chips and said, "Are we going to get back to playing poker, or what? Don't you guys dare quit while I'm up."

Zinnia shuffled the cards and dealt another hand.

* * *

Gradually, something dawned on us.

It was dawn. Literally.

The dining room filled with a generous yellow glow. The sun was rising.

All six of us who were still awake—Ribbons had excused himself hours ago—put down our poker cards and turned to the window in wonder.

"The rain has stopped," Zinnia said.

It was true. There was no familiar patter of rain falling. I'd almost forgot what it felt like to not hear rain around me.

Persephone said, "It's probably just taking a break. People keep telling me it rains a lot in September. Like, for the whole month."

"But it's October now, Aunty P," Zoey said. "It has been for a few hours."

There was a creak and a pop from somewhere within the house.

My father pointed at something behind me. "Was that door always there?"

We all turned.

A new door had appeared on the dining room wall, behind me. It was made of the same weathered wood as the other interior doors. It even had what appeared to be wyvern and cat scratches on it.

When I turned back to the others, Persephone's eyes were wide and her face was pale. "What's going on? Are we in trouble? That door wasn't there a minute ago, I swear."

The others chuckled. Everyone but my sister knew about the house's ability to renovate itself without any encouragement, let alone permission. It was always changing room configurations, expanding and contracting areas as needed. The last time a whole new door had appeared, it had led to my new-old basement.

Zoey quickly explained to Persephone how our house remodeled itself. The door wasn't completely out of the blue. The old gal had been banging away on some secret project through most of September. We'd grown as accustomed to the noise as we had to the patter of rain.

I stood and approached the door. The paint glistened in the orange dawn light as I reached for the shiny brass lever handle.

"Be careful," Zinnia warned.

"Open it," my father urged.

"I'll go first," Bentley said, already at my side.

"As you wish." I yanked the door open. "Age before Beauty," I said, waving him ahead of me.

The door was located on an interior wall, the one that split the dining room from the staircase. It should have opened to little more than a cramped storage spot at the mid-point of the stairs. Instead, it opened onto an impossibly voluminous foyer, and a spiral staircase. The stairs led up two stories, and the treads were made of gleaming, polished walnut.

Bentley and I exchanged a look. "This shouldn't be here," he said. "There's no space for all of this."

"I know," I said. "The basement was different. It could have been there all along, just without a door for access."

He waved an arm through the opening. "Feels real."

"I don't know about this," Zinnia said. "Portals can lead to other times, other worlds."

"A portal?" Persephone let out a nervous laugh. "Stop messing with me. That door was always there, wasn't it? You must have cast some sort of witch spell to hide it until now."

"It's magic, all right, but I didn't cast it," I told her.

"But that shouldn't be there," she said. "I need to check something." She slipped into fox form and trotted out of the room. We heard the tick-tick of her paws on the main stairwell, on the other side of the wall, as she ran up, down, paced to measure distances, and then returned. She was breathless and pink-cheeked when she returned to human form.

"This defies physics," she said. "This stairwell can't be here. It must be a portal."

"I don't know about this," Zinnia repeated. "Hold on a moment." She pulled a vial from her purse, cast a spell, and tossed something invisible into the air.

We all waited.

"It's stable," she said. "And it doesn't leave this world." She looked at me. "Or this time."

"That's enough assurance for me," Bentley said, and he stepped through.

He ran up the spiral staircase, out of sight. There was the sound of a door opening, and then he ran back down.

"Come on, everyone," he said.

Nobody moved. Persephone asked, "Where does it go?"

"To a flaming Hell dimension," he said.

Stunned silence.

"That was a joke," Bentley said. "It goes up to the roof. The house has a patio now. If we hurry, we can watch the sun rise."

"The sun is rising?" Rhys made some concerned hmm sounds. "Are you sure that being out in full sunrise is safe for someone such as yourself, young man?"

Zoey groaned. "Pawpaw, he can handle bright light, and he doesn't sparkle. Those are myths."

"Right," Rhys said. "I knew that."

My sister and I exchanged a look.

Bentley took my hand and squeezed it. "Come on, Zara," he said. "It's beautiful up there. You've got to see it."

I squeezed his hand, stepped through the portal door, and the two of us led the way up the spiral staircase.

Other than the fact I knew the stairwell couldn't exist, it felt completely normal and solid.

The rooftop deck was more of a viewing platform than a big patio. The platform was nestled within the peaked roof in a way that prevented it from being seen from the sidewalk. As long as we didn't stand on top of the built-in wood benches, our heads wouldn't be visible to passersby.

The three of us who were foxes shifted into fox form, and jumped over the railing to explore the renovated rooftop.

Bentley, Zinnia, and I exchanged a look.

"Shifters," Zinnia said with a shrug. "They have their ways."

The black fox had paused her exploration and was looking at me.

I heard Persephone's voice in my head. "Thank you for welcoming me into your family," she said, telepathically.

"It's your family now," I said, then, "You're welcome."

Persephone-Fox winked, then returned to her play, running at full-tilt to catch up with the other two.

When I turned to my aunt, she was watching me intently.

"I picked up something," Zinnia said. "It sounded like static to me, like when Ribbons was trying to get you to help him cheat at poker."

"We have a psychic link," I said. "Persephone and I. It happened in the forest, too. I knew it. I knew I hadn't imagined it."

Bentley frowned. "You and Rose have a psychic link? Is it bad that I'm a little jealous?"

I swatted him on the shoulder. "It's cute that you're jealous."

"I'll get used to it," he said, the frown fading. "And it might come in handy. She can let you know whenever we're tied up late on a case."

"You will *not* use my sister as your personal secretary," I said, swatting him again. "Here's a fun fact: Did you know that the word secretary comes from the term secret-keeper?"

"I do now." He looked at my aunt and said, "She's such a librarian."

My aunt smiled. "She's a lot of things."

Three foxes ran by, chirping excitedly.

The sun on my face was warm. The roof steamed as the rain began to dry.

In the light, my memories of the darkest times of my life felt distant, like old stories contained in a book somewhere else.

In another lifetime, I'd spent so much time worrying that I'd screwed up my life beyond salvage. It had felt to me like everyone but me understood what life was all about. While they made plans and looked forward to things, I stood outside, looking in through the glass as they celebrated milestones I couldn't relate to.

My life had been chaos. Just getting from one minute to the next, always promising myself that any day now I was going to get my act together, but I never did. Whenever good things did happen, they seemed to occur by accident. I was more comfortable with things going badly, because that was what I felt I deserved.

That was how I used to feel.

My life was still chaos, and I was taking things one minute at a time, but it was different now. I wasn't waiting to get my act together. This was the act. The moment-to-moment chaos, with the good things and the bad things, and all the accidents along the way.

The sun warmed my face, and my body, and my spirit.

Daybreak.

We had the future, and we had the past—there was no denying it—but the most important time we had was now.

On that first dawn of October, I turned to watch the sun rise over the town of Wisteria.

Zinnia and Bentley did the same, flanking me. I don't know how it happened, but I was holding hands with both of them, as though we were about to cast a spell.

And maybe we were casting a spell, and we just didn't know it.

Maybe the three of us were hoping that we could hold onto this perfect now, this sunrise, for as long as possible, and that nothing would ever change.

The three foxes bounded back into the viewing platform, changed into human form, and then all six of us were standing together, holding hands, each of us privately wishing that this moment could last forever.

For a full list of books in this
series and other titles by
Angela Pepper, visit

www.angelapepper.com

www.ingramcontent.com/pod-product-compliance
Lightning Source LLC
Chambersburg PA
CBHW071525120726
47907CB00013B/669